PRAISE FOR STEPH

Deliciously suspenseful from the very first line. With characters as intricately crafted as its twists, a break-neck pace, and unrelenting tension, *The Final Scene* is as gripping as it is terrifying.

— NOELLE W. IHLI, AUTHOR OF *RUN ON RED*

Brimming with nail-biting suspense, twists galore, and full of heart—*The Final Scene* is a page-turner that has absolutely everything you crave in a thriller.

— FAITH GARDNER, AUTHOR OF *THE PREDICTION*

Steph Nelson's well-plotted thriller takes a horrifying premise and follows it to the bitter, electrified end.

— DREW HUFF, AUTHOR OF *FREE BURN*

THE FINAL SCENE

STEPH NELSON

Cover art by Mat Yan

Published 2024 by Ticking Clock Press

ISBN: 979-8-9896154-0-7

For NWI

This novel contains child loss, kidnapping, body shaming, manipulation, violence, coarse language, sexual situations, and non-explicit references to suicide, drug addiction, and prostitution. Please read with care.

CHAPTER 1

Brooke doesn't remember her first day at the cabin, but she'll never forget the day he grabbed her.

It was summer in Portland, and the sun set in a warm glow at her back. The sky was creamsicle. She wore a gray pencil skirt and black strappy heels. Her sleeveless white blouse had ruffled edges that the mild breeze kept lifting, tickling her shoulders. A Louis Vuitton bag she definitely couldn't afford rested on her hipbone, because making a good impression at the new job was worth maxing out a credit card.

Brooke usually wore her shoulder-length hair down, but by the end of that long day, thanks to the heat, it had found its way up into a small spout of a ponytail. She blended in with a crowd, and over the years she's wondered if that's part of why he targeted her. Assumed nobody would miss her. But despite being plain, medium height, and a little overweight, she was in her prime.

Thirty years old, newly divorced, a shared apartment with her widowed mom, and shared custody of a baby girl with her ex. Brooke had just landed her dream job working for *The*

Oregonian after years of slinging coffee and freelance gigs that didn't pay enough. She could take on anything.

Anything except him.

He sat next to her on the bench, waiting for the bus. Nothing unusual about that. He was at the other end and seemed to understand the unspoken rules of bench space. Brooke slipped earbuds in and hit *play* on her audiobook. Some domestic thriller. It was dark when the bus arrived, and she and the man approached the folding door to enter at the same time. He moved a hand to invite Brooke to go first, but didn't smile. His face was scruffy, like he hadn't shaved in days, and his eyes were red rimmed. She thought maybe he was high. After all, who wasn't high in Oregon on any given day?

The bus was full, so Brooke took the first seat she came across, midway to the back. She changed out of heels and into city flats, stuffing the black sandals into her big bag. Brooke's thriller was revving up and so she got lost in it, forgetting about that guy as she stared out the window. The bus stopped over and over, which by now was a familiar rhythm to her ride home. The last of the commuters would get off at the same place as her, and Brooke recognized most of them from the daily grind.

The scruffy man from the bench was the first to get off at her stop. He'd moved into a seat near the front. Once outside, he flicked open a Zippo lighter with a flourish and stopped to light a cigarette.

Brooke noticed this in the way any woman keeps track of unknown men in their vicinity when alone and in the dark. It wasn't out of fear or worry. Not at that point. More like keeping tabs to create a cushion between herself and danger if necessary. Brooke still had a bit of a walk to her small apartment, but if she paid attention, she'd be fine.

Just get home to Jessi in time for bath and bed.

The baby stayed with Brooke's mom during the day, but since getting the position with the paper, Brooke had gotten home later and later. It was her dream job, yes, but any new job had a learning curve, and hers was steep. She put in after-hours effort so she could start every day fresh.

Crowds of familiar commuters scattered to their various destinations, and so did Brooke, walking through this man's cloud of nicotine to pass him. He didn't look like someone coming home from work, but what did she know? Just because he was a little unkempt and she'd never seen him on this bus before wasn't any reason to be afraid. Even so, she turned her audiobook off to stay aware.

Soon, hard footfalls from behind punctuated the soft tapping of Brooke's flats on pavement. Her pulse spiked. Was it him? She looked over her shoulder and pretended to adjust her bag to be less obvious. Even in the dark, she could see it was him. Was he really following her?

They were alone in a quiet, empty pocket of the city, the sound of distant car horns here and there. Behind them, along the busy road where the bus had let off, a few street lights shone. But she had to walk away from them, deeper into darkness, to get home.

Alarms went off inside Brooke's body, a heightening of awareness. She surveyed all the open shops in case she needed to duck into one.

Panic climbed up her ribcage until she couldn't ignore it, so she slipped into a little dive bar to let him pass. Couldn't handle him behind her anymore. She watched him saunter right on by as if he hadn't even noticed her.

Relief.

It's all in my mind.

I'm overreacting.

After a few minutes, Brooke walked out of the bar, but there was that man, a short block ahead, looking at a newspaper stand exactly where she needed to walk past. He glanced up, face neutral, then returned to what he was doing. He'd seen her, but the truth was that he still gave her no real reason to be scared. It was only a feeling she had. A feeling that may not have been at all accurate. But still, she was antsy to get home to Jessi and exhausted from the brain drain of her job.

Brooke moved with purpose toward him in order to pass by, and when she was just ten feet away, he stepped in front of her and began walking too, matching her pace.

Relief overtook her once again. At least he was ahead of her. Now she could control her distance from him, so she kept slowing down to create more space.

After about two blocks, the man turned left down a lit alley.

Brooke's shoulders, which had climbed up to her ears, relaxed. It truly was all in her head. When she passed by where he turned off, she glanced down the alley to see how far he'd made it.

He wasn't there.

But whatever. Maybe he worked the night shift at one of those restaurants, and he'd gone in the back door. Employee entrance. What did she know about his plans for the night?

Still, she picked up her pace.

I'm safe. It's fine, she thought, but her nervous system screamed that a threat you can't see is much worse than one you can keep eyes on.

Brooke's palpitating heart pushed the thump of blood into her ears. Her breathing was shallow, her throat tight. But again, her mind reasoned against her body. There was no threat. Just someone new taking her bus and getting off at the same stop, and daring to walk in the same direction. As if nobody could do that. Silly. She was being silly and over-thinking herself into a panic attack. After all, he was gone now.

Still, Brooke clutched her bag and moved at a pace just short of a jog until she was almost to her ground-floor apartment. She only had to pass the row of garages now. Eyes on the front door, she felt for her house key in the bag. She allowed herself an occasional look around, but not enough to signal she was lost and easy prey.

Brooke never got past the garages.

It was as simple as a tug on her ponytail, a huge, warm hand covering her mouth, and then a pinch at the shoulder. The last thing she thought was, *This is it. This is how I die.*

That was ten years ago.

CHAPTER 2

When Brooke finishes telling Kinsey about the day he abducted her, she walks to the front window and stares out into the woods.

She knows it's August because they have a calendar. She knows this cabin is near the Oregon Coast because Mitch told her once. But since she got here, she's only ever ventured a few feet outside. It's as far as they can go.

If they want to stay alive, anyway.

Brooke didn't share with Kinsey the part about her daughter. Something about it still feels too raw, even after ten years.

Ten.

Jessi's age. The same number of years the girl has lived without her mommy.

What does her daddy tell Jessi about Brooke's absence? What does she look like now? Brooke still sees her as a baby.

At least Jessi has Mom.

Brooke's mom would be there as much as Ian would allow it. Brooke won't be. She's never going to escape. But staying alive feels like an act of defiance against being ripped away from her life. It's not hope. Brooke knows exactly what hope feels like, and that part of her is dead. There is no hope.

Kinsey sits on the floor, playing with dolls, not making eye contact with Brooke. If they don't make eye contact, their abductor doesn't know they're talking to each other. There's no audio on the surveillance system.

Kinsey fluffs her Chatty Cathy's dress. It's probably the actual doll that Grace, her abductor, had as a child, because it doesn't work. Its auburn hair is dull, one eye won't open, and the pull string is gone. "Was it Mitch back then, too? Who grabbed you?"

Kinsey knows it was. Brooke already told her that part, but Kinsey doesn't always pay attention very well. She's only been here for two months, and Brooke worries she doesn't have what it takes. You have to accept the boredom of staying on script. Then you have to excel at improvising when Grace shows up and inserts herself into the script. Be on your toes all the time, remembering things that don't seem important. You never know when little details will become life-or-death details.

The cabin's window is open, only a few inches, but it's enough to allow the fresh air in. Brooke closes her eyes and savors the breeze on her cheeks. It smells like wet pine mixed with sea air.

The property is about three acres wide with the cabin in the middle, and surrounded by pine trees except for the front yard, which is full of weeds leading to the roundabout gravel driveway. Brooke can't quite see beyond that. It's just more trees, and another 200 feet or so between the perimeter of the property and the isolated road that she assumes connects them to civilization.

"Brooke? Was it Mitch?" Kinsey repeats. She's one of

those people who can't stifle their exuberance no matter what they do. So, her pigtails bounce when she talks, tips skimming the metal band around her neck. The same one Brooke wears and has worn for a decade.

The band is both what keeps them alive, and what could kill them.

Kinsey's costume is a knee-length yellow dress with a white Peter Pan collar and a knit sweater cardigan. She plays the part of young Grace Hamilton, age nine. Never mind that she's twenty-three.

"Yeah," Brooke says, turning from the window and glancing up at the surveillance camera near the ceiling. She walks back into the kitchen to finish organizing the pantry before someone notices that she's off script. They're being watched during the day. "I'm pretty sure Mitch is the only one Grace has ever trusted. He's been her henchman for the ages."

Kinsey pulls her eyes away from Chatty Cathy and gives Brooke a blank look. She doesn't get the joke about Grace and Mitch having some twisted love story.

Whatever. Not everyone gets Brooke's sense of humor.

Mitch abducted each of them to play a role, and Grace believes that if she can recreate moments from her own childhood, she'll experience healing and be able to find peace. So they act out these half-baked scenes like a perfect family. Nobody knows if any of them were actually from her history or not. It doesn't matter.

Brooke's the only one who has made it this long, and it hollows out her gut to think about the past ten years, all the people who have died. But the tears don't come. Probably because she's already cried them all, and now she saves every single one for the dark of night. For when she's alone, no cameras watching.

She saves them for Jessi.

"Did you ever see Tyson's body?" Kinsey asks.

Brooke stiffens, clenches her teeth. "Not that. Not Tyson." Then she stacks cans of Campbell's soup and turns them so the labels face out. "I don't want to talk about the ones who didn't make it. What else do you want to know?"

"What's the trick to staying alive? How have you done it for so long?" Kinsey asks as if she has questions lined up.

Brooke shrugs. "I follow the rules. It's the only way."

Kinsey lets out a little *hmm*, like Brooke is some prisoner survival guru with profound advice.

"So, for example," Brooke continues, "stop asking for things when Mitch comes by. Stop complaining, and be perfect whenever Grace is here."

Kinsey was a high-end sex worker in her old life. Mitch had posed as a John and drugged her. It was that simple. No learning where she lived, no stalking her on the bus, no figuring out an alternate route to intercept her, no hiding in the shadows, no risk of mistake. It's how Mitch operates these days.

In fact, Mitch has spent the past years kidnapping only those he perceives as nameless to society. Druggies, transients, and the like. *Easy prey.*

When Brooke learned Kinsey wasn't homeless, she was excited. Maybe Kinsey would have people looking for her. Family, friends, anyone. But her family had long disowned her for her choice to drop out of law school and go into sex work, and they hadn't spoken in years. Kinsey was sure her girls would come for her, but Brooke didn't hold her breath waiting for a ragtag group of sex workers to play detective, no matter how smart they might be.

Nobody has ever come. For any of them.

Mitch informed her after a few years here that her mom and Ian had run out of money trying to find her.

So now, Brooke focuses on following Grace's rules. That's the key to surviving, and Brooke has always been good at rules. Come to find out, a survival situation that depends on that very thing is where she shines. It's not like she hasn't paid an emotional price for her compliance, though.

She pays with her own humanity, every damn day.

And Grace is volatile. Even though there are rules to follow, sometimes they change, and you never know when she'll snap. On the one hand, she's just an old lady—in her seventies—but on the other hand, she's a psychopath. She has Mitch, who does upkeep on the property and God knows what else when he's not kidnapping people. Also a psychopath. A well-compensated psychopath, in fact. Add to it that Grace is healthy and spry for her age. Plus, she's extremely motivated to reach the final scene, which Brooke has figured out means her total inner healing. When Grace has successfully relived her childhood through the cast members.

It's insane, but Brooke's done it for so long that she doesn't dwell on the premise of the thing anymore.

Brooke performs as Grace's mother, Helen Hamilton. Tyson, who Kinsey asked about, used to perform as Albert Hamilton, Grace's father. It's always just three of them, give or take, depending on who has been cut from the cast recently.

The roles are mindless and predictable. Household tasks like cooking, baking, and cleaning the cabin for Brooke. Kinsey plays with the few toys she has: the Chatty Cathy, those creepy-ass naked troll dolls with colored hair, and a couple of children's books. Mostly she sits in the living room and pretends to play while Brooke cleans or cooks.

Whoever plays Albert takes care of the outdoor tasks like

clearing weeds and chopping firewood. Otherwise, he must sit and read the newspaper. The same newspaper, dated March 23, 1962.

At random, Grace shows up and inserts herself in the role of young Grace and interacts with Helen (Brooke) and whoever is the current Albert. When she's here, mistakes and missteps can kill you.

It's happened, too.

CHAPTER 3

A situation with one Albert in particular is burned into Brooke's memory. It was in the early years of her time here. He was young, maybe eighteen. New. It was his first day with Grace, even though he'd been at the cabin for a few days. He didn't respond when Grace called him "Dad." He'd been spacing off, or forgot he was supposed to be acting. Brooke doesn't know. Grace broke character and gave him one verbal warning. Her scowl formed deep lines across her forehead, her mouth set in a permanent frown. It had given Brooke the chills. The way she had said it. Kind words, without any hints of kindness. Just those icy blue eyes lasering in on the guy.

A few days later, when she arrived, he did it again. Brooke was shocked. You have only one job here—to act well—and it was like he didn't believe Grace was serious. In seconds, she had the little square remote in her hands, fingers poised over a button.

Brooke had gasped. She knew what it could do, but this guy, like some dumb puppy walking into traffic, didn't. Grace pushed the button on the device once and it gave him a sharp jolt of electricity through the metal band, his collar.

But that was only to get his attention.

Brooke had stood, numb, while Grace shocked him over and over. Tiny jolts.

Maybe she could have tried to intervene. Tackled Grace from behind or something, but she had that remote, and Mitch was right there, hand hovering over the gun on his hip. What was she supposed to do? Then, when the poor guy thought it was over, when he was coming to, Grace smiled, tight-lipped. As the smile faded, she held the button down, repeating, "Your name is Albert. You go by Dad. Albert. Dad. Albert. Dad." The young man jerked and flopped on the floor until he stopped moving.

Grace ordered Mitch to leave his body there overnight. A reminder to the rest of them what can happen. She always did that after cutting a cast member.

Brooke can't think about all the dead bodies that she's spent one or more nights with in the cabin. How many times she's served as a last witness in death. The thoughts that plague her every time it happens.

Could I have stopped this?

I should have tried.

She doesn't bother with those thoughts anymore. There's no point.

The role with the highest turnover is Kinsey's: young Grace. You'd think it would be the easiest to play because whenever Grace comes, whoever is playing young Grace must hide in the bedroom. That's her only task. At first, Brooke wondered, what was the point of having someone in that role, if they never have to do anything but sit in the bedroom? It's like she's a placeholder for the hours when Grace isn't here. Over the years, the old woman has hinted that young Grace's only real purpose will be in the end scene of the whole charade. That she has a crucial part to play in the last act, and until then, she just has to follow the rules. Plus, two Graces in one location at the same time would create what the real Grace calls an *anomaly* and the scene would need to be *reset*.

"Reset" is Grace's word for starting fresh with someone new. Brooke learned that years ago when one girl playing young Grace kept coming out of the bedroom, asking her to make cookies while Grace was there. Grace didn't even give her a warning. No shock to get her attention. She pulled out her hunting knife and drew it across the girl's neck. Her lined face looked almost hungry as life left the girl. That one had broken Brooke, and it was afterward that she let go of hope. Decided not to get attached to other cast members anymore.

But then Tyson came along.

He was sweet and patient. Not her type, physically speaking, but for the first time, that didn't matter to Brooke. It was his heart. So giving. It's only been a month since she lost Tyson, and it seems like she should still fall apart with grief at the thoughts, but she can't cry over him.

Am I really that damaged?

Yes, she answers her own question. Hell yeah, she's damaged. The pain, regret, and terror bubble underneath the surface of her heart. They lurk there, raging, as if biding time until they can explode out of her skin. All the people she didn't lift a finger to help, since it would have meant putting herself in harm's way. Every time she was silent during a killing. Each decision made in favor of her own survival, but a slash into her soul where empathy used to live.

And yet, she got attached to Tyson.

And yet, here she is, coaching Kinsey, the ultimate step one toward growing an attachment.

"When do you think they'll replace Tyson?" Kinsey asks, as if reading Brooke's thoughts.

She doesn't answer right away, and Kinsey looks up. Brooke gives her a glare. How can she not remember that Brooke just said Tyson was off limits? Kinsey straightens up, moves her eyes to her dolls again. "Sorry," she says when Brooke doesn't answer.

"You need to worry more about yourself," Brooke says. "Plus, whenever it happens, it'll be your turn to train the newbie. I'm done." She goes into her bedroom, the one she used to share with Tyson. Where they made love over the years. He was the one and only slightly happy thing she had. Then he was gone.

CHAPTER 4

Tyson had been around for three years and played Albert Hamilton well. Mitch was an expert at finding the scum of society, so most of the men who came through the cabin to play Albert were assholes.

Not Tyson.

It was spring when he arrived. He was a wreck, almost didn't survive the drug withdrawals. His red hair was long and matted, with a gnarly beard to match. Brooke nursed him back to health, even staying up nights to be sure he wasn't alone, the whole time reminding herself that she was only helping him get well. She wasn't his friend. Would not be his friend. He pulled through, and Mitch shaved Tyson's beard, cut his hair. He always groomed the new cast members after abducting them.

Tyson came from the streets, where he'd lived for years, thanks to a strung-out mom and then one poor decision after another. He was young, only twenty-nine. Seven years younger than Brooke at the time. Another factor that didn't put him on the romantic map for her. He seemed more like a little brother.

But Tyson was giving, curious about people, and nice-looking despite the fact that he was small. He was the opposite of Ian, and Ian had been her type. Big, burly. All man. She'd lived the reality of how that turned out.

Tyson started leaving little things around the cabin for her. Flowering weeds from outside, tied together with a long piece of grass. A pretty stone he'd found. It was innocent, childish almost. Yet there was something so pure about him and his gestures. He wasn't jaded, despite having lived on the streets for so long.

One day, Tyson was working outside the cabin. Brooke brought him some of the lemonade she'd made for the girl playing young Grace at the time. Thought she might as well share a glass with Tyson. After all, she wasn't a total bitch.

By that point, it had been months full of bouquets of flowering weeds and other little treasures. Months of Tyson asking about her life from before, about her family. About her dreams for the future. Months of him being shot down out of the clear blue sky for any attempt at friendship, no matter how careful he was with his approach, or how respectful.

"You know, you're kind of tough to get to know," he'd said after thanking her for the drink.

His comment caught Brooke off guard, and she couldn't find a smart comeback like usual. Tyson was the kind of person who didn't register sarcasm, anyway. He would just smile like he trusted you meant everything you said.

Tyson went on talking when Brooke didn't respond. "It seems like you're hard on yourself, so you think everyone else is that hard on you." He guzzled the rest of the lemonade, wiped his forehead with the back of a hand, and smiled. One of his front teeth was tilted, overlapping the other a bit.

"What does that mean?"

"You look for reasons to keep us at arm's length."

"People come and go here. I don't like to get attached."

"Getting attached is the only reason for living. Especially here. Otherwise, why bother?"

It felt impossible to find words to push him away after he said that. Something inside of Brooke just caved. All that time, she'd worked so hard to stay closed off in order to protect herself, and he'd responded by not allowing her negativity to alter him even one bit.

Why was she doing that? What was the point?

She looked down at her feet, only nodding. Tyson reached for her hand, as if he were asking permission. Her first instinct was to resist, out of habit. Instead, she allowed it. His hand, calloused from working outside, brushed her soft skin and that was it. Game over. She was his. Brooke leaned in to hug him and then she cried. He held her.

After that, Tyson showed Brooke what he'd been working on. A spot in the backyard where he'd started digging a hole next to a bunch of wood scraps. When he pulled back a thin piece of plywood covering the hole, she saw it was about two feet deep. He said it was his plan for escape.

"You've been doing this the whole time?"

"Pretty much, yeah. The rain sets me back, especially when it's a downpour, but now that summer's here, I think I'll make good progress."

Brooke had already tried to escape. Or sort of tried. She obsessed about getting away for the first few years, and getting back to Jessi. But she never had the guts to take the plunge. It didn't work out for the others who had the guts. And it was that—the risk that it wouldn't work out, that she'd have to die trying—that made it pointless. She'd definitely never see her daughter again if she was dead. At least this way she stayed alive.

CHAPTER 5

"They're here," Kinsey shouts, pulling Brooke's attention away from the Tyson thoughts. "They were here last night. Why are they coming back so soon?"

Kinsey's right. Grace and Mitch rarely come right back after a full day here. Brooke says nothing, but goes into action, tidying the living room, double-checking that everything is in place for this surprise visit.

Mitch is first through the door, and Brooke is glad. Maybe she'll have a few minutes to find out what's up before Grace reaches the porch.

"You were just here yesterday," Brooke whispers.

Mitch grunts, pushes the door open, and comes inside.

"That's not an answer," she says.

"You didn't ask a question."

Grace is halfway to the front door now. She doesn't even move carefully, babying old hips or knees like a proper seventy-something-year-old might. She swaggers. Seventy is the new fifty, apparently.

Brooke's cheeks grow hot with anger. She hates this woman. Her ego, her toned body, her red lips, her most-likely fake boobs. It's like she's trying to defy death, and somehow she's doing it.

"Why's she here?" Brooke pushes through clenched teeth at Mitch.

He shrugs, takes a drag of his cigarette, then stomps it out on the wood floor. "She does what she wants. You know that." Then his eyes comb over her. He does that a lot, but Brooke ignores it. Instead, she yells out, "Kinsey! Bedroom!"

"Already going!" Kinsey tosses a hand up in the air.

Brooke glances around a second time to make sure nothing is out of place, then she goes into the kitchen and pretends to be busy wiping down countertops.

She can feel Mitch still watching her.

Grace walks in. She wears her silver hair in a tight bob, parted down the middle. Clothes that Brooke can only assume are fashionable, having no idea what's in style anymore. All the characters' clothes are stuck in the fifties, but Grace always looks more modern. Today she wears a knee-length oatmeal-colored jersey dress with Birkenstocks. This stops Brooke for a minute and she has a totally useless thought:

Are Birkenstocks really back to haunt us from the nineties?

Mitch walks into Kinsey's bedroom. He waits in there with her during the visits because his presence would create an anomaly otherwise.

"Hi Mom, I'm home!" Grace goes into character as young Grace, offering her usual greeting for Brooke, like some sitcom. As if the cast is here for fun, and not prisoners, acting for their very lives.

Brooke steels up. Ice queen on the inside, perfect mother on the outside. It's the only way she can get through this.

"Good afternoon, my sweet darling," Brooke croons.

Grace doesn't care as much what you say, but how you say it and whether you can improvise to respond to her. Brooke wipes her hands on her apron and reaches for Grace. It's disgusting to even touch the bitch, but she has to play the part, and her life depends on playing it well. "How was your day at school?"

"Bad. Gerry pulled my pigtails again," Grace says, pouting, and coming at her for a hug. Brooke reminds herself to breathe through it so that Grace can't feel her stiffen at the touch.

"Well, you *know* he only does that because he likes you." Saying this makes Brooke shriek on the inside. It's so wrong, this role she plays, so full of bullshit.

"You think he likes me?" Grace looks up at her with a hint of real childish hope. But no, it's an act. It's all an act.

"Darling, I don't know for sure, but I have a feeling he does. Boys tease when they like a girl. It's a good sign." Brooke wants to barf at this sick, sentimental stuff, but Grace is addicted to it.

"I hope you're right," Grace says. "Brush out my pigtails, Mommy?"

Why the hell is she here again so soon?

This is like feeling around in the dark, waiting for the boogeyman to jump out.

"Certainly, darling!" Brooke puts on a beaming smile and goes into Kinsey's bedroom for the silver-plated brush. Mitch sits in a chair, reading some muscle car magazine. When Brooke returns, Grace is on the mustard-yellow vinyl couch, legs crossed. "Break scene for a minute," she says, monotone, plastic smile gone.

Brooke stands in place, waiting for whatever comes next.

"Mitch has found you a new husband."

A new husband. A new Albert Hamilton. Because Tyson is gone.

Her insides tighten, but Brooke nods, smiles, and it's all she can do to keep from retching.

"This one has to work out," Grace says.

Rage rises like a tide in Brooke's body at the flippant reminder of how many people haven't *worked out*, but she doesn't give in to it. Instead, she changes the subject to take control of all the stray emotion.

"Yes, ma'am," Brooke says, keeping her face neutral, bringing the anger back down to simmering. "Come, darling," Brooke coos, sitting next to Grace on the couch. "Let's get those piggies out."

Grace smiles and leans her head into Brooke's lap. Of course, the old woman doesn't have pigtails, but Brooke brushes her hair with the right amount of pressure all the same. Over time, she's learned what Grace likes.

Soon, Grace is moaning and sighing, and then she looks up and says, "Mommy, I love you." She lays her head back on Brooke's lap.

It's like the woman gets off on this. Brooke doesn't know if it's imagining herself as young that turns her on, or if it's the murder.

"I love you too, my tulip," Brooke whispers, and stares out the kitchen window mindlessly.

CHAPTER 6

Derek's eyes slit open, and it's bright. So fucking bright.

His head screams bloody murder, so he squeezes them shut again. A lot of good that does because the pressure builds no matter what the hell his eyes are doing.

"Slow down. Here's water," some chick says, but Derek can't answer her. His body is heavy and all he can do is groan. When he finally opens his eyes again, it inspires a mosh pit in his brain. Derek toughs it out in order to get some idea of where the ever living fuck he might be. He doesn't remember much. Body's slow, but he manages to prop himself up on elbows in an attempt to sit. He only gets that far—an awkward reclining position on the floor—because something chokes him, and he reaches for it. A metal band around his neck.

"Oh, don't touch that," this chick says, pushing his hand down. "I think you're through the worst of it. Took you long enough. It's been weeks. What's your name?"

Weeks.

Derek doesn't remember much except for the pain gripping him so hard that he didn't even care to ask where he was or who these people were. They floated around dreamlike, anyway. He gives a cursory look around to assess the scene, but he can't move very well. He's in a small, wood-paneled bedroom. Looks like a child's room.

"Derek," he answers with a stunted cough. He puts his fingers on that metal thing again, but he can't even wedge one between the metal and his throat. "What is this?" he asks.

"There's a lot to explain, but first, we gotta get you out of here," the chick says, her shape backlit by a narrow window full of light, like she's some angel of mercy. She hands him a clear plastic glass of water and he takes it, drawing it up to his cracked lips, centimeter by goddamn centimeter. Last thing he needs is to dribble water all over his chest like some infant. But he's shaky. The water is cool, and he drinks it all, suddenly realizing how thirsty he is.

"Where?"

"Where what?"

"Get me out of where? Where's here?"

Derek's eyes adjust a bit more and he sees that this angel of cool water is not a chick. She's a little girl. But no, maybe not all that little, based on her looks. Not that he's checking her out because, God, the last thing he needs right now is *that*, but underneath all that dress fabric, her tits are huge. Her waist is small, but she's got pigtails. When his eyes focus better, he can tell she's definitely not a child. And yet, she's wearing kids' clothes. Like she's straight out of the fifties. There's metal around her neck too, but what's got him nervous is how instead of answering his question, her gaze travels to the left, across the room, eyes almost as big as those tits of hers.

Derek follows to see, and despite how groggy he is,

despite how he can't move without setting off a jackhammer in his head, he startles hard.

A skeleton. The remains of a dead body are within an arm's reach. Not only that, but it's small. Definitely a child. It's got on overalls and a ball cap.

And a metal collar.

"The fuck?" he shouts, scooting toward Angel Chick as fast as he can, but he's so slow. Body won't move like he wants it to.

She stands, then steps away to make room.

He tries to stand too, but falters.

She grabs his arm, and he knows immediately she'll be no help. What's her tiny little grip going to do to lift him? He's not as jacked as he was before his life fell apart, but he's no featherweight either.

"God, he stinks," another chick pipes up from the doorway. "And he's huge. Why would they go for someone so big?"

Derek tries to scramble to his feet, but he has to stop and let the pounding in his head settle every half a second. It's infuriating.

"Maybe he could take on Mitch," Angel Chick says, then adds, "Hey Brooke, can you come over here and help me?"

This itty-bitty girl is still trying to pull him away from the human remains and she's just plain old spinning her wheels.

"Meh, I'm good," Brooke says, and leans against the door jamb. She's wearing a knee-length light-blue dress with a white apron over it. Dark hair, pulled back in what looks like a French twist of sorts, to expose a pointy chin and high cheekbones. Same metal band around her neck. She's got big, brown eyes, and he must be able to see a lot better now because he notices her long, dark lashes. She's pretty.

"Come on. Not like it's his fault he's here."

"It's not my fault he's here, either."

That's when Derek recognizes Brooke, even though he doesn't know her. Never met her in his life. But it's the tone of voice, the attitude, the way her body leans, those crossed arms, set jaw. She's in charge. Or thinks she is.

"And besides," Brooke continues, "it's not like he's unsafe in this room. Just leave him until he can move his own *ripped* body around."

"We can't let him stay in here with . . . " Angel Chick doesn't finish her sentence.

"I don't know." Brooke shrugs, and her voice changes, softens a little. "I kinda like the idea of Cody having some company."

"But Brooke . . . Cody's a skeleton."

Brooke waves a hand and turns away, saying, "Whatever," as she goes.

Derek's not sure which question to ask first, but he needs to establish a baseline. Best start there.

"Where am I?"

"Grace Wakeford's cabin," Angel Chick says. Her words come out bouncy. "Also known as the middle of actual nowhere, and there's nobody for miles and miles."

Not helpful after all, and talking hurts. Derek tries again to stand, and this time he gets on his feet, but he's wobbly. She slips her toothpick shoulders under his arm, gripping half of his wrist with both of her hands. Her effort to support him is admirable, but useless. They both fall to the ground, and he lands on top of her.

She yelps, which drives Brooke back into the room.

"What the hell?" Brooke yells, pulling Derek off the girl. She's surprisingly strong and able to actually budge him, even though she's not much taller than Angel Chick. Curvier though. She releases him the minute the girl squirrels out from under, and his ass drops on the floor.

"Kinsey, just leave him alone. He'll make his own way out of Cody's room. Eventually."

"I think he's through the withdrawals, though."

"Well, okay, but obviously he's still not strong enough to manage himself."

Withdrawals.

Out of this entire shitshow Derek has woken up to, it's this word that finally sends him spiraling. He feels around, patting himself down, looking for his stash.

Nothing.

"Where's my stuff?" He means it as a demand, but it comes out too panicky.

Neither of the women answer right away, until the girl, the one named Kinsey, speaks. "Mitch took it. Welcome to sobriety. It sucks."

"What? Why?"

"Because Albert Hamilton was sober as a cold shower."

"The fuck is Albert Hamilton?"

Brooke groans loud and leaves the room again, but Kinsey is nice enough to answer. "You. You're Albert Hamilton now."

CHAPTER 7

I don't hate men, Brooke reminds herself as she walks out of Cody's room and into the kitchen. Because it's true. She doesn't. But something about this guy just triggers the shit out of her. Reminds her of Ian, and before that, of the first time she found out that she wasn't as hot as her best friend, Sara.

How she got all the way to ninth grade without this knowledge still baffles her. She blames her mom, who always made her feel beautiful. But when the blinders came off, it was like she'd been walking around her whole life with her fly open and everybody knew it, but nobody told her. She never thought she was supermodel material. It was her size. Always just a little too chubby. But somehow, beyond reason, she hadn't let it bother her. Not until that day during freshman year of high school.

It was the Goddess of Beauty ratings that the senior boys invented. Sara was a "G.O.B. 10," the highest rating you could get. She was blonde, thin, had gotten her braces off, and was captain of the basketball team. The boys rated other girls as G.O.B. 7, 8, or 9, but only Sara was a 10, and the boys refused to rate anyone below a 7. As a *kindness*. The rest stayed unrated.

On this day, Brooke was about to round the corner to the locker she shared with Sara when she overheard her name coming out of the mouth of her crush, Scott, a senior. Big guy, football player. She had him in her English class, and he'd always been so nice, and so she couldn't help catching feelings for him.

She stopped and waited out of sight to hear what they were talking about.

"Oh, I don't know," Scott said. "Brooke's all right, but not a 10 like you."

Brooke's heart raced. Sara knew she had a secret crush on Scott. Why were they talking about her?

Sara gave a sweet, innocent laugh. "Well, what is she then?"

A beat of silence as Brooke clenched her math book to her large chest, pressed her back against the wall around the corner to stay out of view but still listen.

"Unrated," Scott said.

Tears welled up in her eyes, and maybe she should have walked away at that point, but she couldn't make herself go. Some sick thing inside her wanted the punishment of continuing to listen.

"Oh, come on, Brooke is gorgeous," Sara had said.

"She's got a nice face. But she needs to cut back on the Twinkies."

Twinkies? Brooke didn't even eat Twinkies. She didn't like sweets at all. In fact, her mom had raised her on a healthy, whole food diet. She loved salads. Brooke looked down at her body, hating it for getting between her and her chances with Scott.

"That's so mean," Sara said with an awkward giggle. "She's not *that* overweight."

Gee, thanks, Sara.

Heat rushed into Brooke's face when she realized Sara was enjoying this. That she wasn't standing up for Brooke, and was probably the one who had brought up the subject of Brooke's rating—or lack of.

"All right, all right," Scott said. "Gun to my head . . . I guess I'd let her blow me."

"Scotty!" Sara laughed, louder now, and Brooke could hear the playful slap of a hand against leather. The sleeve of Scott's letterman's jacket, surely.

Brooke didn't know what to do. Walking up to them and interrupting felt so degrading, even if she pretended she heard nothing.

But she had heard.

It wasn't Sara's fault she was beautiful any more than it was Brooke's fault she was overweight. Everyone is born with the body they're given. But why did Sara have to take plea-sure in Scott's vicious comments? Brooke stopped talking to Sara that same day. Maybe it was an overreaction, but she was so humiliated that she didn't even explain why she changed lockers. Why she didn't return Sara's calls.

She ignored Scott the rest of the year, but it didn't stop her from starting a diet that very day. All the self-control and restriction in the world couldn't make the numbers on the scale budge enough. And daily running, lifting weights, surviving on apples, low-fat Nutri-Grain bars, salads, and sugar-free peanut butter on bagels did nothing but make her insanely hungry and tired.

After the first week of Brooke pushing the food around

her plate at dinner time, her mom asked, "Why aren't you eating?"

Brooke cried. Told her mom about G.O.B. ratings, about Sara, and what Scott said.

"High schoolers can be cruel." Her mom reached a hand across the table to hold Brooke's. "And immature. Your body is beautiful. It's curvy and perfect. You're strong, and you've always been strong."

Her mom's words helped her make peace with her body over the next handful of years.

Then she met Ian.

She was fresh out of college, and he was gorgeous. Huge, bulky, like Scott, but also nothing like Scott. Or so she thought. The way Ian looked at her made her feel seen. As if he liked her for who she was and her dress size didn't matter.

Ian had gotten a job as a police officer, his boyhood dream. He wanted them to move in together, so they did. He wanted Brooke gone during the day, so he could sleep off his graveyard shift. So she was. He wanted to get married, so they did.

Soon, comments like, "I'm not sure you need another helping," and "Evening eating isn't good for you" started, and Brooke knew he was no different from Scott. By the time Jessi was born, she'd had it. She wasn't good enough for Ian, but even worse than Scott, Ian wanted her to try to be. That felt like being untrue to herself, and she'd already done so much accommodating for him, so she wouldn't do this. It was too much. She left him and resisted all of his attempts to win her back. Brooke chose herself.

Still, her attraction to big, hot alphaholes was very real. And it was toxic. Why was it that the type she was naturally drawn to turned out to be douchebags?

This was also why Tyson was such a breath of fresh air. He cared for her, and her size didn't matter. She grew to be attracted to him. And she grew an attitude about men like Scott and Ian. If they could be cruel, well, so could she.

CHAPTER 8

After a couple of minutes, Kinsey follows Brooke into the kitchen. "God, why can't you just be, oh, I don't know . . . human?"

"What are you talking about?" Brooke plays dumb. She gets out two round cake pans and the flour container to put on a show for the cameras.

"You might not remember what it was like on your first day here, but I do. It's not Derek's fault he's not Tyson."

Whoa. Way out of line.

"Tyson has nothing to do with this," Brooke says, but the words come out too tight.

"Yeah, sure, okay. This is all about Tyson. Everything with you is somehow about Tyson now. You're so damn depressed. You won't even talk about escaping anymore. The way you treated that poor guy. You were a dick."

"That poor guy," Brooke scoffs. "You mean the ginormous dude who probably hasn't ever been afraid of anyone or anything in his whole life?"

"Everyone's afraid of something," Kinsey says, going

over to her tiny pile of toys, like she just now remembered she needs to pretend to play.

"Some more than others."

"That's not the point!" Kinsey yells, without looking at her. "God, Brooke, we're all in this together. We're all trapped, acting like as long as we play along with Grace's screwed-up game, we'll go home, when the reality is she could kill us any time. Just like Cody. Like Tyson, too. You can't give up."

Kinsey gives a small gasp after the words pour out, like she realizes she's pole-vaulted over the line by mentioning both Tyson and Cody *again*.

Brooke takes a deep breath to stuff the anger down. Keep it at bay. If she speaks right now, she'll regret it.

The silence expands with Kinsey, who seems too scared to say anything else, and Brooke, who's trying to wait for the spark of frustration to pass.

Kinsey is just afraid. We both are.

Suddenly, Brooke wants to scream about how trapped she feels in this cabin. A decade doesn't make it any better. She'll never get used to it, and sometimes it's just overwhelming. She takes it out on her constricting costume by tearing the white apron off and marching toward her bedroom. If Mitch or Grace are watching, they'll think she's changing her suffocating dress. But she can't calm down enough to reach the zipper in the back. Her arms flail behind her like stupid noodles.

Kinsey follows Brooke and waits for her to stop. Without a word, she unzips the dress. Brooke lets her do it, but she hates that she needs the help. God, if Kinsey keeps throwing it in her face that she fell in love with Tyson and lost him, well then, she's going to . . .

She doesn't know what she'll do. Losing her shit would be an option. But her shit was lost a long time ago.

Down to her bra and skirt slip now, Brooke plops onto the made bed.

"Sorry, Brooke. I shouldn't have said—"

"Kins, please," Brooke puts a hand up because she cannot handle sympathy right now. The roller coaster of emotions is too fast, and it's too soon and Kinsey's kindness might turn her wave of anger into tears. "I've been doing this so much longer than you. Please, just leave me alone. If you want to babysit this dude, go for it. Don't rope me in. I'm way beyond caring—"

"—about anyone but yourself," Kinsey interrupts, folding her arms across her chest. They're on the roller coaster again.

Brooke goes into the closet to find a clean dress. The one she took off is clean, but she doesn't want to chance getting caught off script.

Kinsey furrows her brows in confusion, lets out a little "Oh!" and runs back into the living room to get a book. She sits on Brooke's bed and thumbs through it, pretending to read.

It's unfair. It really is. Kinsey doesn't know everything Brooke's been through. She's hardly been here, compared to a decade. But Brooke was the same way when she was new. Still thought she could escape, that she could have a life. She doesn't blame Kinsey, but she won't celebrate that Grace found her a new *husband*.

Right when Brooke is about to say some version of this, that guy stumbles out into the living room.

"S'there anything to eat around here?" he calls.

Brooke races past Kinsey and slams her bedroom door

shut, closing them both inside so Derek doesn't see her half-naked.

Of course, the huge man-bro demands food. He's probably overjoyed to be trapped in a mid-century cage with two women.

Kinsey's face lights up with a beam of hope at his question. *Someone needs me*, it says as clearly as if she'd spoken the words. She's so naive, but Brooke doesn't call it out. Naivety is hope, and hope—in whatever form—is survival, and just because Brooke is so far past all of that, doesn't mean she should tear it from Kinsey.

Brooke pulls the dress on and spins so Kinsey can zip it. Then Kinsey walks out of the bedroom, talking about making the giant a sandwich, and Brooke slams the door behind her a second time. She doesn't want to be out there with them. Last thing she needs is for this guy to set her off again. Yet, she doesn't want to be in her bedroom all day, either.

Brooke reaches for the only book on her nightstand she's allowed downtime with. *The Count of Monte Cristo*. She's read it at least fifteen times. Kinsey makes fun of Brooke for reading it over and over again, instead of just pretending to read, but Brooke has always been this way. Favorite stories are full of friends to visit when you have nobody else.

At least it's a brilliant book.

"What is this place?" Derek's deep voice grumbles at Kinsey. Brooke hears it through the thin walls.

Tyson's voice was always so tender, much more thoughtful, even when he first arrived. Tyson was always thinking about everyone else.

"Told you, Grace Wakeford's cabin," Kinsey says and Brooke smiles to herself at the barely detectable annoyance in

Kinsey's tone. Like she's already irritated at having to repeat things.

Welcome to my life.

Kinsey goes on. "You're a prisoner here now. Pretty soon you'll learn how to act out the part of Albert Hamilton, Grace's father. I'm young Grace, age nine. Brooke in there, she's Helen Hamilton, your wife."

"My what?" His pitch goes higher.

"Your *wife!*" Kinsey raises her voice, as if he didn't hear because of a volume problem. Brooke pulls her lips in so she doesn't laugh. This has taken an entertaining turn.

"Yeah, I heard you, but it doesn't make sense," he says, defensive.

"Nothing here makes sense. You'll get used to it. Basically, you've been kidnapped by this crazy old hag. The three of us have to pretend like we're living a perfect version of her life until the day she got married and moved out. Nonstop. The skeleton in the room? That was Cody. He played Larry, Grace's brother. But Grace's brother died at nine, so his scene ended. Real Grace—that's the old lady—says even though his scene is over, he's still here with us, playing his part. She says he has to stay or it'll create an *anomaly*, which is sort of her word for anything that doesn't seem *authentic*. Like any of this is authentic," Kinsey scoffs. It's a whole torrent of words coming out of her mouth all at once. No way this guy is getting all of it. "Don't bother trying to figure it out. She's your basic psycho. I didn't know Cody, he died years before I came, but Brooke did. She's been here a long time. In fact, the guy you're replacing . . . "

Kinsey's voice goes quieter.

Shit, she's telling him about Tyson.

CHAPTER 9

Derek takes a huge bite of his sandwich when Brooke walks out of the bedroom. Tries to pretend like he and Kinsey weren't just talking about her. She goes into the kitchen and starts pulling out what looks like baking ingredients, setting them next to a big jar that says *Flour*.

"The fuck is this, by the way?" Derek asks, touching the metal thing around his neck.

Kinsey starts in, talking like a tour guide again. "Oh that, well, you see, it's why we can't escape—"

"It's a bomb," Brooke interrupts.

"What?" Derek says.

Brooke stares, like she's waiting for him to catch up.

"This collar . . . is a bomb," Derek repeats, trying to keep the ridicule out of his voice. He figured it was some method for chaining them up, which would be plenty fucked on its own.

"Correct," Brooke says monotone, not offering anything else.

Derek can't help but feel around the metal at his throat

with his fingers, although he does it more carefully now. "What triggers it?"

Brooke doesn't answer. Instead, she looks at Kinsey to take over.

"There's a perimeter outside the cabin and if we cross it—"

"*Kaboom!*" Brooke interrupts again, and there's a glint in her eye like she enjoys this.

"Where's the perimeter?"

"Out there," Brooke says.

"I assumed it was out there, but where?"

"It's buried, so we can't see it, but it's out pretty far, right, Brooke?" Kinsey walks to the window and points. She sort of jumps, smacks her forehead, and picks up these ugly dolls, then goes to the living room chair and gets a newspaper. Hands it to Derek.

"How do you know?" Derek asks Brooke, making a face at the newspaper. The fuck is he supposed to do with this?

"How do you think I know, dumbass?"

Jesus. Why is she being such a bitch? He watches her, trying to figure out what her deal is. What'd he ever do to her?

"The collar shocks us too. There's a remote," Kinsey adds.

"There's a remote?" he says. Why does he keep repeating everything? It's stupid, but his mind is still slower than normal. He's not sure if that's because of all the drugs he's done over the years or because he's in shock.

"Yeah, Grace can zap us. It's not fun, trust me," Kinsey says, then changes her voice so it's brighter. "That's why we pretend. And you need to pretend like you're reading that right now. There's no audio, but they're watching us, and you never know when they might see you going off script. She can zap any time."

Derek looks around until he spots a small camera in the corner of the room. He opens the newspaper and lays it flat on the table.

"Where you from?" Kinsey asks. Cool that she's being nice, but her peppy tone grates his nerves.

"Portland," he says. He doesn't want to chitchat. Has to think of how to get out of here. There's a faint scent of salt air. He sees an open window, but looking outside, it's all trees. Still, these woods have to be close to the coast. Close enough to get that ocean smell. But why is there a window open if they're being held captive here?

"Yeah, we're from Portland too," Kinsey says, unimpressed. "Everyone who comes through here is from Portland. It's Mitch's go-to hunting ground. What *part* of Portland? What do you do? Or what *did* you do?"

Derek ignores her questions and makes his way to the window. It's only cracked about three inches, and it's the kind with an opener like on an old car. You have to crank it to get it to work, then it lifts instead of sliding over. This is as far as it goes, but he could bust it open all the way, no problem.

"Yep, the window opens," Brooke snarls, measuring something and pouring it into a bowl. "So does the door. That's not the issue. Crossing the perimeter is the issue."

So they can technically leave the cabin, but not cross the perimeter. That's weird, but he's not going to complain. He can work with it.

"Had to check," he says. "How am I supposed to know what you've tried? Or what your skill sets are."

"Well, I can tell you for sure, both of our *skill sets* include trying to find a fucking way out of here, and there isn't one.

And since you won't tell us about yourself, I guess I'll take a stab at it," she says, waltzing over to the old-style refrigerator and pulling on the handle. "Drug dealer who got high on his own supply and ended up homeless."

"You're two for three," he mumbles, opening the front door. There's a distinct humming noise in the distance. Sounds electrical. He stands in the doorway, but he's not ready to go out there. Needs more information first.

"Drug dealer who got high on his own supply and crossed the wrong person," Kinsey says, making those ugly dolls dance on the table. Derek can't tell if she's stupid or just young. Sometimes they're the same thing.

"Colder. One out of three," Derek says, closing the door.

"Okay, we know he's an addict, so that has to be the thing we got right," Kinsey says.

"I'm done guessing." Brooke waves a hand. "You're an addict from Portland, and if you don't want to share any more details, fine." She breaks an egg into the bowl.

"Addict who became homeless . . . or maybe a drug dealer who got addicted, although I think he was homeless by the looks of him. And the smell," Kinsey says and glances at Brooke. "Two for three the first time, remember?"

Derek turns and gives them a look, and Brooke smiles out of nowhere, shakes her head in unbelief.

Fucking hell, she's got a knockout smile. Too bad she doesn't put it to use more often. He goes back to wandering around the room, looking at everything.

"A cop," she says. "You used to be a cop. I can't believe I didn't think of it first."

For a split second, Derek considers denying it, but what's the point? He puts his hands up in fake surrender. "You got me. What gave it away?"

"A cop!" Kinsey shrieks, and claps her hands. "Oh God, Brooke, how lucky. He'll be able to help us escape for sure, right?"

Brooke ignores her, squints her eyes at Derek. "My ex-husband was a cop. I can always spot them, swinging around what they think is a big dick. What I can't figure out though is why would Mitch grab a cop? I already thought it was insane that he tried for someone as big as you. There are so many little men to grab instead, and Grace just needs a warm body to play the role. No likeness necessary."

"Why do you say that?"

"I've seen pictures of the real Hamiltons. Helen, my character, was a redhead, blue eyes. Kinsey is twenty-three, playing a nine-year-old. Cody was actually thirteen when Real Grace decided he had to die 'at age nine.' Appearance, age, doesn't seem to matter to the bitch. We're all just placeholders for her to toy with. You must have been extremely strung out for old Mitch to get the jump on you. A sack of potatoes begging to be stolen."

Derek pretends not to hear.

"So did you lose your job because of the drugs? Or did you get into drugs because of the job?" Kinsey asks. "In the shows, it's usually one or the other."

Derek clenches his jaw. "Those shows are always wrong."

And the real reason is much worse. No way he's telling either of them the truth.

CHAPTER 10

"How are you two not freaking out about all of this?" Derek asks, sinking into an armchair with wooden legs. He needs to change the subject, although what to? The claustrophobia of his situation creeps in fast.

Brooke groans and rolls her eyes. She stares at Kinsey, as if mentally willing the girl to explain things to the new bozo in town. A wave of anger hits his belly, but he can't let it out. Losing control of his temper always makes things worse. Always.

"We've already freaked out," Kinsey says. "I still do sometimes because I've only been here a few months. I try not to think too much about our situation. But Brooke—"

"I've been here a long time," Brooke interrupts again. Interrupting seems like her thing. That, rolling her eyes, and being condescending.

"How long?"

"Ten years."

"You've been here, in this place, wearing that collar for ten *years*?"

This reality settles in, stirs the fury already building inside of Derek. The sobriety they've forced him into. The guilt from his past, the fear, now mixed with this trapped feeling. There's no fucking way he can stay here for days, let alone years. He won't.

When Brooke gives him that stuck-up look instead of answering a simple question, Derek snaps. Knocks over the chair he was sitting in and storms around the room again. He has to get out of here. He opens the front door and looks out, even though he already did that. But here comes the tightening in his chest, his breathing hitches, and it's like he can't get a deep breath at all. *You're freaking the fuck out. Don't do that*, he thinks, but his body is already well on its way.

Kinsey backs up from him, but Brooke holds her ground and stares, unruffled.

That's different, something in the back of his mind flags. People typically have Kinsey's reaction and get out of his way when he's like this. Ex-wife number one called it his *Hulk dance*. Rage floods his veins and now he can't stop what happens next.

He goes into the kitchen, throws open cabinets and drawers. There's nothing useful. No knives, nothing sharp at all. Everything is plastic, flimsy. He stomps into the room with the dead boy and the high window. He moves a nightstand over to it and climbs on top. Has to see what's behind the cabin, but the window won't open and the nightstand breaks, sending him to the floor. He kicks the broken wood, picks up the top of the nightstand and throws it at the window. It bounces off. Polycarbonate windows. Must be. He strides toward the next room, but Brooke blocks him, bracing herself in the doorway.

"Hell no. You're not going in there," she yells.

"You gonna keep me out?" Derek chests up to her and her eye-level is only at his sternum.

"Back off," she hisses, holding her ground and craning her neck up to glare at him.

Interesting, the little voice in his mind says, *she's not afraid of you.* But it's the same voice that tries to get him to calm down, and it's so far past the point of having any say right now.

He shoves her aside, his elbow gashing something that feels like punching a face, and he registers a crash behind him, but he doesn't bother to look. Instead, he enters the room, but after a few seconds, Brooke's at his back, hitting, slapping, yelling at him to get out.

Derek ignores it. She can do her worst and it still won't compare to any number of light beatings he's had in his life. He pulls out the nightstand drawer and finds a few rocks, some dried flowers. This must be Brooke's room, and he should stop, respect her privacy, but he can't. He's not in control anymore. He picks up a fat book lying on the bed. *The Count of Monte Cristo.*

Whoa, talk about irony.

He throws it across the room, and it hits the far wall with a crash. There has to be something around here that will help him escape.

Be more rational, slow down, his mind signals uselessly.

He pulls the white crocheted bedding off, turns the mattress over. Brooke has given up fighting him and he's alone in the room now.

You're acting crazy. Stop!

But he can't. The horror of the situation drives him.

Her closet is full of folded dresses on shelves. June Cleaver shit, and not a wire hanger in sight. Nothing useful. He finds other clothes too. Men's clothes. Overalls, polyester pants, shirts. Wouldn't fit him, stuff's way too small.

He eyes something else on top of the last pile of men's things.

A small box, flimsy, like it's made of paper. His hands shake, and he all but crushes the delicate box. Inside is a piece of what looks like hardware—a hex bolt. Finally he listens to the voice telling him to calm down and he sweats, trying to catch his breath as he fingers the bolt. Too small for him, but it's definitely a ring. A hex bolt filed down on the inside so it's round.

It's special to someone—probably Brooke based on the size—but that's a half-baked thought compared to the other, more pressing one. Whatever filed this down, that's the weapon he needs to find.

He moves back into the kitchen with the ring in his clenched fist, but startles at the sight of Brooke corralling Kinsey behind her with one arm. Her eyes are full of fury, and she bares her teeth. She looks feral. Her lip is swollen and nose bleeding, stray red drops on the bosom of her blue dress.

Shit. He did that to her. He panicked, let his temper go, and he hurt her.

Brooke's other hand is holding—a screwdriver? No. Unbelievable. It's the metal file. She grips it by the handle, aiming the tip at Derek.

"Whoa, there," he says, putting the ring into his pocket before Brooke notices it. He raises his hands in surrender, stepping toward her.

"Get back, motherfucker!" Brooke shouts.

Derek stares her down. "We're on the same team here." He takes another step.

"Stay right there."

"What if they see your weapon?" He nods up at the camera.

"What if they can't see because my backside is in the way?" She stabs it at him like it's a little dagger. "I told you not to go in my room."

"What's the big deal?" He takes another step. Has to show her he doesn't mean her any harm.

"Get back! You might take me down, but I swear to God I'll fuck you up in the process. The perimeter isn't the only thing that can set off that bomb around your neck, asshole."

What the hell does that mean? Now's not the time to ask. Still, he stops approaching her. "Where'd you get that file?"

"Sit down."

Derek's face twitches, but he moves to the chair she's pointing at and sits anyway. He doesn't want to fight them, didn't want to hurt her. He just got a little carried away is all.

"Kinsey." Brooke barks her name like an order.

Kinsey grabs a blanket, as if she's acting out a plan they already made. It's a green-and-white, half-unraveled afghan. She approaches Derek on tiptoe, her face scrunched with an apology.

"Hands behind your back," Brooke commands, stepping closer to him with the file.

The truth is that even that tool wouldn't do much to slow him down if he wanted to take her out. But he doesn't, so he obeys.

Kinsey gets busy unraveling yarn, wrapping it around and around Derek's wrists at the back of the metal chair. He's surprised at how strong a shit ton of yarn can be.

"This isn't necessary," Derek says.

"Look at my face." Brooke points at her swollen lip, blood crusted around her nostril. "It's absolutely necessary."

Derek sighs. He screwed that up royally.

That's when Kinsey yells, "Brooke, his collar!"

CHAPTER 11

Shit.

A single yellow blinking dot on Derek's collar makes Brooke's stomach lurch. They have to get him to the charger and show him how to plug in.

"Five minutes," Kinsey breathes.

"Quick, get the yarn off!" Brooke says, then she looks around and shoves the metal file under the couch so the camera doesn't see.

"Five minutes until what?" Derek asks.

"Until your collar goes off."

"What the . . . ?"

"We have to charge our own collars or it activates a kill switch," Kinsey adds, tugging and pulling at his bound wrists.

Derek doesn't reply and his eyes sort of wander back and forth. Brooke gets it. Takes a minute to wrap your brain around the fact that you have to keep yourself alive by making sure you stay a prisoner. It's an infuriating mind fuck. Still, he better move those mental gears faster.

She joins Kinsey, trying to loosen the yarn.

"Jesus, that hurts!" Derek says.

"Not as bad as it'll hurt if we don't get you plugged in."

"Plugged into what?"

Brooke shakes her head and starts helping Kinsey. They don't have time to waste explaining the entire thing.

"You sure did a bang-up job on this yarn," Brooke says to Kinsey, both of them stabbing and pulling at different strings trying to find a loose or thin one.

A second yellow light blinks on.

"Three minutes," Kinsey says.

"Fuck, fuck, fuck!" Brooke curses under her breath.

Derek pulls so hard his hands become a shade of purple.

Kinsey runs to the kitchen, grabs a handful of plastic knives, hands one to Brooke. It's a lame idea, but they have no other options.

Brooke saws an entire piece of yarn with no luck, but Kinsey parses out one micro thread within a strand and cuts it.

Brooke mimics her.

The third yellow light comes alive on Derek's collar and the yarn is almost loose enough for him to pull free.

"Sixty seconds," Kinsey yells.

"Listen to every word I'm about to say, Derek," Brooke speaks in monotone as she saws. She has to channel any calmness available. They might only get one shot at this.

"Do you see that U-shaped device on the wall across from us?"

"Yes."

"That's a charger. It attaches to the collar at the back of your neck. We'll plug you in. All you have to do is stand and move over there and then spin so you're in position. Don't try to help us. You'll get in the way."

"Understood."

The last few threads snap and Derek breaks free. He's at

the charger in a few huge steps, and Brooke and Kinsey line it up with his collar. Snap him in.

The yellow lights disappear, replaced by green lights.

Charging.

Brooke and Kinsey both release body-collapsing sighs, and Brooke's insides thump with adrenaline. She looks up at the camera.

"Kinsey, back to the script."

It's a miracle they didn't get a shock to the collar for any of what just went down.

I wonder if that means they're on their way here.

Kinsey nods and sits on the ground with her toys.

Brooke goes back into the kitchen and to making a cake.

"What just happened?" Derek asks, his face paler than it was before.

Brooke looks at Kinsey, silently designating her to explain the collar situation to him, so she does.

"You've got to be shitting me," Derek says, after Kinsey gives him more details.

Brooke is too tired for this, and doesn't answer. Kinsey doesn't either. It's already been an exhausting day.

"How long do I have to stand here?"

"Not long," Kinsey says.

"How often do we have to do this?"

"Kinsey and I are on a schedule so we charge one after the other, as soon as the camera goes off for the night," Brooke says. "We aren't supposed to charge up while the cameras are on."

"Why?"

"Grace doesn't want to watch us do it. It creates an anomaly in her little world."

"How long does the battery last?"

"Not sure. We charge every day just in case."

Brooke's hands shake from the adrenaline comedown. It's hard to sift the powdered sugar, and she'll have a mess to clean up. Something to do, at least.

Wheels crunch gravel outside. They're here.

CHAPTER 12

"Kinsey! Get in the room!" Brooke shout-whispers.

Kinsey scrambles away.

Mitch opens the door, but doesn't greet Brooke, doesn't even run his eyes over her like usual. Instead, he watches Derek and there's a sly little smile in the corner of his mouth.

Derek gives him a hard glare back but says nothing.

Mitch has a rolling suitcase, and he walks past them in silence, pulling it into Brooke's bedroom behind him. Sounds like he's straightening up the room, and she wants to protest to keep everyone out of there until she finds the ring. But she's silent, keeps following the recipe in her mind for chocolate cake. The one she's made every week for ten years.

Grace walks into the cabin and looks around. "Where's young Grace?"

"She's in the bedroom."

Like always, dumbass.

"I don't want anyone in character right now," Grace says. "Get her out here. I have an announcement."

What the hell? This has never happened before. Brooke's heart beats out of control as she retrieves Kinsey.

Grace looks at Derek and his collar, flinches away, like she wasn't supposed to see that.

"Why didn't you time it so this was taken care of before I got here?" she shouts across the cabin to Mitch, but points at Derek.

"I'm sure Helen will get him on schedule after this," he shouts back.

"She better," Grace mutters, looking at Brooke as she reappears with Kinsey.

"What happened to your face?" she asks, fingering the handle of her hunting knife, which she wears on a belt around her waist.

Brooke doesn't respond to the question. Instead she inhales, staring at the knife, and in her mind's eye, all she can see is blood on the blade, remembering how little Cody's life drained from his neck with every second that passed. The way Grace wiped the blade using a kitchen rag, lamenting at the spatter on Cody's clothes and how she didn't want to "spoil the costumes any more than necessary." Tutting about how they don't make clothes like this anymore. Sweet Cody's face, the light going out. How Brooke couldn't comfort him as he went, for fear that Grace's dead eyes would fixate on her next. They would have, if she'd so much as moved. She swears to God they would have.

Brooke breathes fast. Too fast. She wants to disappear, just needs a few minutes to compose herself. She won't be able to while the old lady is here, so she takes a deep inhale and pulls herself together to answer Grace. "I tripped on the porch step."

"Clean yourself up when I leave."

Brooke nods.

"Glad to see you sober," Grace says to Derek. "The next

time we meet, it'll be in character. I like you, much closer to Albert's stature, but more muscular." Grace walks up to him, still attached to the charger and unable to get away. She pats his shoulder and smiles. It sends a shiver up Brooke's body. He holds the old woman's gaze, but the second Grace turns her back, he darts his eyes to Brooke, and there's a question there. A request for an explanation, but Brooke wants to be alone. Make sure her ring from Tyson is fine after they've raided her room twice in an hour. But Mitch is still in there. What's he doing?

"Now for my announcement," Grace says.

Brooke's adrenaline spikes again. What's happening? Grace never has them out here together. Especially not young Grace.

"I'd like to announce the engagement of our Grace Hamilton to Gerald Wakeford. The wedding will be soon, much sooner than her parents want it to be. They're so sad to see their little girl grow up." She gives Brooke and Derek each a knowing smile, as if they really are Grace's parents.

Nobody responds.

There must be something in this information to grab hold of in order to make sense out of it.

Then, as if she suspects nobody understands, Grace continues. "Sunday is my fifty-fourth wedding anniversary. Young Grace will marry and leave the cabin for good."

It's a new scene.

New scene, new rules.

Leave the cabin for good.

Kinsey.

Brooke stifles a gasp. Nobody has ever left alive. But then again, maybe getting married doesn't mean getting murdered.

Brooke glances at Kinsey, and the fear she reads in the girl's expression makes her heart clench.

"Excuse me, Grace." Brooke puts on her most polite voice. "Where will young Grace go after she's married?"

Kinsey chews her lip, closes her eyes. She doesn't want to hear the answer to this, but they must know for sure.

Grace scoffs. "She'll move into Gerald's home and they'll start their life together."

So it must be the start of a new role for Kinsey. Maybe just in a different location.

"And Gerald lives there by himself right now? Just waiting for the wedding day?" Brooke pushes. She knows the real Grace moved out of the cabin on her wedding day, and obviously she's lived in other places since. Maybe Kinsey will move and continue to play Grace somewhere else. An older version of Grace. It's a wild hope, but Brooke clings to it.

"Of course not," Grace retorts. "That would create an anomaly. All scenes must be running at the same time."

What the hell does that mean?

"So, there's already someone playing Grace at Gerald's house?" Brooke feels the question out as she asks it.

"Clearly."

No. No, this is bad.

This means there's another location where prisoners are acting out parts of Grace's life. Maybe there has been this whole time.

Brooke gets an idea and gentles her voice to ask, "How can Grace be here and at another house? Doesn't that create an anomaly? Two Graces living out different eras of your life simultaneously? There can only be one Grace, right?"

The woman tightens her lips and Brooke stares at the small remote hanging from a chain around her neck. She went too far. Grace is going to lose it. But instead, she says, "Not if they're in different places. That's the design. The way it must be. Both houses acting out Grace's life continually until the final scene."

"What will happen to Kinsey?" Derek interjects. Brooke stiffens, waiting for Grace's reaction. His tone is too bold, too harsh. Plus, they never use their real names. Grace hates that. Brooke does her best not to glance at Derek or Kinsey, as if by doing so she can make herself invisible.

Grace saunters up to Derek again, looks him up and down. "Here's your warning: We don't use any names here other than the ones I give you." Grace presses a knobby hand covered in liver spots and jewels against Derek's chest. "But to answer your question, her scene will be over."

Kinsey gasps, stifles a sob, and Grace flashes a look at her. Slitted eyes, pursed lips. "Young Grace should be over-joyed at the news of her wedding. She's been in love with Gerald for years."

Brooke widens her eyes at Kinsey and shakes her head, telling her to stop it. But this is crazy. Grace said Kinsey's scene would end—that she's going to die—and now she expects excitement from the girl?

"Excuse me, but young Grace is only a child, and as her father, I must object," Derek blurts.

Impressive. Even if he's being way too blunt.

"We're not in character right now," Grace corrects him with irritation.

"Fine. Still, how can the girl get married when she's just a kid? Were you a kid?"

There's a bold challenge in his tone. Maybe Derek won't be such a burden after all.

Derek's body spasms and his limbs jerk while his neck stays stationary.

Brooke's eyes cut to the remote, which Grace holds and points at him. She hadn't even seen her go for it.

When it's over, Derek blinks, processing the volts his body just took. Hardly anything compared to what Brooke has seen before. Still, she can't help but feel for him. It hurts so damn bad.

And she's never seen someone take a hit while they're charging. She'd always wondered what would happen. Would the kill switch activate? But it didn't. Derek just got shocked like normal. Perhaps a touch of whiplash.

"You got your verbal warning," Grace says. "And that there? That was your real warning. I require respect and don't stand for backtalk."

"I'm so . . . sorry." Derek fumbles the words like he's trying to come back to reality.

Mitch walks into the living room after having been in Brooke's room the whole time. Did he find her ring? She wants to ask, but she's too scared.

"We have to improvise sometimes. That's the answer to your question," Grace says. "I'm coming back tomorrow and I want you in this." She reaches for a clothing bag draped over Mitch's arm. Hands it in Derek's direction. He stretches out a shaky hand. "The clothes in that closet should fit you now. Mitch has replaced them."

Derek doesn't respond. He doesn't make eye contact with her either.

They leave the cabin, but Brooke keeps standing there. She's drained, entertaining a single thought as it bangs against her mind.

Kinsey dies in six days.

CHAPTER 13

Derek's body tingles, pins and needles everywhere. His brain feels like mush again, right when it was getting normal after coming out of withdrawals.

Once they're gone, he squeezes his eyes shut and then flares them wide, trying to get the blur out of the corners of his vision. He rubs his hands together, fingers zinging like crazy. What he wouldn't give to be out of this contraption so he could move around. Or sit. Anything to walk out the soreness from that shock.

Derek slicks a hand up his forehead, only now realizing how drenched in sweat he is. They're right. He stinks. Kinsey sobs on the vinyl couch, and Brooke wraps arms around her, repeating phrases like "It's going to be okay," and "We'll find a way out."

"Who is that guy?" he asks.

The charger at his neck clicks and releases him. Must be done.

"What?" Brooke says, irritated.

Derek approaches her so she can hear better. He wants to get a sense of that guy who was staring at him with a look that'd be a fighting look anywhere else. Needs to know what he's dealing with.

Brooke springs up and yells, "Get back!"

He steps backward with his hands up and sits in the chair they had him tied to. Jesus, he wasn't going to attack her.

"That man . . ." Derek tries to find some patience, speak in a less threatening way. Whatever he needs to do to get information from these two. "What do you know about him?"

"Are you talking about Mitch?" Brooke asks. She's so snappy.

"Yeah, the only other man around here. How long have you known him?"

"He grabbed me off the streets of Portland ten years ago. Grabbed you too."

"Is he from Portland?"

"Hell if I know. It's not like we had tea and biscotti and shared our life stories."

Derek clenches his teeth and takes a moment to push down any anger that might find its way into his voice. Thinks of another question.

"You must know something about him."

"He doesn't talk much. I know that."

For fuck's sake. How in God's name is he going to survive this woman? Let alone the psychopaths?

Kinsey sits up and clears her throat. "Mitch is in love with Brooke."

"What?" Brooke snaps, as if this is news to her.

"How do you know?" Derek asks.

"Well, all right, I don't know about love, but Mitch wants to sleep with Brooke for sure. He's attracted to her. I know the way a guy looks at you when he wants you. It's how he looks at her. Always has. So that's something we know about Mitch."

"Disgusting. Why are you telling him this?" Brooke says.

"I don't know. Maybe the cop can help us. I'm a little more motivated to escape now than I was before today." Then she whispers, "Willing to deal with you being mad at me."

The idea that Mitch is interested in Brooke is something they could use in the future, but Derek needs to think about that longer.

"Okay, anything else about the guy? Why is he helping Grace?"

"She's loaded and pays him well. Probably has something on him too," Brooke says.

"Okay. How do you know for sure that there's actually a perimeter? Has anyone ever tripped it?"

"Now's not the time," Brooke says in a harsh whisper, looking over the top of Kinsey's head as she cradles her, making a face that says he should be sensitive because of the news about Kinsey dying. Derek wants to punch walls. This woman won't talk about anything at all, no matter the topic.

"Actually, now is the perfect time," he says. "We have six days to find a way out."

Kinsey moans and goes back to crying, but her eyes stay on Derek, and he senses a new resilience there. Sometimes people can rise to the occasion.

"What the hell is wrong with you?" Brooke yells.

"I could ask you the same question. What's your play? Tell Kinsey that it's all going to be fine while you sit on the couch and hold her for six days?"

"There's no way out. I've told you that."

Kinsey pulls away from Brooke and walks into her

bedroom, shuts the door like a kid leaving the parents to fight. Perfect. No more dancing around her feelings, thank God.

"Yeah, you told me. But you'll forgive me if I don't take your word for it. Can't be that hard to get out of here. They didn't even lock us in. They could be lying about the perimeter."

Brooke puts her hands in her lap. Her energy goes from hot and feisty to completely deflated. "They're not."

"And you know that because . . ."

When she looks up, there's fire behind her eyes. Pure strength. Something about it catches Derek off guard. "Because the previous Albert Hamilton tripped it."

"How? What happened?"

She shakes her head. "God, you're a real piece of work."

But Derek isn't fucking around. Not anymore. He stands and steps toward her, hands out, like approaching a wild animal. "I just want to figure this out," he says, but as he gets closer, all he can see is her swollen lip and dried blood, which she still hasn't had time to clean. He turns for the kitchen, wets a clean washcloth lying across the perfectly scrubbed sink, and sits down nearby in the upholstered chair with wooden legs. He hands the warm washcloth to her. She hesitates, like she's considering refusing it, but takes it.

"I'd offer to patch you up, but I think you'd shoot me down."

"Damn right I would."

"Tell me more. If I know where it happened, it'll give us an idea of how much leeway we have outside."

"Fine. The perimeter is just in front of the driveway, past all the weeds. Out back, it's about the same distance. A big circle." Brooke speaks in monotone.

"It was Tyson, right? The one who tripped it?" Kinsey had

started telling him about the man, but she never got the whole story out. Still, enough to know that Brooke was close to the previous Albert. The hex bolt ring confirmed just how close.

Brooke glares at him, but Derek can see how her eyes glisten with tears. The venom returns to her voice. "You can't save Kinsey. Just like I couldn't save any of the others." She stares out toward the kitchen.

"I'm not letting that girl die."

"Good luck with that," Brooke scoffs.

"So that's it? You're just giving up?" Derek stands. A bloom of anger sparks in his belly and he clenches his fists at his sides.

Brooke looks at his hands and stands too. She comes right at him, shoves his chest, and it's so out of nowhere that it catches him on his back foot. He falls into the chair again, seat planted. She braces her hands on the wooden arms of the chair and leans down, gets in his face. She's only inches away. She smells like vanilla and citrus.

"Don't talk to me about giving up," she hisses. "Homeless, because you couldn't hack it with life? Probably some cliché, like maybe you couldn't solve a case. And since you were always the one dealing out the blows to everyone else, never taking them yourself, you tucked your tail and ran. All the while, I was here and you, *the police*, should have been looking for me, but instead, you were doing dope on the streets! You wanna talk about survival? I'm a survivor. You're a quitter."

Brooke turns and slams the bedroom door behind her before Derek can say anything. His anger dissipates. It surprises him how quickly, given the way she challenged him. Normally, it'd take less than that to set him off. Not this time.

Not this time, because she's right.

CHAPTER 14

After practically pummeling the keypad with her fingers, Mina finally gets the contraption on her Oregon Coast vacation rental to open. It's one of those non-electronic ones. Buttons like skinny little spikes, and a weird lever you have to squeeze and pull at the same time to expose the hanging key. It seems like unnecessary drama when they could replace it with one of those electronic keypads that only requires a code. Honestly, though, Mina's glad this place was affordable and available during high season even though she booked so late. She has so much work to do.

Mina hasn't been back here in years. But Freeport is still her favorite coastal town, and it's grown. Her family used to come here for their summer vacation every year, back when it was much smaller, less touristy. It's only about an hour from Corvallis, where Mina grew up. Now, she and her husband, Brady, live in Seattle.

But when she was a kid, Freeport was a cheap vacation spot for her low-income family.

Standing on the small porch, a rush of familiar saltwater

scent mixed with fish hits her nose. Then comes that feeling—desperately needing to get down to the beach first thing upon arrival, ripping Salt Water Sandals off in order to chase gray waves barefoot, no matter how cold the water is. She doesn't wear Salt Water Sandals anymore, but the pressure to get down to the beach is alive and well despite the decades that have passed.

Mina ignores it and tugs her suitcase into the vacation rental. A small two bed, one bath home. It's cute, but not updated. The pictures on the website were very generous, doing it more justice than it deserves. The place is a little tract rambler, looks post-World War II. Like the couple others on this street. The front door opens to a living room and a small dining table, along with a galley-style kitchen. The back windows face the ocean and the view is extraordinary. It's not directly on the beach, but the place is high enough that she can see the water over the rooftops of properties with a better view. Mina unlocks the sliding glass door that leads to a small spit of deck and makes her way out to the lone, faded-wood gray Adirondack chair. Now she questions if she wants rosé on the deck first or if she wants to stick to her original plan: feet in the sand.

She goes with rosé. Might as well take advantage of the moment since it's not raining out. She doesn't mind walking on the beach in the rain, but sitting on the deck? No way. Rain could start up at any moment, although it's supposed to be pretty warm during the month she's spending here in this little rental. Still, a storm or two will find its way into the forecast at some point. It always does. August has been nicer than usual on the coast the past couple of years. Mina blames climate change for that, but still, she'll put on sunglasses and soak it in.

Just as she relaxes into the chair, the sky produces a massive, low cover of clouds out at sea. Mina lifts her sunglasses to examine. It's a blockade of incoming storms, covering the sun by inches and transforming the blue water into a shade of charcoal.

She takes a big sip of wine. She'll sit here until either the wind or rain forces her inside. But it's hard to ignore her freshly written book pushing up against her mind. *Hello, it's your crime novel calling. My revisions are the reason you're here, remember?*

Mina chuckles to herself and imagines for a minute that her novel actually could speak. Truth is, she wouldn't want to hear its opinions.

Her phone dings with a text message.

Arrive okay? It's from Brady.

He's being sweet, but part of the reason Mina came here was to get some time away. From everything. Even him, and even over text.

Yep, drinking wine on the patio and ogling the sea.

Lol. Well, it's a good start. You need to relax more than you need to edit that book.

Incorrect, Mina thinks, but doesn't type. She can't truly relax until the book is done, and anyway, Brady always thinks she's "overdoing it" when she's just living her life. He also thinks Mina drinks too much, but a couple glasses a day doesn't make her an alcoholic. In fact, it's a shock that he hasn't fired back a comment about the wine yet.

I know what I'm doing, but thanks, she types.

Well, I'll be here when you get back.

God, I know, she thinks, but doesn't type. Instead, she gives him the laughing emoji and sets the phone down next to her on the chair. It's not that she wants him gone, or that she doesn't love him. It's not that simple. If it were that simple, they'd divorce. A nice, clean break. They've been through so much that should have driven them apart. Statistically, they should be long over. If they were going to divorce though, it would have been when they lost Paxton, or during the months that followed, where they saw how differently they handled grief. Brady wanted to move through the pain, maybe try for more children, but Mina refused. No way she was ever going to bring another beautiful, innocent baby into this hellish world. She took her pain out on him even though he was as much a victim to loss as she was.

That feels like something one of their many therapists would say.

Mina and Brady brushed up against divorce again when she cheated on him five years ago. Another wound to their marriage, now scabbed over. Instead, here they are, stuck in some deranged angle of repose, unable to change the past but unable to move forward, either.

Now they're more like roommates. No kisses, no snuggles, definitely no sex. When her friends ask why they're still together, she says they're too lazy to get a divorce, but also too set in their ways to reimagine life and start over with someone else. The truth, however unspoken, is that they love each other. It's just that things are different now. They don't talk about this, even though Brady wants to. He tries hard to revive the relationship, but Mina's focus is on building out her career as a novelist after leaving the corporate grind where she slaved away for so many years.

The first rain drops patter on the deck and Mina takes her phone and wine inside. She tosses back what's left in the glass and pours another. It's about dinner time, and she has a whole box of Wheat Thins and enough energy to start working, but she stands there, looking out the front window at the rain coming down, graying the entire street.

She works so much better in the mornings. Maybe she should call it a night and get trashed, but then she'd be proving Brady right, even if he never finds out.

Across the street, the neighbor is getting what looks like a grocery delivery by the way the overweight, middle-aged man snaps a photo of a group of white plastic bags on the doorstep. Then he returns to his blue Toyota Tercel, and leaves.

Nothing about it seems out of the ordinary. Perhaps it's curiosity about the neighbors, perhaps the wine is already slowing her down, but she stares. Nobody comes out to bring in the bags. Is there any milk in there? Any frozen foods that need to be put away?

What Brady calls Mina's "second-hand anxiety" lays delicate fingers on her heart. God, is anyone going to bring those groceries in? *It's not yours to worry about*, Brady would say, and he'd be right. But still, those bags, sitting on the porch—it's like fingernails on a chalkboard.

Mina goes into the kitchen to pour another glass of wine, thinking she should slow down if she wants to work tonight. Writing while sloshed is fine. Interesting, and even productive at times. But she's not writing anymore. She's revising, and it's just plain moronic to edit while drinking. She'll make the story worse and have to undo all the damage when she's sober.

Who is she kidding, anyway? She's not getting anything done tonight, but she could at least get her laptop out, so it's ready in the morning. Feels like a step in the right direction. She looks around and realizes it's still in the car. Her little

SUV is visible out the front window, even though it's dripping wet. Mina imagines it trying to be brave against a downpour of rain.

Those white bags are still on the porch.

Mina considers going over there and letting them know, but that would be overkill and she's much too lazy to do anything about it but bitch to herself. She chuckles, thinking about how delectable that statement would be to Brady's ear. The admission of her own lazy neurosis.

A silver Jeep Cherokee pulls up to the house, and an older man ducks and runs to the front door, as if he can somehow dodge the rain.

He picks up a few of the bags, unlocks the door with a free hand, and goes inside. He leans out for the other bags, bringing them in too.

Grocery delivery beat him home. That's all it was.

Now it's Mina's turn to dodge the rain in order to retrieve her laptop from the car, and she does it while holding her blue Patagonia jacket over her head like a makeshift umbrella.

With her whole upper body inside the SUV, the back of her black leggings get wetter by the second. Mina reaches across the driver's seat for the laptop bag, which rode shotgun from Seattle. By the time she tucks it underarm and resituates the coat over her head with one hand, the man has come out of the house and he's already leaving again. Then a curtain peels away from the corner of one of the hallway bedrooms and a little girl's face peers out. Her eyes find the Jeep, and then land on Mina. Her hair is parted down the middle, short, and she wears no expression. But there's a lost look in her eyes that rips at Mina's heart with surprising strength.

And something else too. The girl wears cherry-red

lipstick. Mina squints through the rain to see better. Maybe her lips are just chapped, but no. That's a red lip.

The girl lifts a hand as if to wave and presses it against the glass, only allowing her fingertips to touch.

Mina doesn't have time to free a hand in order to reciprocate the wave because the girl disappears.

CHAPTER 15

Brooke's ring is gone. Totally gone.

She found the little paper box Tyson made for it, crushed up, but no ring. She can't lose it. That feels like Tyson dying again, which is stupid, but there it is.

It's after seven at night now, and the cameras are off, so Brooke removes her dress and changes into lime-green polyester pants with an elastic waistband and a brown-and-orange striped turtleneck, the closest thing she has to comfy clothes. She doesn't bother wishing for leggings or oversized sweatshirts anymore.

In her closet, the pile of men's clothes looks different. She picks up a button-up shirt and brings it to her face, smells it.

Something breaks inside of her and thick tears materialize for Tyson. She clamps a hand over her mouth so Derek can't hear her from his spot in the living room.

Tyson's scent is gone. Another part of him, dead.

She stumbles to her bed, and sits on the edge. Mitch must have made it up after Derek destroyed it. A warm tear trickles down her swollen, hot lip, and she remembers Derek's assault. Another stupid brawny man, this time kicking the daylights out of her. It was a new low. Usually, they only humiliated or tried to control her. Why does the universe hate her so much? She's been stuck here with a lot of assholes over the past ten years, but this is worse. This asshole triggers her so much, even though she shouldn't assume he's just like Ian.

She should give him a chance.

Ian never hit me.

But Derek didn't hit her on purpose, and it's not his fault that he triggers her. Still, she can't get past how much he reminds her of her ex.

She pounds the mattress with a fist. Pissed at herself, pissed at Grace, at Mitch too, but mostly pissed at Derek.

Can't let him push me around.

She remembers the ring.

That's what she needs to focus on right now, so she wipes her tears and stands to check her appearance in the small mirror in her room. Puffy eyes. Swollen lip. Splotchy face.

Awesome.

Brooke pushes a stray hair away from her forehead, sticks her chin up, and walks out into the living room. Time to face him.

Derek is still in that chair. Elbows on his knees, holding his head in his hands. He looks small and vulnerable, probably due to the pain. The start of an instinct to feel sorry for him creeps in, but no way. He doesn't get her sympathy just because he suddenly seems like a lost little boy sitting there alone in the living room.

"Did you see my ring when you were tossing my bedroom like a madman?" she asks.

He looks up, pushes the hair out of his eyes. "What ring?"

She exhales a huge breath because she's not going into the entire story about the ring with him. "It's a simple question. I had a ring in my room. And now I can't find it. Did you see it when you were in there?"

"No, sorry. Must have been Mitch."

He looks down and rubs his hands as if they're cold and he's trying to warm them up. Probably still zinging from that shock to the collar.

Brooke stands there, watching him.

He scratches his forearm.

Kinsey should get him some Advil. Maybe some Allegra. Antihistamines offer some relief for the itching that happens after a jolt like that. Derek is Kinsey's newbie, after all. But Kinsey is still in her room, and considering the news she just got, Brooke won't bother her with this.

She could just not help him. Let him suffer with the after-effects. They don't last forever, and nobody was around to baby her the first time she got shocked.

What are you? A sociopath? Get over yourself and help the human being.

Brooke goes into the small bathroom and flips open the mirrored medicine cabinet. She grabs two bottles and pours pills into her palm. Two Advil and some Allegra.

She appears in front of Derek again, one hand full of pills, a glass of water in the other.

He looks at her hands, her face.

"You gonna poison me before the old woman gets her shot at homicide?"

Brooke feels her eyebrows shoot up to her hairline. "Are you for real? I'm trying to be nice. These help with the pain."

"I'm fine," he mumbles, looks back down at the floor.

"Pfft, see if I care," she says and sets the pills and water down on the kitchen counter before going back into her room.

CHAPTER 16

The next morning, when Brooke walks into the living room about an hour before the camera comes on, she notices the pills are gone and the water glass is in the sink. Derek sits in that chair still, and Brooke half wonders if he moved out of it at all last night. She imagined he would sleep on the couch. That's where all the Alberts who are not Tyson have slept. Cody's room has no bed.

He's showered and wearing the suit. When he looks up at her, a stray thought cruises into her brain.

Damn, he's gorgeous.

She dismisses it and gives an exaggerated glance at the spot where she set the pills and water last night. He shrugs, but doesn't say thanks. Because of course he doesn't. She starts the coffee and puts on some hot water for instant oatmeal.

Derek comes into the kitchen and Brooke hands him a bowl.

After minutes pass with ear-splitting silence between them, Kinsey walks out of her room mopey, but when she sees Derek, she makes eyes at Brooke behind his back and then fans herself to show that he's hotter than hell, all cleaned up and in a suit. As if it doesn't matter that she's dying in five days, at least there's eye candy.

Brooke rolls her eyes, but feels a stab of guilt for shaming Kinsey when she just came to the same conclusion herself.

Mitch shaved Derek's beard and cut his hair before Derek was conscious. He's got stubble growing now, but his brown hair is short, a little longer on top. Brown eyes and a good mouth. He's exactly Brooke's type. Her toxic type.

Kinsey pours herself a cup of coffee and moves toward the head of the small table, motioning for them to join her. "I have an idea."

Neither of them speak, but Brooke and Derek sit across from each other with their bowls of oatmeal.

"You guys are going to hate it, but it's the only thing I keep coming back to in order to get out of here."

Brooke hardens. What she hates is this process. The bit of hope an escape idea offers, and the eventual disappointment that follows. This was daily life with Tyson.

"Mitch is hot for Brooke, we've established that—"

"—What the hell, Kins?" Brooke interjects. Kinsey puts a hand up to silence her with such force that it surprises Brooke, and she actually complies.

"And Grace is hot for you," Kinsey says to Derek.

"Gross," he grunts, but he doesn't seem surprised.

Brooke noticed the way Grace lit up at the sight of Derek. He must have caught it too. She's never done that with previous Alberts. But then she shocked him, so who knows? There's no figuring that psycho out.

And where is Kinsey going with this, anyway? Brooke takes a bite of oatmeal and doesn't make eye contact with either of them.

"So, I say we have a competition. Like, who can bed the villain first." She smirks. "You two are already vying for Alpha status around here, anyway. My money's on Brooke getting into Mitch's pants first, but the way Grace came on to you yesterday, Derek, I don't know. You might be able to win."

Brooke laughs. Kinsey can't be serious.

"I'm not kidding," Kinsey says. "Get them off and see what you can find out about the perimeter, or about the collars, how to disarm them, anything we can use to blow this joint. People—men *and* women—like to share secrets after sex. Trust me on this."

"*You* bang Mitch then!" Brooke says.

"I would. Easy. Hell, I'd do Grace if it meant saving my own life. Thing is, neither of them want me."

"You'd do that? You'd have sex with a serial killer? Willingly?" Brooke asks.

"Yeah, if I could figure out a way to seduce one of them, screw their brains out in order to literally save my life? Hell yeah. I've done more for less, remember? And besides, do you think she'll keep you guys around forever after I'm gone? Spoiler alert: She won't."

Shit.

Albert and Helen Hamilton died in a house fire after Grace's wedding. Brooke has always felt that as long as young Grace was only nine, she had at least a decade to figure things out.

"She's right," Brooke says to Derek. "Albert and Helen died a year after Grace married."

"That could be tomorrow in this fucked-up time warp," Derek says, then they hear the truck pull up.

Out the window, Mitch appears crossing the yard first, followed by Grace.

"Just put feelers out, both of you. What do you have to lose?" Kinsey says, shoving the newspaper into Derek's hand.

He groans, rubs his forearm as if remembering his introduction to Grace.

By the time Grace walks into the cabin, Kinsey is in the bedroom. Mitch is on his way there too, but his eyes find Brooke's face. He doesn't smile, and she holds eye contact, which she never does, but he looks away. His ears turn red.

Whoa. Maybe Kinsey is right. She gets the heebie-jeebies at the thought of it though. Brooke didn't think her situation could get any worse, but here she is, leaping right into worse. She moves around the kitchen to look busy with Helen Hamilton tasks.

Grace stands in the living room in a pair of tight skinny jeans and a cropped tank top. Her hair is sleek as usual, and damn, she looks good. She's always been pretty and thin, but her energy is next level. She slides right up to Derek and touches the lapel of his suit, as if brushing off a piece of lint. It's like Brooke isn't even in the room.

"My, oh my, you sure clean up well," she says.

Derek makes eye contact with Brooke over the top of Grace's head. Brooke shrugs, nods. Might as well try Kinsey's idea.

Derek's hard-lined face morphs into a soft smile, exposing white teeth, and he reaches for Grace's hand so that his covers hers on his chest. "You look fine yourself, Grace."

Grace pulls her hand away and steps back. "Break character. What are you doing?"

Derek's eyes go wide.

He doesn't realize that she can break the rules and come on to him, but he can't do the same.

"Were we in character?" he asks.

Grace glares at him but doesn't answer.

"I was complimenting your appearance," he says. "Does that create an anomaly?"

Brooke cringes. He's not smooth at all. Nothing sexy about the word "anomaly."

"Albert never came on to his daughter," Grace spits out through clenched teeth.

A rush of fear sharpens Brooke's mind. This feels like free fall and nobody knows what Grace's expectations are. Not even Brooke. No way in hell Derek can keep up with this. She has to bail him out.

CHAPTER 17

Derek is about to argue because he wasn't coming on to her. Not yet at least. He was just trying to play along like he's supposed to. But he doesn't get the chance because Brooke swoops in with that sugary voice aimed at Grace. "Darling, you look so lovely today. It's all right for Dad to notice how pretty his favorite girl is. Are you getting excited for the wedding?"

The fuck. This whole thing is ridiculous, and Derek hates pretending. He's always hated pretending, which is part of why he flunked out of life. No good at playing the stupid games people seem to need in order to function in society.

"So excited!" Grace says, clapping her hands. "I brought over a magazine. Thought we could flip through it and find a dress."

She doesn't have a dress yet? Is that real or pretend? Didn't she already get married like a hundred years ago? Derek can't keep up with all of this, and he's getting a headache, despite the Advil he finally caved in and took in the middle of the night.

"Honey." Brooke looks at Derek now, calling *him* that.

He squints, trying to catch up constantly. She smiles at him. That nice smile. It makes something inside of him light up. And her voice is so kind that for a minute he believes her. "Why don't you go outside and see what flowers you can gather for our little girl's bouquet?" Brooke reaches for Grace, to pull her into a hug.

Derek stands there, wondering why the hell they need flowers right now. They'll just be dead by the time the wedding comes around, anyway.

Leave, Brooke mouths to him over Grace's shoulder. Normal Brooke is back.

"Oh yeah, sure," Derek says. "I'll just go out and look for flowers in this fancy suit I'm wearing."

Brooke's eyes get wider than seems possible. She's mad again. He can't do anything right around here. But he can't hide his annoyance, either.

Grace faces him and says, "Dad, you're right. You should change your clothes first."

"Grace, why don't you go with Dad and help him pick out an outfit?" Brooke says, smiling as sweet as ever.

Derek looks at Brooke, and he can't hide the surprise, but she gives an airy wave and laughs. "You know how awful men are at fashion. Can you do it for me this time, tulip? Go pick out something better for him to wear and I'll get you lemonade to drink while we look through your magazine." Brooke bounces up on her toes, like she's thrilled to be doing this. It's opposite of how she normally is, but Derek can see how she could be a nice person if she tried harder.

Grace smiles and walks into the bedroom, giving Brooke and Derek a split second alone.

"Be sweet." Brooke whispers the order. "Smile, and take off your shirt, but nothing else. Let her approach you."

There's no time to push back because Grace is talking inside the bedroom, probably from the closet where Mitch laid out Derek's new clothes. He removes the suit jacket and starts unbuttoning the shirt on his way to the bedroom. Brooke smiles, nods.

Derek pulls off the long-sleeved shirt when Grace turns around from inside the closet. She's a few feet away from him. He likes to wear an undershirt with a suit like this, but Mitch didn't provide him with one, so he stands there, bare chested. Grace stares at his skin. He swallows hard.

Don't think about how fucked up this is.

"What's your favorite flower . . . darling?" he asks, surprising himself with how real it sounds. Like he sincerely cares.

Grace shuts the door. She actually shuts them inside the bedroom, then turns and smiles.

"I knew you were the right one." She approaches him. "From the first moment I saw you."

"Are we still in character?" he asks. Grace touches his shoulder, but is he still her dad right now? "Wait, the right one for what?"

"The perfect choice for my very last Albert."

The gold chain peeks out around the back of her neck, but the remote is tucked under her shirt.

Derek has never felt fear in the presence of a woman. He could overpower her in one motion, but not if she can shock him to death, or detonate his collar. Maybe he should try to do it, anyway. Take his chances.

Then, as if she reads his mind, Grace takes the remote off and holds it in her hand.

She controls this moment, and all of his moments unless he can get out of here.

Or unless he can somehow win her over. Overpower her another way. Not physically, but emotionally.

God, the task feels impossible. Two ex-wives in his wake are proof of it. He's shit at romance, but this woman definitely wants him and doesn't seem to care about romance. Maybe he can swing it.

When he's about to make the next move, Grace breaks away. "We should go out of character more often." She taps his chin and opens the door.

Brooke stands there with the wedding magazine and a glass of lemonade. She and Derek make quick eye contact. Brooke smiles and nods. She seems genuinely happy with him.

CHAPTER 18

Definitely the right call to get Derek shirtless.

Brooke tries not to notice, but it's impossible. He's got a five-alarm body. Her stomach flips a bit.

Butterflies? What the hell?

He puts his shirt back on right away.

Once Grace and Mitch are gone, Kinsey comes out of the bedroom. There's something different about her. A little harder, or maybe just more serious. Analytical.

"How did it go with Grace?" she asks Derek.

"Fine. Don't we have to pretend like we're doing our roles right now? The camera is on."

"We have a little bit of time once they've just left. Nobody else monitors but them."

"They don't record?"

Brooke shrugs. "If they do, they've never punished us for being off script while they're driving back." Then to Kinsey, "It didn't just go *fine*. I'd say it even went well. Grace was in the bedroom with him, she closed the door, and he came out shirtless."

"I knew it," says Kinsey. "Shirtless! Wow, you're better at this than I thought you would be."

Brooke watches to see if Derek will give her some credit. It was her idea, after all, but he just smiles and takes the compliment for himself.

"This is our way out," Kinsey says. "But you're still in the game, Brooke. Grace seems plenty willing, but she might be harder to crack information out of. Mitch might be more difficult to get into bed because of twisted loyalty to Grace. But maybe he'd be open to betraying her if we can just press on the right spot . . ."

Brooke feels her mouth hanging open, so she closes her lips and tries to act unsurprised. But she's baffled. It's like Kinsey has turned into some escape strategist. She would have made a good lawyer. An excellent lawyer.

"Mitch is a man though," Derek says. "You really think he'll be hard to get into bed? Harder than a *woman*?"

"Wow," Brooke says. "Your sexism knows no bounds."

"What? How much experience do you have trying to get women into bed?"

"How much experience do *you* have?" she claps back. "You were horrible at it. I had to tell you what to do!" Brooke's voice rises, and it looks like Derek's about to shout something back at her, but Kinsey steps between them.

"Enough. Look, Derek, you wanted to know what our skill sets are? Brooke is perfect at following the rules. She's brilliant, quick on her feet, and tough as hell, and she'd probably sacrifice both of us in order to stay alive—"

"No I wouldn't!" Brooke protests. But shame flares up inside to silence her.

"Whatever." Kinsey shrugs. "Me? I'm optimistic. To a

fault. And I'm pretty good at reading people and situations, especially when it comes to sex. Never imagined that would come in handy here, but I taught all the girls how to feel out the dangerous ones, and how to get out of a bad spot. I can tell what people want in bed just by looking at them. You wouldn't believe how much drama that sort of anticipation can avoid."

"Pretty sure that's not a skill set," Brooke whispers.

"It is this week, when my life is on the line."

Brooke already tried being friendly with Mitch before, early on. Not coming on to him, but still, he was nothing but a concrete wall. Would it be different now?

After some time passes in silence, Kinsey speaks again. "Come on, you two, quit clutching pearls. It's just sex. Do you have a better idea?"

"No," Derek says. "Not so far. And Brooke's right. She called me 'the very last Albert' while we were in the bedroom. Could be why everything's different now. Why she's coming here more often, why she's catching you two so off guard from the way things were before. We thought her timetable for ending this whole thing could be sooner than a year. Well, it is."

———

"She said we're dying in six days?" Brooke asks.

"No, she didn't *say* that. But still, she said it, you know?" Derek can read between lines. It was necessary on the job.

"I can't sleep with—my kidnapper," Brooke whispers.

Derek scoffs. "You're a real piece of work. Our lives are on the line, and Mitch is our best shot. I could probably fuck that old lady every day for a week and still get nothing out of her."

"At least you won't die pent up. Might make you more livable around here," Brooke mutters.

Derek kicks the metal garbage can. It happens before he even registers the anger, and trash goes flying across the room.

Not helpful, reel it in, he thinks, but it's too late. "What's your fucking problem?" he shouts in Brooke's face.

Kinsey lowers herself on to the couch, trying to hide that she's cowering, but Brooke stands there, holding her ground like usual, eyeing him with that look. The one that is equal parts exasperating and goddamn attractive.

"Does that usually work?" she asks. There's no emotion in her voice. Only the simplicity of a question. "The whole big guy freaking out and kicking things? Does that get you what you want in life?"

It stuns him. That she's so blunt, but also that she's not afraid to ask it right now in the height of his *tantrum*, as ex number two used to call it. He doesn't have an answer for her. Because no, of course it doesn't work. He rubs the stubble on his chin.

"Well, does it?" she presses him.

He sighs, sits on the chair, which feels like his official spot now. "I was jobless, homeless, and full of dope when Mitch picked me up. I hadn't spoken to anyone I care about in years. So use your best guess."

Kinsey stands. "Great, so we've established that you both have real anger problems. Now, can we focus on the plan?"

"Fine," Brooke says.

"Fine," Derek says.

CHAPTER 19

Mina hasn't made much headway on her book revisions. It was so nice out that she couldn't sit still long enough, so she spent the bulk of the day down at the beach with a chair and a book. Some rosé in a Hydro Flask mug. Now it's late, but since there's still daylight, it's time to work. She hasn't even been sitting at the kitchen table for fifteen minutes when something catches her eye.

White bags on the porch across the street.

Again?

She puts on sunglasses and Adidas slip-on runners and goes out front, making like she's getting something out of her car. But her eyes, hidden behind the glasses, shift a little to watch the neighbor's home instead. The food sits there, same as the last time. But now, instead of letting it give her second-hand anxiety, she walks across the street. She can see frozen meals poking out of a couple of the bags. She leans over them to knock on the door.

No answer.

Mina knocks again, harder this time. "Hello? Your food's out here." It's nosey and not something she'd normally do, but she can't stop thinking about that little girl with the red lip. It wouldn't hurt to meet these neighbors, if just to put her mind at ease and silence the gnawing in her gut.

Something moves in her peripheral vision, and Mina steps back to see better. That same curtain, opening. The little girl's face peers out, still no expression. But no lipstick this time, either. She waves at Mina. Then the girl breathes hard on the glass to fog it up, but only gets a space about as large as a mouth, which shrinks right away. She makes a capital "H" in the fog with a small finger, wipes it away, is about to fog it up again when the sound of tires crunching gravel makes Mina turn around. It's the silver Jeep, and the man is looking right at her. He gets out of the car.

Mina peeks back at the window to see what the girl was trying to say, but like before, she's gone.

"Can I help you?" the man asks once he's almost to the front door, almost to where Mina stands. He sounds annoyed.

She smiles. "Sorry, your grocery delivery was just sitting out here, so I came over to ring the bell and let you know."

The man lifts his phone. "I have the app."

Mina forces a laugh, touches her forehead. "I'm so sorry, you're right. You know when your own groceries are arriving, of course you do. My husband always says I worry too much about things that are none of my business."

He peers down at her, and Mina regrets saying it. She's basically admitted to being snoopy, and now that he's this close, she wants to take it back. Needs to get away from him. It's something intangible about him. His vibe. Now she's super aware of being alone on a vacant street with him. Just an arm's length away, too.

"None of your business is right," he mutters.

She steps past him, making sure to smile and look down.

89

Be unthreatening. She walks down the path through the Xeriscape yard, which is identical to hers. Some coastal theme with sea grass and little bushes dotting small rocks. No lawn grass in sight.

She holds her breath until her feet reach the blacktop. Her gut tells her not to go straight into her rental. Don't let him know where she's staying. It might be overboard, but she obeys the little feeling and turns down the street instead, aiming for the path to the beach, where there's bound to be people. She makes a point to look at her fitness tracker and then jogs even though she's not wearing a bra. Maybe if he thinks she was just on a run, he'll put her out of his mind.

Brady would call the precaution ridiculous. But Brady's never been a woman.

He's never had randos approach him in the grocery store under the pretense of needing help to find something, only to comment about how pretty he is. He's never had a man follow him into a deserted CVS parking lot at night when he's picking up milk, then tag along into the store. Never had to slink behind an endcap to hide as the man looks around with determination. Never had to wait for the man to leave in order to finish making a purchase. Only to find that the man is sitting in his car, idling, waiting for you to leave. You find this out because his car pulls out right after yours does. Follows you. You take a different route home when that happens. You settle it in your mind that you might not even be going home for a while. You'll just drive around the city, staying in public places until he turns off, praying to God you'll have enough gas in the tank to outlast him.

This is what Mina thinks about as her feet hit downhill pavement, as the roar of the sea grows louder, and her out-of-shape lungs scream *What the hell are you doing to us right now?* Her breath is quick because of that, or because she still hasn't turned around to see if the man with the silver Jeep is following her or not.

Once on the public beach, she slows to a walk, but her body demands rest. She stops and puts hands on her knees, hangs her head so that her long, blonde hair almost touches the sand. She cries to release it all. The fear, the energy from her fight-or-flight (flight) response, but it's more than that. Somehow this cry feels like grief, as if what she went through so many years ago with Paxton is mixing with the panic of this moment. It all washes up against her heart and she sobs, grateful that the sound of the ocean waves mutes the noise she makes. The misty sea air wets her face and coaxes her wavy hair into tight curls around her hairline as it mingles with sweat.

And then, Paxton's face comes to mind. Blonde curls, dimple in her left cheek, big hunter-green eyes. It only makes Mina cry harder.

CHAPTER 20

Mitch arrives the next day without Grace in tow. This doesn't strike Brooke as too odd because he does that sometimes, to make repairs, bring them deliveries, whatever.

He's in the cabin before the three of them even realize he's pulled up, and nobody knows what to do. Derek wears the suit again, and he's sitting in his chair with that newspaper. When Mitch enters and closes the door behind himself, he checks Brooke out while she irons her dresses and Derek's shirts. He sighs.

"You don't have to do all that. She's not watching right now."

"It's fine," Brooke says, continuing the task. She's channeled all of her nervous energy into cleaning the house, and so everything is done. These don't even need ironed. But there's no way she's going to take his word that Grace isn't watching them.

"You guys need anything?" Mitch puts one foot in front of the other, tucks his gun into his waistband like he's some old Western cowboy holstering it. Or maybe he stands that way to accommodate his knees. Brooke has noticed his gait is stiffer than it used to be.

They don't answer because what the hell? Of course they need stuff. Starting with freedom. Why is he asking?

"Recognize me yet?" Mitch asks Derek when nobody replies. "I figure if you did, you'da come at me by now."

When Derek doesn't respond, Mitch laughs. Brooke doesn't know what any of this means, and she's over it.

"Are you here to see what flavor of ice cream we'd like you to pick up while you're at the store?" Brooke says, unable to hide the sarcasm.

Mitch looks at her, but it's Kinsey, off to his side, that Brooke notices. Kinsey purses her lips and shakes her head, as if telling her to remember her goal. She has to seduce Mitch, not piss him off.

Mitch steps closer to Brooke so that his stale cigarette smoke scent hits her nose. She stiffens.

"I'm not gonna hurt you," he says in response to her movement. "Wasn't even gonna touch you, Jesus Christ."

Her mouth feels like it's stuck closed. It was just a visceral reaction to him getting into her space. She couldn't help it.

He stands there a minute longer, and it's awkward. They still don't know why he's here, but it's like he doesn't know why, either.

"Hey, Mitch, how deep into the ground does that perimeter go?" Derek asks, and Brooke wants to hit him. Is he that stupid? Why would Mitch come out and tell them?

Mitch laughs again. "Nice try. Maybe you could ask your *wife* here that question. She could tell you better than I can." Then he walks out, laughing like it's the funniest thing he's ever heard.

Brooke clenches her teeth.

Derek glances at her like he's requesting an answer, but Kinsey speaks up. "Go after him," she tells Brooke. "You have until the driveway. This is your chance to win him over while Grace isn't here."

Brooke shakes off the reaction to Mitch's comment and throws the door open. She calls his name.

He's halfway across the weeds to the driveway, but when he hears her, he stops and whirls around. Her stomach turns over, and she has no idea what she's going to say.

"It was good to see you." She squints because the sun is so bright.

Mitch pulls out a pack of cigarettes, tamps it down on his hand to get one out, and lights it with his Zippo. It's a long, awkward silence, but Brooke doesn't think she should leave. Not yet.

"You know why I picked you up all those years ago?" he asks, takes a slow draw from the cigarette. Brooke's gut drops and there's no way she's ready to hear this, whatever it is, but she plays along, shakes her head and smiles.

"Thought, *If I gotta look at the same damn woman for the next however many years, I'd like it to be that one.* Who knew you'd last so long?"

Wow. Romantic.

The line works about as well as a punch in the face. But Brooke is following a new rule. The rule of getting Mitch to trust her enough to betray Grace.

"That's really sweet," she coos.

"Sweet my ass. Nice try though," he says and walks to his car without looking back.

When Brooke returns to the cabin, Kinsey stands glaring at her, arms crossed. But Derek laughs.

"That's *really sweet*," he mimics.

94

"Shut up," she growls.

"Uh, Derek's not wrong," Kinsey says. "You can't slather on the honey like you do with Grace because, obviously, Mitch sees through it." Then to Derek, "How the hell do you know him, by the way? You need to figure that out, and fast, because maybe we can use it."

"No idea." Derek shrugs. "Might be one of my informants, might be someone I knew from high school. Although he seems older than me. Hell, I have no clue!"

"Well, apply yourself and *try*." Then to Brooke, "And you need serious work. When was the last time you came on to a guy?"

Brooke flops her shoulders. She hadn't come on to Tyson. That wasn't how things went with them. And before that? Maybe Ian after college when they met. So yeah, she's rusty.

"Show interest, but you can't throw yourself at him or act totally different than usual. Mitch likes you as a smart aleck. He knows you're kind of a bitch—"

"Thanks a lot," Brooke interrupts.

"Okay, fine, you're not a bitch, but you don't take shit. He knows it. You can't suddenly be the sweetest thing since cotton candy. My hunch is he likes you because you don't take shit. So you gotta walk the line between that and pushing him away."

Brooke nods. Kinsey's right. She hates to admit it, but she's right.

CHAPTER 21

Brooke is grumpy because of her strike out with Mitch, but there's no time to dance around her moods. Derek has to come up with a fallback idea because neither of them are making good headway with Kinsey's strategy.

The perimeter. He'll start there.

Derek doesn't mince words. "What did he mean, that you know how deep the perimeter goes?"

Kinsey inhales sharply and goes into her room, as if his words shooed her away. So this must be another topic Brooke doesn't want to talk about. What's new?

Brooke sits on the yellow couch and moves her neck side to side, like she's trying to crack it. She looks right at him with those fierce eyes. "It's what Tyson was trying to do when he died."

He nods, understanding now why she's so cagey about it. Why she stiffened when Mitch said it.

"Oh," he says. "Like in *The Count of Monte Cristo*."

Brooke's head bounces left to right, like she's weighing what he said. "Not really. In *The Count of Monte Cristo*, they tunnel to each other and then the old man dies and the Count hides in the body bag and they toss him out to sea."

He shrugs. "There was tunneling for a lot of pages."

"True."

They're having a conversation without her flying off the handle, so maybe she's open to more questions. His comment about *The Count of Monte Cristo* should have pissed her off, considering he flung the book against the wall the other day.

"You know how far Tyson got?" Derek asks.

"At least fifteen feet down."

"Shit," Derek whispers. "And when he tried to dig forward?"

Brooke nods, looks down.

That's when it triggered the explosion. He's smart enough not to ask more about that.

"Where along the perimeter?"

"Mitch filled it in. But it was out back." She stands and points to a spot that doesn't look any different from the rest of the area around the cabin.

"Where did you get that metal file?"

"Tyson found it."

Derek had looked under the couch where Brooke had shoved it when they were trying to untie his hands, but it was already gone. She'd somehow retrieved it without him noticing. He was pretty out of it from that jolt to the collar.

The hex bolt ring burns hot in Derek's pocket at the mention of Tyson again. It's taking all the patience in the world to not tell her he has it, even though he lied when she asked, and like a heartless dick, he listened to her crying in her room. But one thing the job taught him was to keep his cards close, and to save important chess moves for when he can call checkmate. He squeezes his eyes shut. Stupid game metaphors.

"What's wrong?" Brooke asks.

"Oh, nothing. Where's the metal file?"

"It won't help us. The perimeter and these goddamn collars are the problem. Not to mention the remotes."

He knows this. He's already thought of it, but still, he needs to gather up every tool that might give them a fighting chance. What if the file can remove the collars?

"Still, I'd like to have it," he says.

"No." Brooke holds his gaze. Man, she's got some balls on her, this one. "But I can show you something." She waves for him to follow her outside, then goes behind the cabin and there, in the grass, is a small metal bowl.

"You want tools? This is what Tyson used to dig."

"Fifteen feet? With *that*?"

"This and the metal file, yeah." She smiles while handling the bowl.

Derek would be stupid not to notice the pride in her response. For good reason. Digging down fifteen feet with a small metal bowl is impressive. Derek nods, eyebrows up to show appreciation. She smiles at him this time.

It makes his stomach feel warm.

"Kinsey knows best," Derek says, "but if you want my two cents, our best chance is that smile of yours. You should put it to work more with Mitch." He's just trying to be helpful. Wave a white flag, but her whole countenance hardens.

"That's so goddamn patronizing. Like me smiling more would help a single thing? Do you know how many times I've been told to smile more? But newsflash, smiling doesn't get shit done, and—"

Derek puts a hand in the air and it's a miracle, but she stops.

"I know," he says. "One of my exes used to rant about that all the time, and I actually agree. Smiling doesn't get shit done. But you know what it can do? Seduce an idiot."

She lowers her chin and stares him down with those eyes. Those damn eyes, so full of life and energy.

"I'm just sayin', if you want tips for winning over that bastard, it's this: Use the smile."

He doesn't tell her to use the eyes too, even though she should. If he says that, it'll sound like he's coming on to her. And he's definitely not.

CHAPTER 22

Mina's had a productive day: thirty pages, revised. They're good pages too, and she doesn't think they'll need more than a proofread before publication.

This, despite the hangover.

She got trashed after coming back from the beach yesterday. All the thoughts about her daughter, the pain she's staved off for the better part of eight years barreled her down there on the sand.

Mina hasn't been able to cry over Paxton for years. In fact, the tears dried up a few months after Paxton died. That had shocked her. Brady was still crying, still a mess. Mina thought she'd outrun the grief. It seemed too soon, but she couldn't force the tears. She hadn't actually cried over Paxton again since yesterday.

The girl she saw in the house across the street had brought it up for her somehow. Had to be. She's monitored that house all day, but nothing has happened. No movement. That little girl may be trying to tell her something, but also Mina may be overreacting.

Her phone dings with a text message. It's Brady.

Been down to the beach yet?

She sucks her teeth and sets the phone down because what she really wants right now is a bath. And another glass of wine. No way is she telling Brady about her experience at the beach. About how much she's been thinking about Paxton. Although she should. Her inability to share his grief is a constant sticking point for them.

Instead, she ignores the text and runs a bath. She's about to step in when another one comes through. Brady again.

You okay?

He says that a lot and it always feels like a "question behind the question" situation. Like he wants to ask something else but knows better. For example, right now it's like the question he really wants to ask is, are you drunk?

I only had a couple glasses of wine. I'm fine. Heading to bed soon, she types.

Bed? At eight-thirty?

Mina groans like a teenager dealing with a nagging mom and turns her phone on silent. *I thought you wanted me to relax*, is what she wants to say.

She definitely can't do this with him all month.

In the bath, Mina closes her eyes. She couldn't find a candle, so the lights are off and she settles for darkness. It's exactly what she needs, and her wine-fuzzy mind drifts. But it's not long before her phone lights up and shines against her closed eyelids. More texts from Brady.

I miss you.

Hope you're having a great time.

Oh, for God's sake. She wipes her hands dry and reaches for the phone to type a response.

I need this time to focus so I probably won't be looking at my phone much, Brades. Don't be worried if I don't text you back.

She puts her phone on airplane mode, not only so she doesn't get the notifications but also so Brady can't see her on location sharing. It'll cause a fight, her going dark like that, but she just needs to know she's truly alone for a few minutes. Not being watched.

Mina's friends say she's a bitch to Brady. That he's madly in love with her, willing to stay with her even after she cheated, and what wouldn't they give for their partners to offer even a fraction of the fucks Brady gives.

But Brady's version of giving a lot of fucks is suffocating.

After the bath, she gets into her comfy clothes and is about to close the computer for the evening when she sees the silver Jeep parked in front of the house across the street. She ducks down on the couch, out of sight.

When the man comes out of the house, he's followed by an older woman with short gray hair styled into a clean bob. He gets into the driver's seat. She goes for the back seat door, and looks toward Mina's rental. Mina only knows this because she can't resist peeking to see if they're still there.

When she steals a look again minutes later, they're gone. But the curtain in the little girl's window is pushed to the side. The girl's not there. The window is empty, but she wrote something in . . . is that toothpaste?

HI

Mina stares at the two capital letters, trying to comprehend what it means. A greeting, yes, but it also must mean that there's nothing to worry about across the street. The girl is just being friendly. The bad-vibe guy is just a bad-vibe guy.

So, why doesn't she feel better?

Maybe because this brings up more questions. Why write

something in the window at all? Why use toothpaste if you're going to do it? Kids don't always think things through, but the effort it would take to use toothpaste to write on the window is extra. Wouldn't even a child switch to a crayon and paper?

It's like the little girl is trying to get her attention without . . . what? Raising alarm?

She's coming to the wrong person for that, because Mina goes immediately to alarm in any given situation. It's her superpower.

She gets an idea. The girl isn't there right now, but the next time she looks out the window, she'll see a message from Mina.

Mina squirts a bit of toothpaste on her finger and, in the corner of the front window, she writes:

U OK?

But as she finishes, there's a flash of movement across the street. In the girl's window, a huge hand wipes the *HI* away with a washcloth and closes the curtains.

It was a man's hand. The little girl is in there with a man.

For some odd reason, once again, all Mina can think about is Paxton. Not that this is Paxton. It's not. Paxton's gone. But still.

CHAPTER 23

When Grace and Mitch arrive early the next morning, Derek feels ridiculous standing in that suit again. But it was Kinsey's orders.

This time, Grace doesn't even acknowledge the suit. He might as well be wearing sweats, but those are nowhere to be found either, and the overalls Mitch left for him are still too small, so they ride up his ass.

Mitch disappears into Kinsey's bedroom like usual, and it's Derek, Grace, and Brooke. Derek is determined to do his best with Grace today and so when she goes to hug Brooke, turning her back to him, Derek gives Brooke a *get-out-of-here* nod and a shooing hand. She glares back.

"Hi, Daddy," Grace says, now facing him. God, this is weird, and every minute feels like tiptoeing through a minefield.

"Hey, Grace."

She takes his hand and comes in for a hug. Derek holds her and glares at Brooke until she finally sneaks into Kinsey's room.

With the gentle tap of Kinsey's door closing, Grace pulls back. "Break character."

Yes, please. This is painful.

Grace says nothing else, but slides her hand under Derek's suit jacket to remove it and presses herself into Derek's personal bubble. That remote touches his chest, and he cringes, like he could accidentally shock himself with the pressure.

"Let's talk for a bit. Get to know each other. What do you say?" He takes her hand and tries to lead her to the couch.

She doesn't move forward. Just stands there. Face set, her eyes empty.

So, the woman wants to be in charge. Fine, but God, can't she give him a minute to get used to the idea of sleeping with someone the same age his mother would be? His captor.

"Just for a second." He tries to be reassuring. "You're the boss. I just like to know the person first."

Not necessarily true, but true today.

She doesn't respond with words, but joins him on the couch.

Derek folds his hands in his lap and realizes he doesn't actually have anything to say. At least, not beyond asking her for information to help them escape, but he can't lead with that.

"What do you want to know?" she asks, but her voice is flat, like she's irritated.

How do I short out the perimeter?

How do I get this damn collar off?

How far away from civilization are we?

Why are you such a fucking psycho?

Derek clears his throat. "Well, I already know where you

grew up." He forces a laugh, but it doesn't land. She stares at him.

"How did you . . . come up with the idea for . . . this?" He waves a hand around the cabin, grateful that a question materialized, even if it's a stupid one.

"Does it matter?"

"Matter? Oh, I don't know. I'm curious, is all. It's quite . . . creative."

Talking was a bad idea. He's going to piss her off.

When she says nothing, he reaches over to lift her shirt and get down to business

But a jolt of electricity courses through his neck, zings down his torso, and into his limbs.

When it stops, his head pounds, body throbs.

"What the hell are you doing?" Grace shouts. "You think my father was a sicko?"

Derek blinks. Weren't they out of character? Isn't that what she said? He doesn't reply.

She stands up. "My father never did that with me. And if you think that's what I want, I need to find another Albert!"

Sweat beads on his forehead. But he thought that's what she wanted. She was the one who came on to him. More than once! She sent all the right signals. Did he misread them?

Grace holds that remote, pointed at him. What's he supposed to do now?

"Jesus Christ, I'm sorry. I thought we were out of character."

Grace smirks. "You think I would sleep with you? When you could crush my windpipe with one hand? You're nice to look at, nice to touch even, but I'm not stupid. Now, back off."

Derek stands, takes a few retreating steps and Grace

stands too. "You're lucky we're so close to the last scene because otherwise, I'd get rid of you and find a new Albert. You're more trouble than you're worth."

He puts his hands up in surrender. "I swear, I won't be trouble again."

CHAPTER 24

Brooke walks into Kinsey's room to make another attempt with Mitch. Kinsey sits on the bed, hands not tied.

"Hey," she says to Mitch, her tone low, casual, not overly nice. "Not tied up?" She nods toward Kinsey. Brooke assumed Mitch tied Kinsey up in here. She's never checked before.

"Nah, she doesn't cause a lot of trouble, and besides, it's not like I couldn't put her down if I needed to."

That's dark, but Brooke takes a deep breath and stays the course. "Generous of you," she says, still keeping her tone slightly sarcastic but far from sticky sweet.

He looks at her but doesn't respond. It seems like he's trying to decide what to think about this change of pace.

She remembers what Derek said about her smile and flashes him one.

Mitch's eyes soften.

Derek was right. It did something to the man. Why didn't she know about this so much sooner in life? This tool at her disposal.

Brooke sits on the bed next to Kinsey, but Kinsey moves

away, facing the back wall. Maybe to give them privacy? Now she's back to back with Kinsey.

"Ten years here and we've never really talked," Brooke starts, trying not to wince on the outside because that was such an awkward line.

Mitch flips the page of his magazine without looking up. "Why would we? I ruined your life."

Exactly. He knows exactly what he did, and it makes her harden inside, makes this whole thing that much more difficult to pull off. Kinsey elbows her in the back. Brooke turns and bares her teeth, as if to say, *I know, I'm working on it.*

"Well, whether or not I like it, this is my life now," Brooke says. "And considering I see so few people anymore, I thought it might be nice to strike up a conversation. Even with you. Call me desperate."

Mitch likes you as a smart aleck.

Surely that one made Kinsey happy.

"Grace needs you out there," he replies.

"Oh, trust me, Grace is fully distracted by the guy you pulled off the streets."

"Why do you say that?" There's a sharp edge in his tone, and he looks up. Is he defensive because she thinks Derek is distraction-worthy, or because he's actually jealous of Grace's affection?

"Just that she seems to really approve of your selection this time."

Mitch mutters something unintelligible and Brooke cannot believe she's flirting with this man.

"*You* approved of my selection last time." His eyes turn down and the words come out in monotone. But Brooke can spin this. Her mind is already fast at work.

"I did. You gave me the only happiness I've had in a decade, and I owe you for that."

She can hear the audience clapping in her mind. An award-winning line.

"You're being nicer than usual." Mitch's tone lowers. He's still wary.

"Well, I guess when you're in my shoes, you decide to make every minute count."

"Hmph," Mitch mutters. He seems to buy it.

She waits.

"Your daughter's doing fine," he says.

Brooke's breath hitches, and she loses her cool, almost shouting, "You've been in contact with my family? Watching my daughter?"

Kinsey elbows her again, but she elbows Kinsey back. Because right now? Screw her.

"Not in contact, but I've kept tabs on her. Your mom too. Jessi's a pretty little girl, just like her mommy. But I'm sorry to say that your mom's in hospice care. The cancer's got her."

Brooke cannot do this. The first news she's had of her family in all this time and it's that this creep has been watching her baby girl? That her mom is dying?

All of her senses cascade inside of her and threaten to come out in a volcano of rage and tears, but she chokes it down. "Stay away from my family," she hisses.

"Well now, there's the girl I know." His lopsided smile curls up.

Brooke wants to throw up. He's attracted to her, sure. But there's no way in hell she can get anywhere with him, not after he said that about Jessi. Even if Kinsey's life depends on it.

CHAPTER 25

Walking out of Safeway this afternoon, Mina notices a sandwich board sign on the pavement next door.

Happy hour: Wine half price every day until 5:00

That sounds like exactly what she needs. She deserves a reward for so much progress on her revisions. Plus, she has nothing in her reusable bag that needs refrigerated. She only stopped for some coffee and another box of Wheat Thins, Goldfish crackers, some melatonin.

Standing in front of the small wine bar, hugging the obnoxiously-colored Trader Joe's bag that holds her Safeway items, it happens again. Her nose runs, eyes fill with saltwater. Why? This is completely out of nowhere, as if just because she cried over Paxton the other day, now tears have an open invitation to show up whenever they want to. Apparently, they don't even need a reason.

No way she can go in for happy hour wine like this. But she stands there anyway, thinking about her baby girl. About the four years that she was actually a mom, and hard sobs climb up through her chest. She has to get to the car before she falls apart like she did at the beach, so she speed walks across the parking lot.

Inside the car, Mina releases it all, reaching for a tissue from the glove box. She takes a deep breath and blows her nose, looks at herself in the rearview mirror. "Eight years late, but here comes the grief train anyway," she says, wiping the mascara from under her eyes.

She remembers her phone is still in airplane mode.

Shit. Brady will definitely notice that he can't see her on location sharing. It's been hours.

When her phone is back online, text after text and some missed calls from Brady show up.

Where are you? The first one says.

Then the second: *You okay?*

Jesus Christ. *Are you cheating on me?* is the question behind this one.

Mina takes a deep breath, doesn't even read the other texts. Maybe Brady is concerned because she went dark and he couldn't get ahold of her. She shouldn't go to the worst-case scenario right away. After all, she was the one who agreed to share her location twenty-four-seven after the affair. But only if he didn't watch it obsessively. He did at first, and they had a fight about that too. Afterward, Brady agreed to only check it when he was expecting her at home, and only to estimate how close she was. This seemed like a good alternative to him constantly asking for her ETA after work in order to time dinner right.

Mina can hear her book club friends in her mind: *He makes you dinner every night! What's wrong with you?*

What is wrong with her? Brady is sweet, really the perfect husband in so many ways. Why can't she open herself up to him? Things would be a lot easier for both of them if she could get past this hardness in her heart.

Mina wipes her eyes again and texts: *I'm here, I'm fine. Had the phone on airplane mode while I slept and then I forgot about it.*

It's sort of true.

Oh, no worries, I just wanted to check in to make sure everything was good.

Mina closes her eyes and takes a deep breath, but before she can respond, he texts again.

Sorry, babe. Not trying to hover.

And then, *Has being back there brought anything up for you about Paxton?*

Interesting. *Hovering* was exactly what Mina assumed he was doing. Hovering and growing more pissed and stressed by the moment. It's what he's been doing for years. Actually, she expected him to get emotional about not being able to contact her for a few hours, but he seems fine.

Fine, minus this bombshell question about Paxton. But she can't help but note the progress: he either trusts her more than he used to, or he's trying to manage his trust issues without exploding drama all over her. She'll take either.

Mina's lip quivers, and for a moment, because she feels this little nudge of softness in her heart toward him, she considers telling Brady about the girl across the street. About her outburst at the beach, and the one just now. But it's too much. Too much for text and too much for her to share. And yet, this is a chance for her to connect with him, something she's been so incapable of. Something he's constantly trying for.

I miss her, Mina types and waits before sending it. She

adds more. *It's been eight years and suddenly, I miss her like it was yesterday. I cried for the first time in forever over her, and I've cried twice since. I don't know why. It all feels so fresh.*

She stares at the paragraph. It's more words strung together than she's texted Brady in eons. Her finger hovers over the little blue "up" arrow. One tap to send it and she will have made an effort. More effort than she's made in years.

Something hardens inside and she deletes the whole thing. Types, *Not really.*

Mina hits "send."

Regret fills her heart. She turned down an easy opportunity to show him she's making progress. But she can't take it back. She can't text something else. Moment's gone. Fresh tears fill her eyes because she realizes that she actually wants to be open with him. She wants them to have a good relationship, but it's like something inside of her just withered up and died with Paxton. And now, it's been so long that she's not sure she can find her way back.

When Mina pulls into the driveway of her rental, she sees that the little neighbor girl is back in the window. Sitting there, her arms on the ledge, one cheek resting on her little hand. Mina scrambles out of the car and waves. The girl presses her hand to the window, and in her face, Mina swears she sees it again, that lost look, but this time, the girl mouths something. Mina cups a hand around her ear to say that she can't hear, and can't understand, but the girl turns around in a quick motion and her blonde hair whips the window.

She's gone.

A man's face appears in her place.

He has a beard and bushy eyebrows. Looks old enough to

be her father, but Mina knows better than to assume this is the case. Kidnappers always try to pass as the father.

Before she has time to analyze whether it's a good idea, Mina crosses the street. She has to find out what's going on once and for all. Has to know why they never come out, why the silver Jeep shows up. Why the girl keeps trying to get her attention, because it isn't just to say *HI*. Can't be.

Mina pounds on the door three times.

Nothing. No footsteps, no shushing noises from inside.

She knocks hard again, over and over. She rings the doorbell, which is either broken or silent.

Still nothing.

She's about to give up and leave, when a man's voice comes through on the other side of the door. "Go away."

Mina stiffens. "I just wanted to ask you a question."

"Lady, please go away."

"I'm concerned about you and your . . . daughter. Do you need anything?"

"No. I'm disabled, but we get food delivered."

Mina stands there. She's intruding and should mind her own business. But she has to push a little harder because what if something bad is happening over here and she didn't try? How could she live with herself?

Paxton.

"Doesn't your girl need to be in school?"

"It's summer." The man's voice is softer now.

Right. Duh. Mina isn't totally satisfied that everything is fine, but it's enough for her to think, once again, that maybe she's overreacting.

"Okay. Sorry to bother you. I'm just across the street. You can send her over if you need anything. Anything at all."

"Thank you," the man whispers.

When she turns to leave, something catches her eye. A tiny red light blinking high in the corner. It's tucked under the home's eaves, so she didn't notice it at first. She stands on tippy toes and peers closer. It's a surveillance camera.

CHAPTER 26

Kinsey's back to that annoying, frenetic state she was in when Derek first arrived. That grating eagerness.

"How'd it go?" she asks the room once Grace and Mitch leave.

"I can't do it," Brooke says.

"Mitch only said all that stuff to rile you up," Kinsey says.

"What happened?" Derek asks, rubbing his arms again. That goddamn ache. He'd just gotten rid of the itching, too.

"Oh, he told her he's been keeping tabs on her family."

"My mom has cancer," Brooke adds.

Derek doesn't respond.

"Thanks for your sympathy," she says to his silence.

Why do I suck so much at basic courtesy?

"God, I'm sorry. Sorry about your mom. But unless we escape, she's going to outlast us all."

"How'd you do?" Kinsey asks Derek.

"We misread Grace. I got another jolt to the collar for coming on to her."

"No," Kinsey breathes. "No way. She wants you. I can tell!"

"Well, even if you're right, she's not willing to be vulnerable with me, or let me get that close in proximity. Which honestly is smart because I'm pretty sure I could snap her neck before she could push that button. If she were good and distracted."

"Well, that sucks," Kinsey says, and chews on her thumbnail. "It's all on you then," she says to Brooke.

Derek goes into the kitchen for a glass of water. Pours one for Brooke too because how shitty to find out about your mom like that.

Brooke sighs when he hands her the glass of water, but she takes it. Doesn't say thanks. "I don't think I can. He's already taken so much from me."

"You can." Derek forces his voice to be tender and sits on the other end of the couch.

She has to. So far, it's their only real idea.

Kinsey nods at him like she's encouraging him to keep going. Keep talking like this. Problem is, he kind of wants to shout at Brooke. Shake her. She's been here ten years and she can't screw someone if it means getting free? But he stuffs all of that down. Getting in a screaming match with her right now won't help.

"No I can't," she says. "Even when I try, he makes it impossible by pushing my buttons. He's a monster."

"So you're going to let him take your life?" Derek surprises himself at how even his tone is. Somehow, miracle upon miracle, he's found his interviewing voice. The one that was money when he needed witnesses to work with him, or see the error of their reasoning, to come around to his perspective. It's been a long time since he's spoken this way. But he can't think about how long. Can't face the wash of guilt and regret that follows.

Kinsey sits in silence.

Brooke looks up at him, leans away a little and makes this face like she bit into a lemon. "You know, I actually hadn't thought about it that way."

"You're fucking with me." Derek grunts. She's being sarcastic and his patience is already so thin.

"I'm not. But what if I give him *that* and he still doesn't tell us anything useful?"

He shrugs. It's a risk, that's for sure.

Minutes pass in silence. "I have to try harder," she says.

"It sucks shit, but so does everything else about this situation," Derek says. "I'm going to wander around outside and see if there's anything I can learn about that perimeter."

"Be careful," Kinsey says.

"Yeah, yeah." Derek motions with a hand and walks outside.

Outside, there's a little drizzle starting up, but that's the Oregon Coast for you. Much more typical than all this heat they've had. Derek hears the humming from the perimeter.

He stays close to the cabin. He's seen Kinsey wander around outside, which she does more often than not, and they said it's right before the driveway. Plus, he knows where Tyson was digging when he hit the perimeter. So he has a bit of a leash. He approaches the spot Brooke pointed out. Kicks the dirt and weeds around with his feet.

C'mon, think of something.

Why is his mind a total blank whenever he thinks about escape? He always imagined he'd be so great in a survival situation like this. But there are only a few ways out of here. First, by removing or turning off the collars.

So far, doesn't seem possible.

Second, by getting past the perimeter.

Tyson's way didn't work and we can't sprout wings and fly over it.

Last, by turning off the perimeter. That's the angle they're trying to work with Mitch, but Jesus Christ, it's not going anywhere.

He could straight-up tackle Grace, but Mitch has a gun.

And a remote!

Brooke said Mitch has a remote too even though he's never seen it.

And anyway, if he went after Mitch instead, he'd get shot or Grace would have a heyday electrocuting him.

The three of them in the cabin could work together to subdue those two. But if there was one slip up—if Brooke couldn't get the remote away from Grace, or he couldn't get to Mitch at the exact same time—all bets would be off. The margin of error is way too wide.

For now, he'll have to settle for helping Brooke get to Mitch. And maybe another—better—idea will come to him.

His mind drifts to Brooke. How interesting it is that she stands up to him. That she's not intimidated by him at all. All the other women in his life—including his own mom— responded by stifling their own personalities until he barely recognized them. Soon, all that resentment poured out at once, and it'd been festering too long to fix. This always damaged the relationship. He told them not to do that, that they could talk to him before losing their minds. But it was like they couldn't help it. They always said they felt like they had to be perfect around him, that anything they did would set him off. But that wasn't true. The times he got angry, it was never directed at any of them. He has all of this big energy that seems to barrage him and he doesn't know what to do with it. Not that he's ever admitted that to anyone. He's just an intense dude, and it bugs him to no end that the people in his life—women *and* men, honestly—constantly misread him and assign him bad intentions. They don't feel like they can be themselves around him.

But not Brooke.

Then again, she kind of hates his guts.

That's fair since he attacked her on their first meeting. She's got a chip on her shoulder though, and he's pretty sure that's bigger than the fat lip he accidentally gave her. Too bad, because they could probably be good friends.

Maybe more.

But whatever. What does it matter? If they don't find a way out of here, they're all dying in a few days, anyway.

I have *to come up with something.*

CHAPTER 27

Morning coffee in one hand, phone in the other, Mina's destination is the beach. She steps out onto the porch and pulls the front door of the rental shut, but unlike all the other times she's done this, there's a little snick. She gasps and immediately turns the knob to get back in. Locked.

No. She peers through the front door's window and there's the key. Sitting inside on an end table. *Damn it.* She always has her phone in one hand when she leaves, and the key in the other. But this time, because of the coffee, she forgot to grab the key. As if having both hands full was good enough.

Mina sets the coffee on the porch and navigates to the Airbnb confirmation in her email inbox, finds the owner's phone number and dials it.

It goes to voicemail after a few rings. Some generic robot voice telling her to leave a message after the beep.

"Hi there, my name is Mina and I'm staying in your vacation rental on 'J' Street in Freeport. I locked myself out accidentally. Is there any way someone can come and let me back in?"

She ends the call and sits on the top concrete step. At least it's not raining.

Her phone vibrates within minutes. A private number.

"Hello?" she says.

"Yeah, there's a second lock box on the side of the house. Code is 34213," a man says. No greeting, no bothering to verify it's even Mina on the other line.

"Okay, thank you," she says.

He hangs up.

That was weird, and rude, but people are assholes a lot of the time, so Mina lets it go and walks across the yard full of small rocks, dodging bushes and plants. There's no actual path to the side of the home, so she makes her own, enters the code. It's the same damn analog key lock as the one on the front door. The metal piece you have to pinch and pull at the same time has some give, so she knows she got the code right, but it's like the key box is old, and it's been out here exposed to salty air for too long. Almost looks corroded from exposure and it won't budge.

She tries again. Her fingers hurt from the narrow, pointy buttons and from squeezing the opening so hard. Nothing.

Mina picks up a rock bigger than her own fist and tries to use it to unjam the holder after she enters the code. That doesn't work either.

Shit. She'll have to call the owner—or property manager, whoever he is—back.

She redials the number.

Please answer this time.

Straight to voicemail.

"Hi, it's me again, Mina. The second lock box is jammed shut. Can you send someone to let me into the house, please? I'm so sorry for the hassle."

She ends the call and groans out loud, still so annoyed with herself for forgetting the key inside.

Her phone vibrates. Private number again. She answers.

"What do you mean it's jammed?" the man says.

God, this guy is rude. He better not be the one who shows up to help because he's a prick.

"It's stuck. The code seems to work, but the box won't open."

"Give me an hour."

"An hour?" she blurts out.

"Yeah, lady, an hour. It's not like I'm sitting around waiting for you to lock yourself out so I can come save you."

Mina raises her eyebrows and lowers her chin. Rude, he's so rude. Definitely warrants a shitty Airbnb review later, but she doesn't want to say anything else to make him mad and leave her outside longer.

"Great. Thanks so much, I truly appreciate your time," she says, as perky as possible.

She looks at her phone to calculate when an hour from now is, and it's plenty of time to walk down to the beach instead of sitting on the doorstep all morning.

Her phone rings while she's on her way, and she stops to check it. What if it's that rude guy again?

It's not. It's Brady. And amazingly, there's no groan of annoyance queued up inside of her. That's new.

"Hey, Brades," she answers, slowing down her walking pace so she can breathe well enough to speak.

"How's it going?"

Mina chews her cheek. Brady will worry if she tells him she's locked out.

"Great! Just heading down to the beach for some morning coffee and then I'll start working."

"Oh, nice. Hey, I had a dream about Paxton last night."

Mina thinks again about sharing what she's been feeling about their daughter, but now isn't the time. "Oh yeah?" she says.

"I don't know if it's you being back there or what, because I haven't dreamed about her for years. But this was weird. She was older, and she was lovely, Means. Just . . ." He chokes up, and while Brady's displays of emotion would normally harden her, this time she feels like she might cry too. She bites her lip, walks faster, and lets him talk.

"She was an adult. Still had those blonde curls but her hair was long. Full, beautiful. It looked exactly like yours, and she was wearing this white dress. A wedding dress, I think."

The tears well up in Mina's eyes and all she can think is, *Oh God, oh God, I can't do this right now.* And yet, she keeps listening.

"We were there with her, you and me. But this man—I couldn't see his face, but in the dream it seemed like he was her groom—he took her by the hand and they ran away. We couldn't catch up to them, but we laughed as they went."

Mina covers her mouth with the back of her hand holding the coffee. As if that will somehow stave off these tears.

"And then it was just us," Brady says, sniffles, and clears his throat.

There's a long pause and Mina's gut prompts her to say something, but she can't. Can't open her mouth. Even if she wanted to, everything she's held in over the years feels like Mount Everest to climb now.

Brady breaks the silence. "You there?"

"Yeah." Her voice cracks when she says it. "I'm here. Thanks for sharing that."

"Sorry, maybe that was too much for you, being back in

Freeport and all," Brady adds, composing himself. "But she was happy, Meens, and that's why I wanted to tell you about it. I think she's okay, wherever she is. Whatever happens to us after we die, I don't know. But it was like she was telling me not to worry. It wasn't our fault."

Mina looks out at the water. The ocean roars loud. The tide's out, exposing a huge boulder, covered in barnacles. Probably star fish too.

It wasn't Brady's fault.

It was Mina's fault.

It would always be Mina's fault.

"I gotta go, Brades. Love you," she pushes out, and hangs up the phone.

A text from him comes through almost immediately. *You okay?*

This time she can tell that he's not asking a different question, masked as concern. He's truly concerned.

I'm fine. Thanks for telling me your dream. Need to focus on my book. xo, she types.

Even though it's not a lot, she's proud of herself for thanking him for sharing instead of getting mad or steeling up. Little win. It doesn't keep the tears at bay though, and after half an hour at the beach, each second full of so much sobbing that her throat hurts and her mouth tastes almost metallic, Mina finally composes herself and makes her way back up to the house.

What if this is me, processing Paxton's death?

The idea feels scary on one hand, but also, she's ready. Ready to do what it takes to move forward. If only she knew how.

Climbing the hill to her street, she checks the time on her

phone. It's been close to an hour. As she rounds the corner, something sits at the end of the little lane.

A silver Jeep.

But it's not parked at the neighbor's. It's in her driveway, blocking her SUV.

CHAPTER 28

Mina creeps up to the rental, her mind whirling. Why is the bad-vibe guy at her place?

He's standing on the porch when she gets within earshot. She waves, smiles, even though she doesn't feel like being nice. "Hey! Can I help you?"

He narrows his eyes, holds up a key. "I'm here to let you back in. You already forget?"

What? Bad-vibe guy is rude-phone guy is bad-vibe guy?

"Oh! You own both houses?" She motions across the street.

"I'm not the owner."

"Do you work for the owner?"

He nods.

"Like a property manager?" she asks. He's not very forthcoming.

"Sort of," he mumbles, turns the key, and pushes the door open. He walks inside. And *what the hell*? screams across Mina's mind. Why is he going inside? It's not her house, sure, but it still somehow feels like a breach of privacy and it weirds her out. She doesn't know him.

Mina stands on the porch, scared to be inside with him. What if he's coming right back out and then he'll go away?

"Hey, lady," he shouts from inside.

She squeezes her eyes shut, grips her phone, and gets an idea.

"Yeah, head on over," Mina says, projecting her voice into the phone as she approaches the man. He stands in the kitchen, eyes trained on her.

There's silence on the other line because she's not really on the phone with anyone, but still she says, "That sounds great. We could grill burgers here."

Pause.

"Yep. So how long you think you'll be?"

Pause.

"Oh, five minutes? You're closer than I thought. That's perfect. See you soon." Mina pulls the phone down and says to the man, "My brother's on his way. He lives in town and we're doing lunch here today."

"No grill," the man grunts.

"What?"

"There's no grill."

"Oh." Mina touches her forehead. "I didn't even check that! What an idiot. But that's okay. We'll figure something else out when he gets here."

"Sure, whatever," the man says like he doesn't believe her. This sends a shrill panic through her core. She wants to ask why he's still here, but doesn't want to set him off, so she raises her eyebrows and shrugs, trying to signal the awkwardness so he leaves.

"You had any problems with the carbon monoxide monitor beeping?" he asks.

Mina furrows her brows. "What?"

"Previous renters complained about it. I fixed it, but wanted to be sure you hadn't noticed anything."

She throws her hands up in a frustrated shrug. "Nope, haven't heard anything."

He looks around, into the living room where her laptop is charging on the coffee table. "You here working?"

What the hell. She's not telling him anything about herself. No way.

"Something like that."

"You're here for a month," he continues. "Problems at home?"

Sharp panic hits her chest. How does he know how long she's here? But, of course, he knows. He has access to her rental records. Mina's eyes widen in surprise but she catches it and switches to a smile. Tries not to let on that she's scared. "Why do you ask that?"

He shrugs. "Pretty lady like you, all alone for such a long time. Just seems odd."

The downy hairs on the back of her neck stand on end. It's the way he says it.

Pretty lady.

Feels like a threat.

She has to get out of here. If he won't leave, she will. "Well, I better get back to it," she says and walks to the front door, praying he'll follow. Pick up even a single hint.

He does, and now they're standing at the threshold, the door still wide open.

"Get back to grilling with *your brother*, right?" he scoffs, and smiles. His smile is ten thousand times creepier than his normal face.

Mina forces a flat smile and he walks out, tosses a hand up in the air behind him without looking back.

She goes inside and locks the door, leans up against it, and then double checks the window locks too.

CHAPTER 29

Just when Brooke was all psyched up to go hard after Mitch, the whole day passes by and it seems like he and Grace are going to be no-shows.

Now she has to live with this anxiety simmering in her stomach for another twenty-four hours. It's nervous energy, like she drank way too much coffee. She can't sit still, but like every other time when she's stressed, her chores are all done, and she needs something to do with her hands that will free her mind up to wander in a better direction. Maybe she could write a letter to Jessi.

Tears fill Brooke's eyes and she wipes them away.

Can't do that. Can't think about Jess.

But it's not only that. There's a steel wall in her heart at the thought of having to say goodbye. She's not ready.

Strange. When it comes down to it, she's not willing to admit defeat. This gut response means she's still hoping to escape. Must be, and this thought makes her want to cry harder because escape is so impossible.

Okay, so no goodbye letter. Not like anyone would ever find it, anyway. Make cookies? Seems so stupid to do that when her life is going to end in a few days and she doesn't like them anyway. Then again, screw it. She used to make cookies for one girl who played young Grace before, and it always calmed her down. Maybe it'd calm Brooke down, too.

It'll have to be raisin because they're out of chocolate chips, and it's doubtful Mitch will do any shopping before . . . the wedding. Kinsey's last day. And after that, her own life will be a big, black hole.

Can't think about that either.

Derek comes inside and goes for a glass of water. Brooke tries to dodge him because the kitchen is small and he doesn't make any effort to avoid her, just bowls through like all big men do. All space is their space. His pants are too short for him, hitching up around the tops of his ankles, and Brooke would laugh at the sight if she wasn't so strung up with anxiety about all the things.

"I was thinking," Derek starts. "What if we could reverse engineer the remotes? Instead of detonating, maybe they can unlock." He sets his glass down on the counter right where she's working.

"You see an engineer around here?"

Derek exhales. It's an attempt to channel patience, and this makes Brooke question if she's being too hard on him. He's trying. But still, here he is, doing the thing big dudes like him always do. Act like they own everything. He hasn't budged out of the way despite Brooke reaching past him to grab the bowl she set down. It's like he thinks he belongs wherever he wants to be, and damn everyone else. Must be nice way up there at the top of the food chain.

"No. It's just a thought," he says.

"We'd have to get the remotes away from them in the first place," Brooke says. "That alone is impossible."

"But if we could do that, it's progress toward escaping. Then we'd just have to take them down."

"Mitch has a gun," Brooke reminds him. She's not trying to wet blanket the idea, but he's not being very realistic.

He runs a hand through his hair. "And Grace has that goddamn knife."

"Mm hm."

"Where's Kinsey?" he asks out of nowhere.

"I think she's out back. As long as she has her books to pretend to read, it's fair play in Grace's mind."

Brooke cradles the bowl in one arm and goes up on the balls of her feet to look out the back window to find her.

"What are you doing, by the way?" He watches her stir batter when she turns back around.

"Making cookies." She glances up at the camera. "Speaking of which, you should be doing more than just standing here, getting in my way."

Kinsey walks in the front door, looking flushed from the sunshine.

"The fuck is wrong with you two?" Derek pounds a fist on the counter and Brooke startles, annoyed with herself for the reaction. "We have two days until Kinsey dies. Then us. And you're sunbathing!" He throws a finger at Kinsey. "And you! You're making cookies like some off-brand Betty Crocker!"

Brooke slams the plastic bowl down. "You'd rather we all sat around and cried?"

"No, I'd rather you thought up a way to escape because the plan to screw our way out isn't going anywhere."

Brooke purses her lips and shakes her head. She's tired of telling him how useless it is to waste energy on escape. How much time Tyson spent on the effort and where it got him in the end.

"For the love of Christ, you two," Kinsey says, "I wish you'd just hit the mattress and have the fuck of your lives. Get it over with so we can have some peace around here." She stands in the open doorway.

"Sex isn't the answer to every problem, Kinsey!" Brooke shouts.

"Whoa! Not saying it is. But I think it's the answer to this one." Kinsey waves a hand between Derek and Brooke, who are super close to each other in the kitchen still.

"He's not my type," Brooke lies.

Derek watches her, and one eyebrow raises. There's a smile playing at the corner of his mouth, like he doesn't believe her. It pisses her off. "What?"

"The remotes," Derek says, ignoring the comment, but staring at her still. "We need to get our hands on those. Grace is a no-go, so our best hope is getting hold of the one Mitch has. That might do more for us than trying to get him to talk."

"Great, so why don't you manhandle him and get it?"

"Because he can end me."

"And he can't do that to me?"

"Not if you steal it without him knowing. But it'll require you to at least undress him."

"Well, that's not new information." She's playing tough, but inside there's a tiny burst of something. Is it hope? This is an angle Tyson never tried. What if Derek is right? What if there is something to them having control of the remotes? It's a step in the right direction and even though it feels impossible, it feels *less* impossible than trying to get Mitch to tell them how to escape.

CHAPTER 30

When he's done at Mina's rental, that man goes across the street instead of leaving. Of course. Even keeps his car parked behind hers so that if she wanted to go somewhere, she'd have to hunt him down and ask him to move it.

It's like he's trying to call her bluff about her brother coming over.

Anxiety stokes her pulse and makes her a little shaky, but is it stupid for her to react this way? He's not done anything to her except let her back into the rental after she locked herself out.

She could walk to the beach again and say she's meeting up with her brother down there. Or she could ask him to move his car and then leave, saying they're meeting at a restaurant since she doesn't have a grill after all. They're both just craving burgers, you know.

Mina watches out the front window, takes a deep breath, allowing her cheeks to balloon with air, then blows it out. It's already lunchtime, and she hasn't sat down at her laptop yet.

That's what she'll do. Work. She goes to the couch and opens the computer. But after twenty minutes, she's read the same two lines a zillion times because she can't stop looking over at the house.

Finally, the man comes striding out. Looks both ways before crossing, which is asinine because there are no cars, and this is a dead end. He glances up and catches Mina's eye. She doesn't duck this time. What's the point? He makes a show of turning his wrist over like he's checking the time and taps his pretend watch three times. Shrugs.

Bastard. He's asking where her brother's at. Mina doesn't respond but turns her back and sits on the couch in front of the window. Types to pretend she's busy.

His engine starts. Tires crunch the driveway gravel. He's leaving. Damn, it's about time. But now he knows where she lives. Hell, he knows how long she's here for. Her full name, her home address, too. She swallows the urge to cry and tells herself it's fine. He's just an asshole and she'll make a point not to cross him.

She goes to open the window and let some of this ideal Oregon Coast weather in, and her eyes go right to the house. The little girl is in the window again, and she's writing something with toothpaste, but this time she's gotten more than *HI* written. In fact, it's not *HI* at all.

It's *HELP*.

What Mina thought was the "I" in *HI* was actually the start of a capital E.

Shit. The man is gone, but Mina's too afraid to go over there now. It's too soon after her run-in with him, and she's exhausted from the interaction. But this girl is asking for help.

Mina pulls her notebook out of her work bag and tears a piece of paper.

Are you in danger? She writes, holds it up to the window.

But the girl's head whirls around, like someone is calling her, and she disappears again.

That's it. Mina's calling the cops.

The 911 operator answers and she explains what she saw. How the girl asked for help, how she's never seen either the girl or the man outside of the house, but she spoke to the man through the door. How a creepy guy keeps coming over there and about the grocery deliveries and—

"What's the address, ma'am?" The operator interrupts her.

She flings open her front door and strains to see the house numbers across the street. "35 'J' Street."

A long pause on the dispatcher's end.

"Thank you," the dispatcher eventually says. "Do you believe a crime is being committed?"

"A crime? Like . . ."

"Has a crime been committed, or is a crime in the process of being committed? Or is someone in imminent danger?"

No. Mina can't say that any of that is true, but something is weird and that little girl is asking for help.

"I don't know, but can't you send someone to come and check on them?"

"It doesn't sound like there's any reason to believe they need a wellness check."

"She's asking for help!"

"It's not enough, unfortunately."

"It is. You're supposed to send an officer out when someone calls 911. That's how this works." Mina can't comprehend this. At the very least, it would be a reason for a check-in. What's up with this dispatcher?

"Well, here in Freeport, the department's too small to send cops out willy-nilly every time someone snoops on a neighbor. If there's a crime being committed, I'll send someone out there. Otherwise, good day."

"Arc you kidding me?" Mina shouts. She's not snooping. The girl wants help.

But there's nobody on the other line anymore.

911 just hung up on her. Is that even a thing?

It was a whole lot of messed up. But she's not surprised. This town has always been a little strange, even if it is where she has a ton of wonderful childhood memories.

That girl.

Paxton.

Mina's mind scrambles, her body is restless. It's a feeling she knows well. The sense that something is wrong, so horribly wrong, but you can't do anything about it. You can't fix it, and you can't get past it. You can't move forward. You're stuck, suspended in dread, this loop of thinking that maybe if you had been in the right place at the right time, you could have prevented it. You could have done something.

It's what put her in the hospital after Paxton died.

CHAPTER 31

Derek is so relieved when Mitch shows up alone the next morning. What luck! Brooke gets the bastard all to herself and if she can steal his remote, Derek would take his chances mano a mano. He's bigger than Mitch. Younger. He could take him down, and with a little luck, steal that gun, too. And then when Grace shows up, he'll give her a not-so-friendly welcome. With Mitch's pretty Glock 19. A quick bullet to the brain once she's close enough to the cabin for them to . . .

His mind screeches to a halt.

The collars.

So they kill both Grace and Mitch. Then what?

They're still stuck wearing these goddamn collars they can't disarm.

Whatever.

Killing those two window lickers would still be a good first step. Or maybe he wouldn't kill Mitch. Maybe he'd save him for later. Make him talk once Grace is out of the picture.

They'd be free and if Derek can get out of here, help Brooke and Kinsey get out of here, it would be some sort of redemption for all the ways he's screwed up. Too little too late to change the past, he knows, but maybe he can somehow put the shards of his broken life back together. Use it as a boost to keep going. Maybe he'd even go to a shrink, like his last ex was always telling him to do. Sort his shit out.

"Where's Grace?" Brooke asks Mitch, bold as ever, the minute he saunters in.

"Not here."

"I see that, but why?"

"Has other things to tend to."

"Why are you here?" Derek asks.

"Thought you all deserved a warning." He shoves his gun into the back of his pants and lights up a smoke with that silver Zippo. "She's going to kill you two. Not long after Kinsey. A day maybe. I came to tell you that. Thought you deserved to know. Especially you," he says, and his eyes soften when they land on Brooke. "You've been here so long, done everything right."

"Not everything," Brooke says, her expression changing when she turns her face to Mitch, and it's those eyes. That look. Derek watches Mitch's face change too, and he swears Brooke could manipulate him. Get everything they need out of him, probably. Hell, the man might hand his remote over to her if she just asked with those eyes.

"Far as I can tell," Mitch says. "You didn't even get in the way every time she came for the others."

Brooke's face falls.

Why'd he have to say that? She's right. He knows precisely how to get to her. She's not focusing anymore, and it's like whatever gumption was there, working the plan, has retreated into a cave.

But Mitch is wide open. He wants to talk.

She needs to jump on that.

Derek tries to make eye contact with Brooke when Mitch isn't looking at him. She needs to see how close she is to having him. She needs to give him that one-two combo of smile and eyes and who knows what else he'll tell them? The woman probably wouldn't even have to compromise her dignity for it. This guy likes her, and not just to screw. Derek thinks Mitch might genuinely care about her—and only her—in his own way. Men do stupid things when they're into a woman.

Mitch turns toward the front door, as if to leave, and it's like everything moves in slow motion. Kinsey makes faces at Brooke to not let him go. Derek tries to get Brooke's attention too, somehow tell her she's almost got him.

Mitch twists the knob, and Brooke drops her hands to her thighs. It makes a clapping sound like she's given up hope. But she catches Derek's eye and there's that fire. She's got this.

"Hey, Mitch," she says.

He looks back at her.

"There's something I wanted to ask you, but in private. Would you come into . . ." She looks around and stalls. No way she'd ask Mitch into her own room. "Kinsey's room with me?"

"Why?"

She gives an exasperated sigh. It's perfect. She couldn't work Mitch any better, even if Derek was coaching her. "Just shut up and come here for a second." She walks into the room, expecting him to follow.

He does.

CHAPTER 32

As soon as she's inside the room, Brooke goes for it. "You want things and I want things. Let's meet somewhere in the middle."

"What are you talking about?"

His face is hard, but as long as he doesn't set her off, she can stay the course.

"Not interested in violating you, if that's what you mean," Mitch says, and Brooke wants to laugh. This is the moral high ground he's taking? Even though he's a kidnapper, and probably a murderer, even though he's no doubt watched her undress over the camera a thousand times, sleeping with her is somehow beneath him.

"Then what do you want from me?"

He stares at her, says nothing for a minute. "This a joke?"

"No. I don't do jokes anymore. Haven't for years. Surely you can understand why."

"Well, if you're serious, truth is I wouldn't mind looking at you in person."

In person.

Her stomach turns over. Why does he want this when he's

likely already seen everything? Brooke looks at the camera in the corner of Kinsey's room.

"Is Grace watching?"

"No."

Brooke will know if he's telling the truth based on what he does next. Whether or not he goes for it.

"Okay, but if I have to undress, you do, too. At least your shirt," Brooke says. She's trawling for that remote at the end of the chain around his neck. It's always tucked under his shirt and she's never seen him use it. He has the gun, so why would he need the remote?

Mitch gives a little chuckle, and it makes her skin crawl, but at least he's amused. He pulls his T-shirt off and what she thought was the remote, what Mitch has threatened her with for years, is just some military dog tags on a chain. The metal rests against gray chest hair next to a series of tiny scar lines.

She stares at the dog tags.

"No remote, I see," she says.

"You thought this was a remote?" He taps it, smirks.

She wants to scream at him for making fun of her. But no, she can't do that. Has to keep working him. She looks at her feet in mock shame.

"Hey." His voice is shockingly tender. "I won't let her do anything inhumane to you. You been through enough with her."

What does that mean? Grace has done inhumane things for years and he's never been able to stop her. Her spark comes back.

"What can you do? You think you can get in her way at all?"

His mouth twitches. Was that too much sass? He doesn't

answer, instead spins her around by the shoulders and drags her zipper down. "You said I could look."

Brooke steels up inside. This is happening, and she's going to do it. But he won't win the long game.

Her dress falls to the floor, and she stands there in her bra and skirt slip. She turns to face him. Grits her teeth.

"I always liked the curvy ones better. More to hold on to," he says, running his tongue along his bottom lip.

Mitch tries to reach for her bra strap, but she swats his hand away. An idea has landed. It's a long shot, but she feels like squealing with delight that she can improvise this well. "No. *You* give *me* something now."

He unbuttons his jeans.

"I don't want that."

Mitch's hands hang limp and there's no expression on his face. She can't tell if he's enjoying this or if he's angry.

Then he chuckles and reaches for her bra again.

She slaps his hand away, harder this time. "No. Not until you answer something for me. One question for every piece of clothing."

Yes, Brooke. Genius.

He cocks his head to the side and gives a hard shrug.

She has to be smart about her questions. Ask ones he's most likely to answer because she has exactly three questions until she's naked. Bra, slip, underwear.

"Do you have a remote? Or does Grace have the only one?"

Mitch narrows his eyes like he can't figure out what Brooke's play is, but it doesn't seem like he'll look a gift horse in the mouth.

"That's two questions. You wanna rephrase or you taking two things off?"

"Rephrase. How many remotes are there?"

She knows for a fact Grace has one.

"What makes you think I don't have one? Just because you thought it was here, and it's not?" he points to his dog tags.

No, because you told me it was there, dumbass.

"Answer my question," Brooke says.

"Ask something else."

Brooke sucks her teeth. He doesn't have a remote. That has to be why he's being cagey. But it would be so Mitch to confuse her like this, when he has a remote the whole time. She changes gears. "Why the perimeter? Why not just lock us in the cabin?"

"Two questions again, but I'm feeling generous. Because Grace wanted you guys at this location to be free. To have the freedom she experienced as a child. Before she got trapped in a marriage."

"I don't feel fucking free," Brooke says in a mock-sweet voice.

"Her ways don't always make sense. I'll give you that. Now . . ." Mitch reaches for Brooke's bra strap again, but she dodges his hand.

"I get to choose."

Since he wants her bra off, she pulls down her slip instead, so it falls to the floor and she's in her bra and underwear.

"Well, hell, you're a tease," he says, giving her that menacing half-smile.

Brooke stands there, waiting for him to make another move so that she can fend him off, but he sits in the chair he occupies when he babysits Kinsey. Rubs his chin.

"You gonna ask me something else?" he says.

This is stupid. It's not working. The first question gave her nothing definite.

"Yes, but if you give me another lame-ass obvious answer, it doesn't count."

Mitch stands and in a few steps, he's in her personal bubble. "Maybe you need a reminder about who's in charge."

Brooke holds her breath and summons all the courage she can find and touches the scar on his chest. Mitch shoves her hand away. Much harder than seems necessary.

"So sensitive," she says.

"Don't want you touching that."

"Why?"

There's a pause and then a glimmer in his eye. "Is that your question?"

"Will you give me an actual answer?"

He stares at her chest, and rolls his teeth over his bottom lip. She wants to cover herself, but doesn't. Instead, she sticks it out and takes a step forward. "Yeah. That's my question. What's the scar from?"

"Surgery."

"What kind?"

She doesn't care, but his overreaction makes her curious. It seems important to *him*.

"I gave you an answer, now come on." He waves a hand to tell her to take something off. But he's already showing his cards a little too much. Brooke feels a light shifting of their power dynamic. She may be wrong about it, but it's worth pushing to find out.

"I said no lame-ass answers. Doesn't count."

His face twitches, and again, she can't tell if it's a smile or disgust, but it's emotion, that's for sure. She shifts her approach. Has to find *something* out.

"You don't have a remote. All these years you've been bluffing."

Mitch shrugs. It's an answer. He doesn't have one. Without using words, he points at her, asking her to remove another piece of clothing. He's still staring at her chest, so she removes her underwear instead. The way he looks at her is sheer predator. She's a thing to be stalked and consumed. Fear resurfaces, but she already has her next question in mind.

CHAPTER 33

"Is there a way to turn off the perimeter?" Brooke asks.

"Might be. That was your last question." His tone is hard, eyes fixed on her exposed body.

But no, that was definitely a lame-ass answer.

"Give me something specific about how the collars or the perimeter works. How do we shut it down? Or we're done here." Brooke reaches for her dress.

"Fine. Yes. You can't turn off the collars, only she can. Only I can. The way I turned Cody's off. But yeah, there's a way to shut the perimeter down."

Brooke had always wondered why Cody's collar didn't need to be charged anymore, and it didn't detonate either. But she focuses on the second part of the answer.

"How?"

"No more questions. Take it off."

She stands there, staring at his scars. People are funny about scars, but these look like knife slashes, not surgical. Why did he freak out? It's not until Mitch comes toward her that she snaps out of her thoughts.

"No, I got it," she says. He steps back.

Brooke unclasps the bra and lets it fall down her arms and to the floor. She stands in front of him with her hands to her sides. He looks her up and down, taking his time, like he's savoring it.

There's a way to shut down the perimeter. She has to find more out.

"You sure you only want to look?" she whispers, trying hard to make her voice sultry, but cringing on the inside. "Answer more questions and I'll let you touch, too."

He grunts, turns, grabs his shirt, puts his arms through and then pulls it over his head.

"Maybe when I come back later," he says and leaves the room.

He's coming back again today?

While she's dressing, Brooke hears Mitch's truck start up. She looks out the window of Kinsey's bedroom in time to see him peel out, sprays of gravel and dirt in his wake. She hurries into the living room where Derek and Kinsey sit at opposite ends of the couch like patients waiting for a doctor's update.

"There's only one remote and Grace has it. He's been lying this whole time," Brooke announces.

"That explains the gun," Derek says. "Why would he need one if he had a remote? Anything else?"

"There's a way to turn the perimeter off."

"Yes, and . . . ?" Kinsey pushes.

"I couldn't get it out of him. He got spooked. I need more time."

"We don't have time. The wedding is tomorrow," Kinsey whispers.

"He said he's coming back later today. With *her*." Derek's voice lowers.

"If you can keep Grace busy, and if Kinsey can stay out of sight, I might get further with him."

"How do I keep her busy? She zaps me every time I get too close," Derek says.

"I don't know, get the remote away from her. Just take her down," Brooke says.

"You can take *me* down," Kinsey says to Derek. Her flirty tone stuns them both.

Brooke looks at Kinsey. That came out of nowhere. But Kinsey shrugs. "What? I'm just saying."

Derek rolls his eyes at her. He must have picked up on Kinsey's half-baked crush in all of this.

"I'm almost twice your age. You know that, right? I could be your father," he says.

"So?"

"So, you're a little young for me."

"I'm twenty-three!"

"And I was already drinking age by the time you were born."

"All right, all right, let's stay on task here," Brooke says. "When they come back, Derek, you're on."

"I'll have to disarm her before she gets to the remote and before she can pull out that knife," he says, raking a hand through his hair. He looks at the ceiling and shakes his head.

"I know it seems impossible, but if Mitch isn't around when it happens, you might get away with it."

This is dumb. It's a dumb plan that relies way too much on chance and good luck. Derek's right. He has to get two weapons out of her hands and if he doesn't, he's probably dead. But they're desperate.

"You have to get close enough to go for the remote first.

Seems like if the remote is gone, she's just an old lady with a knife," Brooke says.

"At that point, I'd take her off the board, no problem. I've thought it through. As long as we still have Mitch to tell us how to turn off the perimeter, we have a shot."

"Yes," Brooke says, excited now. Even if it's a long shot, it feels good to try. "I'll talk Mitch into sending Kinsey outside or something, and then I'll see what else I can get."

"Like I'm the pet dog," Kinsey mutters.

"You're slated to die first." Brooke whirls around to face her. "What's the big deal?"

She shrugs, softens. "Yeah, sorry."

Kinsey was so steady the past few days, so clear-minded. It's like she's the old Kinsey again. But irrational. She's probably trying to cope with the idea of dying, but still, why is she trying to get Derek to sleep with her? Of all the things to care about right now.

Derek moves toward the door, says something about checking outside again. That maybe there's a simple way to turn the perimeter off they haven't found yet.

There's not. Brooke and Tyson already covered that base, but she lets him go.

"What's gotten into you?" Brooke asks Kinsey when Derek's gone.

Kinsey shrugs and a tear runs down her cheek. "I'm not ready to die."

"You won't die," Brooke lies. No sense in making this worse by telling the truth. "And anyway, why did you say all that stuff to Derek?"

"I don't know. I guess I want to be close to someone. It doesn't even have to be sexual, although that'd be nice. He'd be a great lay, and you know I can tell these things. Also, I miss my mom."

Brooke sighs and reaches for her. What a random string of thoughts to process. "You're not alone. I'm right here."

Kinsey lays her head on Brooke's lap and cries.

CHAPTER 34

The next day, the only way for Mina to get her mind off the neighbor's house, off the weird phone call with the 911 dispatcher, and off Paxton, is to work. To do the thing she came here for, so that's what she's been focusing on today.

It's almost lunchtime and she's soared through fifty pages, many not even needing a correction. She's also cleared out a bag of Goldfish crackers, somehow avoiding the wine, but it's calling her name, so she keeps looking at her phone to see what time it is.

Anything before noon is just too early to start. Even for her.

Plus, she's greedy for more headway on her revisions. So, Mina sits at her laptop at the kitchen table, where she can't see out the front window at all. No distractions. So far, so good.

On the way back from the bathroom though, she notices the grocery delivery guy pulling up across the street. Again. The same dude as before.

They sure get a lot of groceries delivered.

She should keep walking. Through the living room, plop

her ass back down in the wooden kitchen chair, put fingers to the keyboard and work. Instead, she stands there, watches him get out of that little blue car.

Before Mina can stop herself, she's out the front door, her rental key in hand, because she won't make that mistake again. He's walking back to his car, and she waves her hands to flag him down.

"Hey! Sorry to bother you." She smiles. "But have you ever noticed anything weird about this place?" Mina points to the neighbor's house.

"What do you mean?" The guy speaks in clipped words, probably in a hurry to get to his next delivery or get away. Sweat drenches tendrils of his unkempt hair beneath a Trail Blazers ball cap.

"Like, have you ever seen anyone come out, for example? Maybe to take the groceries in before you're gone."

"No?" His voice goes higher, and he looks down like he's holding something back.

"Yes you have."

"Really, I haven't. But this house is strange. I don't know what it is, but it gives me the willies. Plus the order is always just frozen meals. Rarely anything fresh."

Mina already noticed the frozen meals. "The little girl. Ever see her?"

The guy looks over his shoulder, down the road. As if he expects the man in the Jeep to come rolling up. This raises Mina's hackles. The man does usually show up after an order arrives. They don't have a lot of time.

"She looks out the window sometimes," he starts. "Wearing this red lipstick, which is creepy."

Mina knows this already too, but she refuses the instinct to cross her arms and tap a foot. Maybe there's more. "What else?"

"I always take this order because it's close to my house."

Mina shakes her head.

Don't care about that.

He glares at her, and she realizes how strange it could seem that she's asking, so she gives him more details. "I'm worried the girl is in trouble. The cops won't come unless there's some proof of a crime."

"You called the cops?" His eyes narrow even more.

The ridicule in his voice slows Mina down. She's coming off like a nosey, emotional woman now. In his mind, it could cancel out any of her valid concerns.

"The little girl wrote 'help' in the window, so yeah, I called the cops. What else about this house? Anything you've noticed about the people inside? Or about the tall guy?"

"He tips really well. That's the other reason I always take this order."

Mina crosses her arms.

"I don't know much. Just what they order and whose name is on it."

"Okay, what's the name?"

"I can't give you that information. I'll get in trouble."

"Come on, grocery delivery isn't HIPAA."

"I know, but I really need this job. We have school debt, a second kid on the way—"

Mina waves him on to show she doesn't care about any of that.

He takes off his ball cap and wipes his wide forehead with a hand. "Fine. The names on the order are always the same: Gerald and Grace Wakeford."

Maybe that's the dad and little girl?

Or maybe the tall guy and older woman?

She has no idea, and as this awkward moment expands into silence, the guy shuffles his feet. "Lady, I need to go."

She thanks him and then immediately questions her instincts.

What if everyone else is right about this and I'm wrong?

It's a strange situation, sure, but just because a little girl writes *help* in the window, it doesn't mean there's an impending tragedy.

Not a tragedy like your daughter's death sending you into a mental break that puts you in the hospital for far too long. That girl is fine, fed, seems taken care of, although yes, the lipstick is weird. But what if it's all she has left of her mother, who must be dead or out of the picture, and she's trying to be close to her?

This sounds like a narrative Mina would write in a story, not real life.

She's spending too much time fixating on this. And while, yes, she'll keep an eye out and call the cops again if anything else happens, she really needs to focus on her damn book.

As soon as she gets inside the rental, she pulls the blinds closed.

CHAPTER 35

When Mitch and Grace arrive later in the day, Derek is ready. He's in the suit and he's showered. He even combed his hair. No razor, so he couldn't shave, and his stubble is growing soft, but he's tried to look nice, and hopefully it'll be enough to entice Grace to get close to him.

Kinsey is in the bedroom by the time the truck pulls up. The plan is for Brooke to keep Mitch occupied, asking him more questions about the perimeter, while Derek tries to steal Grace's remote. Or kills Grace, whichever is easiest. Brooke must wait for Derek to succeed before letting Mitch leave the room. Whatever it takes, because if Mitch hears them fighting, he'll come to Grace's rescue and the entire plan gets shot to hell.

Grace's eyes lock right on to Derek the moment she walks in the door. Nerves dive bomb his gut. He can't read her expression, but he thinks she likes what she sees.

This plan is such a long shot, but it's all they have. Even if he can rip that necklace from Grace, Mitch still has a gun.

God, they are so royally fucked. But one thing at a time. First up: this impossible task with Grace.

"Hi, tulip!" Brooke starts in, acting like Helen Hamilton.

Grace doesn't even look at her, then she waves her off like some annoying insect. She stares at Derek.

Brooke stands there watching, as if she's scared to make a wrong move, but after a moment, she goes into Kinsey's bedroom.

"Would you come in here? I want to show you something," Derek says, his hand motioning to Brooke's room. He needs to get her as far away from Mitch's earshot as possible. This could get loud.

"No, Daddy," Grace says. "I want you to take off that suit so we can go outside. Today, you're going to show me how to chop wood."

He stares at her. Is she serious? But hey, outside is even farther from Kinsey's than the other bedroom. Maybe Mitch won't hear a thing.

And an ax? Hell yeah.

"Sure, let me change my clothes. I'll be out in a minute." He tries not to let the eagerness show.

"I didn't say change your clothes." A small smile creeps across her face. "I said take off that suit."

The fuck.

He takes off the jacket, the shirt. And she watches. He stands there, hoping that's good enough.

"Pants too," she whispers.

This is so humiliating. He's not sure he's ever felt this way before. It's not the fact of being in his boxers, it's the way she's going about it. A total control play. Derek clenches his jaw so he doesn't say something to get himself electrocuted, and unzips his pants, kicks them off.

"You're not into this, huh?" Grace says, looking right at his boxers.

"Do you want me to be?"

She shrugs. "I don't care. Let's go."

He follows her like some brainless idiot in his underwear, but stops when she gets closer to the truck. He doesn't know how far the perimeter goes. She opens the trunk and out comes an ax.

Go time.

"Obviously, you don't get to use this, so you'll have to tell me how to chop the wood."

"Where's the wood?" Derek asks.

"Go get a few pieces from the trees over there."

He doesn't move. Again, he has no clue where the perimeter is at. There are a few trees near the cabin, but most of them are beyond.

She smiles. "Oh, come on, you don't think I'd lead you across the perimeter with only two days to go, do you?"

Bitch, I have no clue what you wouldn't do.

She's out of character, talking to him, Derek. How should he interact with her?

He looks at the gold chain around her neck. Thinks about how fast she can get it into her hands. Lightning speed. He's seen her do it.

He stretches his neck and moves toward the trees nearest to the cabin. Feels the cool wind on his bare skin, her gaze on his ass. It's nice out, but not that nice. He wants to cross his arms and try to stoke some warmth, but won't give her the satisfaction of seeing his humiliation and the way the wind chills his skin.

When he reaches the first little stand of pine trees, there's nothing large enough to chop. No downed boughs, and none of the trees themselves are small enough to hack down with just an ax. Not unless he spends all day on it.

He turns to the side to get a view of Grace in his periphery without her noticing he's trying to find her. She's in the same spot, near the driveway with the ax.

This is some test, and he doesn't know how to pass it.

"Go to the next tree," she shouts.

He looks up and behind the cabin, is the next tree. But it's hella close to where Tyson was digging. No way he's doing that.

CHAPTER 36

Brooke kicks Kinsey out of the bedroom right when she walks in.

Mitch sits in that chair, like usual, right by the door, and against the wall. The dresser is on the other side of him and his gun is there, on top of it.

"Ready for round two?" she asks Mitch.

"Round two starts where round one left off," he says, setting down his magazine.

Naked. Round one ended with her naked.

"Fine. I have four questions to get us to where round one ended."

Dress, slip, underwear, bra. Why should she undress for nothing?

"All's you got is a day or so before you die. Now strip." He reaches for his gun. What's he going to do? Sleep with her while holding a gun?

She stands right inside the room, and the door is still open, so she closes it. Then moves farther into the room to create some distance from him. She stands at the foot of the bed.

Who knows how long Derek will take to get close enough

to Grace to hurt her. Brooke wants to stall, but Mitch holds all the cards right now. If she spooks him again, it's over.

Brooke takes everything off and forces herself to make eye contact, but it's pointless. He gropes her body with his stare.

"You going to do this fully clothed?" she asks.

He sets the gun down, kicks off his shoes, pulls his shirt off, and moves to unbutton his jeans so fast that she almost wants to laugh.

There he stands in his tighty-whities, and he reaches for the gun again.

"A gun? Really?"

He looks at it. Shrugs. "I guess I could overpower you if you tried anything." He sets it back on the dresser, moves toward her, but she puts her hands out to stop him.

"Questions first." Truth is, she doesn't have questions. None that he'd answer. But she has to stall somehow.

He hangs his head to the side like he's irritated.

"How do we shut off the perimeter?"

Mitch laughs. "Not telling you that."

"How do we get these collars off?"

He narrows his eyes. "These are stupid questions, and you know I won't answer them. But you're not stupid."

All right, helpful questions are out. On to Plan B: Easy questions. Go through the motions so Brooke doesn't look too eager, but get this moving along too. She'll have to stall another way.

"Is Grace really going to kill Kinsey?"

Mitch grins. "Yes."

He approaches her and she steels herself while he palms her breast and then lets out a nasty groan.

This is horrible. She'd rather just get on with it than drag it out like this, so she slams her body into his. He gasps out of surprise. Eyes peering over his shoulder, Brooke tries to find the dresser, the gun.

A new idea perks to life.

She tries to spin him around so she's the one closer to the gun—it would be right behind her—but he doesn't budge.

He's still skeptical of her actions.

"What? I like being on top," she says to explain the change of position. "Think you can handle that?" His eyebrows raise, and he lets her spin him. Now her back is to the gun, good. But his eyes are wide open, and he's still not distracted. He's really hard too, which makes bile rise in the back of her throat.

That's when she knows for sure she's doing this. She's going to have to do the deed in order to get that gun.

Go all in.

She pushes him down on the bed, and climbs on top, straddling him.

Brooke closes her eyes as they get going, but slows down enough to put on a show, caress herself and be certain she's making all the right noises to trick him into believing she's super into it. God, the way she's moaning, he probably thinks she's having the romp of her life. She hates giving that to him, but it's more important to get him lost in the moment.

His age shows in how long he takes to finish, which is torturous, but convenient since she needed to stall, and when it's over, she falls to the side of the bed closest to the gun. Closest to the door. She's one quick leap away from it, but she's also less than an arm's length from Mitch. He's lying there, panting, like he just sprinted down the driveway.

Disgusting.

Another idea comes to mind, so simple it's almost unbelievable.

She stands and pads toward the gun.

"What are you doing?" he asks, sitting up in a rush.

"Getting your smokes. Don't you like a cigarette afterward?"

She passes by the gun, not even looking at it and reaches for his pants on the floor.

She roots around in his pockets and finds his lighter in the front, smokes in the back.

Mitch doesn't seem to know how to respond, and he still combs her naked body with his eyes. If Brooke didn't know any better, she'd think he believes her. That she's trying to serve him, take care of him. The confidence of a less-than-mediocre white man.

She pulls out the cigarette and holds it like she's handing it to him. He leans over to get it, but she pulls it back, like a tease.

"Let me," she says and smiles. Maintains eye contact and channels any ounce of seduction into the look. He lets her put it in his mouth. Then she strikes the Zippo, and lights the cigarette. He takes a big pull, and she stands still with the flame still glowing in her hand. As he tips his head back a bit, letting his guard slip just barely, she tosses it in his lap and lunges for the dresser.

Mitch yelps, curses. But he's got both the lighter and a lit cigarette to deal with. He flings his arms to put out the flame, while trying to move away from it. Brooke's hand stretches out for the gun. She can see him in the corner of her vision, his rough hand reaching for her hair.

She ducks.

He misses.

Her fingers touch cold metal and she wraps them around the grip of the gun.

"The hair grab again? Really?" she says, turning and pointing it at Mitch. "Just like day one. You're so predictable."

He steps back. "Fucking bitch. Knew this was too good to be true. Give me that."

Brooke laughs. "Hell no." She checks the safety. Flicks it off. She doesn't know a lot about guns, but she knows that. Figures the rest she can learn on the fly.

He puts his hands in the air.

She tosses his pants at him. "Nobody wants to see that. Cover up."

He obeys.

Brooke reaches for her dress and, without taking her eyes off him, steps into it and pulls it up and over her arms. It's clumsy, trying to do this with one hand, and the back gapes open, but it'll have to do for now.

Mitch laughs. "You think you're gonna get away with this?"

"Yes."

Brooke backs toward the bedroom door. She needs Kinsey to help her tie him up. She can't do it with only one free hand.

"I could just yell for Grace," he says.

"Why haven't you then?"

His face twitches.

"Ahh . . . You're gonna be in deep shit, that's why."

His jaw clenches.

She keeps the gun pointed at him, far enough away that she could shoot if he made a move toward it. But what's she supposed to do now? Stand here like this until Derek gets Grace's remote?

She can feel Mitch growing bolder. He's stronger than her. What if he tries to tackle her? Even if she got a shot off, it might not be enough to stop him. Kinsey needs to be in here. Two are better than one even though neither of them are as strong as Mitch.

"Kinsey!" Brooke shout-whispers through the door.

The door opens, and Kinsey smiles.

"Help me tie him up."

A woman's voice cuts through the cabin. "What are you doing in the living room, Young Grace?"

Kinsey's breath hitches in panic.

Brooke glances over Kinsey's shoulder and it's Grace, standing behind her, holding the remote in her hand.

No.

Derek emerges in boxers behind Grace.

Kinsey steps aside.

"Come out," Grace snarls.

Brooke points the gun at Mitch and waves him on ahead. He can face her first.

"For Christ's sake, Mitch," Grace says when she sees him half-dressed.

Derek was unsuccessful. It's over. This was their last chance and they blew it.

"Give it to me," Grace says about the gun. She could end Brooke right now. But could Brooke shoot her first? No. She'd have to move the gun's barrel from Mitch over to Grace, and Grace would have already pushed the button by then.

But she can't just hand the weapon over! Not going to happen.

Brooke whips the gun toward Grace and squeezes off a shot.

It's premature, and the bullet hits the paneled wood wall above Kinsey's head.

"Fucking hell!" Kinsey shouts.

A piercing sensation runs through Brooke's body. Every single goddamn cell. She can barely breathe.

She registers hitting the floor, but nothing else.

When she comes to, she's on cold wood. The brightness of the room makes her head pound. But what sends terror in shockwaves through her body is Grace. The woman is on top of her, the cold metal of her blade pressing against the tender skin of Brooke's neck.

The room is quiet. Nobody speaks. Grace's dead eyes bore into Brooke's, which are watery and hard to see out of. A warm tear courses down her cheekbone and across her earlobe toward the floor. "I'm so sorry," she breathes.

This is the pose and the face Brooke has observed in Grace for so many years. Just before a cast member dies. Now, it's her turn.

Grace's lips flatten, she groans in annoyance, but keeps her eyes trained on Brooke, the blade pressed.

Brooke has never seen Grace take this long with a killing. Maybe she won't do it.

Of course she's going to do it.

Then, a release. Grace takes the blade away and stands. Brooke exhales, but stays lying on the floor, unsure how to process what just happened. Grace didn't kill her.

"Goddamn it," Grace mutters.

Brooke sits up, but can't find words to say. She doesn't trust that Grace would let this go. And then Grace raises the gun and Brooke's insides drop. She isn't letting it go.

Grace moves the gun over to aim it at Mitch and shoots.

She misses. Definitely on purpose, the way the bullet winged by his head.

Brooke's mind is in free fall. There's no way to make sense of this, but one thing is a consolation: the look on Mitch's face. It's pure shock. He ducks and puts his hands up, and greasy strands of thinning hair fall over his forehead. He doesn't say a word, but cowers there in front of them all.

"If we weren't so close to ending this scene, I would get rid of all of you and start with a new cast," Grace says. "But I'm eager to be done. This has been a lot of work for me. My life's work, my passion, yes, but I don't have the energy to start over fresh. I need to make do with what I have."

As if she's being put out by them trying to escape with their lives.

"Come on, you stupid bastard," she says. He scrambles into Kinsey's room for the rest of his clothes.

"Tomorrow is young Grace's last scene," she tosses over her shoulder on the way out. "And then it'll be time for the final scene."

Mitch sulks, following behind her, and he seems a hundred years old. Disoriented, his gray hair gone wild.

Kinsey goes into her bedroom and slams the door. She screams, and there's a crashing noise, as if she's overturning furniture.

Brooke and Derek make eye contact, but she can't conjure any words, so she goes into her own room and closes the door.

CHAPTER 37

Mina slept maybe two hours last night, and this morning she's groggy. Doesn't think coffee will do it for her, but she drinks her third cup anyway. It's not even six a.m.

She dreamed that when they'd buried Paxton, she wasn't actually dead, and in the dream, it was like Mina experienced everything from Paxton's perspective instead of her own. Trapped in a dark coffin, screaming, fists pounding on the inside. Tears, and the horror of knowing that you're going to die anyway, no matter what you do, but still, you try. The clawing need for air, but the knowledge that it will run out. The stubborn survival instinct to conserve your breaths.

This was not how it happened for Paxton. Mina saw her daughter at the funeral home, even dressed the girl for her viewing. She was absolutely gone by the time they lowered her into the ground, but still this thought lingers like pine sap residue you can't quite wash off. The desperation her daughter might have felt in her last moments; Mina felt it too. She wants to tell Brady because it's strange that they both dreamed of Paxton this week. But hers was so much darker than Brady's, and she doesn't know how he'd respond to it.

Sure, it might bring them closer, but Brady might read into it and somehow equate the dream with Mina's mental state. She doesn't need that. Especially when her mental state has been stable for so many years.

Now that it's getting light outside, Mina opens the blinds and she's discouraged to see there's no sun. The sky is full of bloated, ashen clouds that'll dump rain any minute. Then again, it's a perfect opportunity to stay inside and get some work done.

Her eyes find the little girl's window, and she almost drops her cup of coffee.

Blood. There's a bloody smear across the glass, like someone had a cut on their hand and wiped it.

She gets her phone and calls 911 again. There's a reason for someone to check on this house now! Whether or not a crime is being committed, they need help.

"Blood! There's blood on the window!" she shouts as soon as the operator asks for her emergency.

"Slow down. What's the address?" a man asks.

"35 'J' Street in Freeport."

A long pause again, identical to the last time she called.

"Are you there?" Mina asks.

"Yes, ma'am, I'm here. Blood you say?"

This is a different dispatcher than the first time, and yet he's just as inept.

"Yes! Blood. Get someone over there to check on them."

The sound of tapping comes through. Like fingers on a smartphone. Is he texting? What the hell?

"Hello?!"

"Still here, ma'am. I'll send someone over."

"Damn right you will," Mina says, ending the call. Weird. So, so weird!

Mina sits by the window, her heart climbing up her throat, like it's trying to escape. She bites a hangnail, and before she realizes it, she's chewed all of her fingernails down.

What if she's too late? What if the little girl tried to get her attention while bleeding? If it was a large cut, she could have passed out. Depending on how disabled the dad is . . . Oh God, what if she's lying there dying right now?

Ten minutes pass, and time feels like a watched pot.

That's it. Mina's going over there again. What is taking the police so long in this tiny town?

She pounds a fist on the door, but there's no answer.

Before she can try again, the silver Jeep pulls up to Mina's rental.

What the hell?

The door opens and the man gets out. She can't believe her eyes. That man is in a police uniform.

This man is also a cop?

"Hey!" she waves as if he's a normal cop, as if they haven't had multiple unsettling interactions. She walks over to her place again.

They stare at each other in her front yard. His name tag reads "Moore." She doesn't know what to say, so she keeps pretending like this is normal. "I called 911 because there's blood on the window." She points, crosses her arms.

"Hmph," he grunts. "How do you know it's blood?"

"Look at it!"

His eyes shift in that direction, but he doesn't really look. "Could be lipstick."

"That's not lipstick. And what the hell is going on around here? You're a cop, too?"

"Part time. Only when I'm needed. Small town with lots of jobs to do."

"Well, go check on them!"

"Right." He smirks and walks past her. He pulls out the house key and goes in without even knocking.

Isn't that illegal entry? Or maybe not, because he's the owner or property manager or whatever. But still, they can't just walk inside. He's been doing that the whole time.

Mina finds a tiny sliver of skin around a fingernail and works it with her teeth while she waits. A drop of rain lands on her cheek, another, and then it's a drizzle. Why is she still standing here? Who knows how long he'll be inside. She goes back into her rental, sits on the couch at the front window to watch.

He's not even in there for five minutes before he walks out to his Jeep. He opens the door to get in. Without even updating her? What is wrong with this person?

Mina flings the front door open and yells through the rain, "Well? Is everything all right?"

"Course," he says and slams his car door, drives away.

The situation is no more resolved than it was before he came. Not only that, but she doesn't believe him. It feels like he's hiding something, and . . . what if Mina only got the little girl in trouble by sending him over there?

The thought feels like a rock dropping in her stomach.

Mina's phone pings with a text message. It's Brady.

Good morning, beautiful. How's the book coming along?

Great! she texts back.

She could call the Portland police. Maybe they'd do something. But no, she's seen the shows. They'll just tell her it's not their jurisdiction.

Another idea comes to mind.

I'm going into Portland today for some research, if you notice that on location sharing, she texts.

Sounds good. Thanks for letting me know!

That was different. She expected him to ask a million questions about why she needs to do that and where she'll be in Portland. But, surprise upon surprise, he reacted normally. Affection for Brady grows inside her heart again.

Despite the fact that her text to him is only half-true.

Mina pulls on her raincoat and slips into Hunter boots. She's going into Portland, yes. But not for research.

CHAPTER 38

It's a downpour outside today, and Kinsey is an absolute wreck. Full on muttering to herself, crying on and off. She's wandering around in that vintage wedding dress Grace brought over.

Brooke understands why, and tries to be comforting, but after being shot down a few times, she gets angry and gives up. It's not like Kinsey is the only one whose life is on the line. The only one who will die this week. Steel moves over Brooke's heart, and with it, shame. She doesn't want to harden up against the girl, but what else can she do? Kinsey's going to die today. Brooke's compassion won't change that outcome.

Derek, bless his heart, tries to calm her down, but she snaps at him, then disappears into her room.

Brooke opens a can of tomato soup to warm up on the stove. They're down to the pantry food now. Everything fresh is gone, another reminder of their ticking clock.

Derek approaches Brooke, manages to get in her way like usual. She groans, motions for him to move.

He doesn't seem to pick up on her impatience because he

only takes a fraction of a step back. "I can't sit around and wait for this to happen. There has to be a way."

"You're so thick-headed. I've told you from day one, there's no way. I tried with the last plan, and it failed."

I can't try anymore.

That's what Brooke wants to say, but doesn't. It sounds stupid. Who gives up when their life is on the line? But she's emotionally drained and can't conjure up the energy or the hope it takes to plan another escape. She pours the soup into a small saucepan.

"You want some?" she asks, only now realizing that one can won't feed all three of them.

He goes to the pantry and grabs another can without being asked. He hands it to her.

That was helpful. She wants to thank him, but he's too quick to speak.

"Maybe there's still a way to get to Mitch."

"I'm not sleeping with him again. He wouldn't trust me now, anyway."

She turns and Derek's *right there*. So close she runs into his chest. He smells like soap and deodorant. A hint of something earthy that she likes, but can't place. A rush of warmth courses through her body.

What the hell.

She takes the soup from his hand.

"That's not what I meant," Derek says. "Maybe he'll give us something. She dressed him down right in front of us. He's got to be pissed."

"Mitch is loyal to Grace. He made it pretty clear." Brooke pushes Derek away. It's not rough, just a signal for him to scoot back again. Her insides light up at the touch.

Jesus Christ, what is wrong with me?

Derek clears his throat. "I'm not saying—"

"What are you guys fighting about this time?" Kinsey comes out of her bedroom and the first thing Brooke notices is the dopey, almost absent look on her face. It's obvious what that means.

"Are you high?" Brooke asks, even though it would be impossible.

Kinsey gives a ridiculous smile. "Maybe."

"How?" Derek asks.

Kinsey shrugs.

"No, really, Kins, how the hell?" Brooke asks.

"Mitch gave me something last time we were in the room alone. Said to save it for a rainy day. And it's fucking raining to high heaven today." Kinsey staggers to the couch and sits. Stares at nothing.

"What did he give you?" Brooke asks.

"Not sure, but it feels good."

Then Kinsey seems to zone out, fingering her collar. Her face changes, like she's realizing something. "Guys, can you help me get this off?" Like she's asking them to help her with a jammed zipper.

"Can't take that off," Brooke says, stirring the soup and trying to fend off the irritation in her voice. Kinsey knows. Why is she trying?

"I want it off."

"We all do, Kins, but you know it doesn't come off."

Kinsey keeps messing with the collar.

"Stop doing that!" Brooke says, growing concerned. Derek puts a hand on her shoulder and when she looks at him, he's shaking his head. Telling her to stop. Or to calm down? Who knows?

Kinsey goes into Cody's room and Brooke returns to the

soup.

"She's hallucinating," Derek whispers.

"You think?"

He nods.

"Shit. What do we do?"

"Get it off!" Kinsey yells, coming out of Cody's room only seconds after she went in. She has the metal file. She saws at the collar with it.

"Help me!" Kinsey screams, her neck red from pulling at the metal. There's a bit of blood from where the tool has nicked her skin. "I can't breathe."

But she can. Brooke sees her chest heaving, along with the tiny space between the choker and her skin. Derek's right. She's hallucinating.

"Kinsey, you're tripping balls. Just listen." Derek puts out his hands trying to calm her, but Kinsey responds by pointing the file at her own collar, as if she's going to jam it in.

"Stop that!" Brooke yells, backing toward her bedroom. There's no rear door at this place, or she'd run outside. No way she's running past Kinsey to get out the front. Brooke has never seen a collar go off, and she's not willing to find out what happens.

Derek steps *toward* Kinsey, but she points the file at him. "Get back. Unless you're going to help me take this off."

"Yes, I'll help. Just give me the file."

She shakes her head and returns the tool to her collar, wedging it into the metal with more force than before.

Red lights appear all around Kinsey's collar.

"Derek!" is all Brooke has time to say, but in that split second, he sees it too.

He lifts Kinsey in one motion, throws her over his shoulder and she thrashes, the white dress and her loose, wild blonde hair swishing. He launches the front door open and runs outside into the rain. Brooke takes shallow breaths. It's the start of hyperventilating.

Kinsey.

Derek.

Brooke's legs wake up, so she sprints into her bedroom and hides in the closet. Closes the door and sits in the dark. Covers her head with her arms and sobs. Like she always does. Protect herself first.

There's a sound like a loud pop coming from the front yard.

CHAPTER 39

When Derek opens Brooke's closet door and sends light into the darkness, he's drenched. Rain with tiny blood flecks across his chest. His light blue button-up shirt sticks to his skin, wet hair hangs in swaths across his forehead. He grips the metal file in one hand.

They stare at each other in silence. He reaches a hand down to where she's crouched.

The soup burbles over in the kitchen and hits the burner with a hiss. Burned tomato soup and rain on clean skin. That's what this moment smells like.

She takes his hand to get up, then pushes past him. Runs into the kitchen to move the saucepan to a cold burner as if that's the most important thing right now.

When she turns around, Derek stands in the living room, still watching her. Brooke covers her mouth with both hands and screams into them with wild horror. It's a delayed reaction. Shock surely. She takes a sharp breath in and whispers, "Oh God, Kinsey!" She starts toward the front door.

Derek intercepts her. "Don't go out there."

"She might be alive. She needs us!" Brooke yells, moving to get away from him, but he's got her by the shoulders.

"She's gone." Derek's voice cracks.

Brooke rips away from his hold and sits on the couch, shaking her head. "How did that happen?"

Derek doesn't answer. It's as if he knows it's a rhetorical question. Instead, he sits against the door, knees up. He seems to be somewhere else. Both of them face the kitchen.

But Brooke has to see. Has to know for sure. She moves to the window and there, halfway between the front door and the perimeter, lies Kinsey.

Blood smothers the wedding dress, her arms and legs outstretched. Where her neck is, it's red. So much red bleeding out in tiny streams from her immobile body. Mixing with the deluge of rain.

"Oh God, the blood," Brooke gasps.

Tyson's collar had gone off underground and Mitch had to dig through the collapse to retrieve his corpse. But she never saw, didn't know what would happen.

Derek nods, doesn't look at Brooke. "It ripped her throat open."

"How did you . . . get away without it hurting you?" she asks. "You were so close by."

Derek bites the inside of his cheek, and doesn't answer right away.

"Did you hear me?" Brooke asks.

He looks over. "I threw her. I had already set her down, and she had that file at her neck, fucking around with the collar and it was still blinking red, and then it made a noise. A click. I shoved her away from the cabin and ran." His mouth twitches like he's trying to hold back tears.

Brooke can't think of what to say. Derek gets up and hands the file to her. She returns it to Cody's ribcage. She's numb, moving like an automaton. Derek seems distant.

They sit in the living room all afternoon in silence as they wait for Grace to arrive for the godforsaken wedding. What happens next? There's no bride. What if Kinsey's death has bought them a little more time? Grace may need to find another girl to play young Grace for the wedding. But she said she doesn't want to start fresh. Brooke has no idea what to expect.

———

The sound of a car approaching seems so much louder than usual, probably since Brooke has been both dreading and straining to hear it all day. It's late afternoon. Her stomach lurches at the pure uncertainty of what will happen when Grace sees Kinsey.

The door opens, and it's her.

"What the hell happened?" Grace demands.

Brooke stands. "She tripped her own collar . . ." She hesitates because it occurs to her that Mitch could get in trouble here. He's the one who gave Kinsey the drugs that made her lose her mind. Brooke keeps that to herself. It could be useful to manipulate Mitch.

"And why would she do that? How?" Grace asks. She's close to accusing them, holding them responsible for Kinsey's death.

"She said she didn't want to be a part of the cast anymore," Derek says.

Brooke looks at him.

When Grace doesn't respond, he clears his throat and goes on. "Said she'd rather take her own life than let you take it. We tried to talk her out of it, but that's why she ran outside. So she wouldn't hurt us if it was an explosion."

"Well, she hurt my wedding dress," Grace mutters. "And now I have to find a new young Grace."

Brooke gasps, but swallows down the jolt of hope. They have more time. It took Mitch a month to bring Derek in after Tyson died.

"No matter, Mitch's got it figured out. He already has someone in mind," Grace says.

No.

When Mitch shows up, he doesn't look so good. Is he grumpy or sick? Brooke can't tell. He walks back outside.

"Well, since we can't have a wedding today, I guess we should chop wood," Grace says to Derek.

Random.

They go outside, and Brooke stands in the cabin alone.

She peeks out the front door. Doesn't see Grace and Derek. They must be in the back, where the only trees inside the perimeter are located.

Brooke corners Mitch. It's still pouring out, but she steps into it, anyway. Kinsey's body is gone, but there's still a smear of diluted red where she fell.

Water courses down Brooke's face, drips into her eyes and mouth, but she doesn't care. She has to find him and see what else he'll tell her if she threatens to rat him out about the drugs. Where is he?

The perimeter hums loud over the sound of rain, reminding her how little time they have left. Sheets of water fall from a gunmetal gray sky. Mitch appears, using a small towel to wipe his hands off near the car. He's across the perimeter from her. Brooke stands there, hoping he'll notice and come over.

When Mitch sees her, he shakes his head and approaches.

"What the hell do you want?" he says.

He's still mad about yesterday, of course he is.

"Hey, sorry about the gun thing," she says. "I had to try. You understand that, right?"

"I understand that you're a fuckin' bitch."

"You gave her drugs," Brooke says, ignoring the insult. "That's why she did it. She was hallucinating about the collar. Messed with it until it exploded."

Mitch sighs and rubs an open palm against his gray stubble. "Dammit. You tell Grace yet?"

Brooke shakes her head. "Doesn't seem like Grace missed that shot on accident yesterday. Wonder what she'd do to you if she found out about Kinsey? Tell me how to get past the perimeter and I'll keep it to myself."

He pauses for a minute, sighs again. Brooke crosses her arms. It's not freezing out, but she's soaking wet and the wind is taking advantage of it, turning her skin cold. Grace and Derek could show up any minute.

"Let's go inside," Mitch says, and takes her by the arm.

Brooke shakes him off. "No. Tell me how to get past the perimeter. You think she's going to hang on to you for much longer? She wants to be done with this. Didn't you hear her?"

Mitch grunts. "She needs me."

"Like hell she does."

He flattens his lips, but doesn't reply. He must have thought of this possibility already. Why would she keep paying him after this is over? How can she send him off to live happily ever after with everything he knows?

Mitch looks at the spot where Kinsey died and says, "There's a flaw in the perimeter design. Too bad you didn't know about it when that one offed herself. Grace doesn't even have a clue."

CHAPTER 40

"The fuck does that mean?" Derek says, watching out the window as Grace and Mitch drive away through the rain.

Brooke is sopping wet, shivering with cold, but she's already told him the news.

"No idea," she says, "but something about the perimeter doesn't always work right."

"He didn't tell you more?"

Brooke shakes her head. "I pressed him, but he said that if I was as smart as he thinks I am, I could figure it out."

"And Grace doesn't know about the flaw?"

Brooke shrugs. "That's what he said."

"What do you think it is?"

She throws her hands up and they slap her wet thighs when they come back down. "It has to have something to do with the collar detonating. Because why else would knowing about it after Kinsey died matter?"

"Fuck," Derek breathes. Runs a hand through his hair. "I heard something when I was out there with her. With Kinsey."

Brooke's eyes fix on him. He continues, "You know that

constant humming that the perimeter makes? Well, it went silent right when her collar made that *click* noise."

"And you didn't tell me this?" Brooke yells.

"How could I know it meant anything?"

"What if it means the perimeter goes off?" She pauses. "Cody's collar," she whispers with excitement, looks at Derek. "We could toss Cody's collar over the perimeter and see what happens!"

"Cody's collar is dead. It'd be no different from tossing a piece of metal over."

"So, we charge it."

Derek can't think of a reason to argue with this idea. If the perimeter shuts off when a collar detonates, that could be the way to do it.

But then, no.

One of them would still have to walk across the perimeter to test it out. So, even if Cody's collar works, there's no way to act on the idea without tremendous risk.

"One of us would still have to take the leap of faith across the perimeter since we aren't sure the detonation turns it off," he says. If it's up to him, neither of them is going to be the lab rat who tests it out. End of story.

"That has to be it. What else would it be?"

Derek shrugs. It's a strong possibility, but not a sure thing.

Brooke seems to consider this, and any excitement she had about this idea drains from her face. "Mitch said he turned Cody's collar off. It probably needs to be turned on and I don't know how to do that. I should change my clothes," she whispers, and goes into her bedroom.

Derek sits in his living room chair, mind whirling as he thinks of other possibilities. Every time he comes up with something, his brain spins out again. Cody's collar may be a way to trip the perimeter, yes, but it's still a gamble. And it may flat-out not work.

There's always the chance that Mitch is lying to them, anyway. Then again, they're out of time. It could be a matter of days at the most before those asshats come back for the wedding.

When she comes out of the bedroom, Brooke is in dry clothes and back to her normal, hardened self. She heads into the kitchen and wets a red-striped washcloth at the sink as if nothing happened today.

"What are you doing?"

"Cleaning."

"Why? What does it matter?"

Brooke throws the washrag down. "It doesn't matter, okay? Nothing matters. Nothing has ever *mattered*. Not in this little world. But I don't want to stare at this burned soup mess anymore." She wipes her nose and tries to hide that she's crying.

He approaches her in the kitchen. "We can't give up," he says, bracing for the impact of her anger. But it doesn't come.

"Part of me just feels ready to be done," she whispers. She stares past him, detached. This bothers him more than her anger does. "Stepping over that perimeter, even if I die, feels sort of like freedom. Taking control of my life for the first time in so goddamn long."

"No way," Derek says. "That's not happening. We have a little more time than we thought we did, so let's use it to come up with another idea."

Brooke screams. She actually yells like some Viking warrior, all teeth, and sprays of spit, and Derek flinches.

"No! No more ideas. No more plans!" She moves around the island and away from him. "I can't handle it anymore. I'd rather spend the last of my time alive in peace, thinking back on my life—about my daughter whose entire childhood I've missed, my mom, my family, the job I loved, which I'd just gotten before I was taken. I'd rather prepare myself for the end. Not scramble to do some impossible thing. Only to fail."

"You have a daughter?" Derek says. He had no idea, and this puts Brooke into a different category in his mind. He can't help it. Those damn protector instincts that drove him into police work in the first place. He has to get her out of here.

"Never mind." Brooke closes down so fast.

"Okay, what if we come up with a plan that doesn't fail?"

Brooke throws her hands up again. "I don't know. But I'm done."

"You always say that." Derek tries to soften his voice.

"I mean it this time."

"Look," he says, placing his hand on the countertop for emphasis, "when I first got here, you pinned me correctly. Nailed it. I am a quitter. I know everything there is to know about giving up. It's what I've done my whole life. Except since I've been here. No clue why I had to wait to learn this damn lesson until now. But having tried both ways, I'm telling you it's better to go all in and try. Even if it means you might fail. I'd rather go out like that than live a nothing existence."

CHAPTER 41

Brooke sighs and seems to soften. She bites her top lip, and Derek takes it as a sign that she's willing to hear him out. To listen to his sob story.

Here goes nothing.

It was three a.m. when he got the call, and Derek's first thought was that he didn't want to disturb his wife, even though she'd left him weeks prior. But that's how out of it he was. Couldn't sleep unless he drank himself blind. Even then, it'd be four hours tops, and he'd be awake, head pounding, still spinning. This was Derek's first night of actual sleep in a long time.

On the other line, his supervisor said they'd found the body of a little girl hidden in a ditch and he needed to come in.

Derek worked in Homicide. Had been a detective for a few years, and his record was unbelievable. Impossible, really. He had solved every case assigned to him. The job was every-thing. In fact, it was more than a job. It was a calling. You're with people on the very worst day of their lives. They don't need you there unless that's the case, and maybe you can do some good. That's how he used to think.

This little Jane Doe had been dead for at least a week and dumped by the side of the road, wrapped in a tarp. Who knows why the hell anyone walks their dog at three a.m., but that's how they found her. Something about her case hooked Derek deep in his soul. It wasn't gruesome. There were no signs of sexual trauma. She was simply a dead little girl. Still, he had to solve it.

Problem was, evidence was scarce. Testing said all traces of blood were hers, and had been contained inside the tarp. This likely meant she wasn't attacked where they found her, but if someone dumped her there, where did they kill her?

For months, they couldn't match her with any missing girls in Portland. But then they got a tip from a woman a few hours away. She sent a picture of her daughter, and sure enough, it was their Jane Doe. The Rodriguez girl, that's what they called her around the office. They hadn't seen her in the database as a missing person, and later found out it was because nobody inputted her. Someone hadn't done their job. No matter, at least they knew who the victim was, and Derek was eager to find the son of a bitch who could snuff out a young life like that.

The police in the city where the girl disappeared started looking around, and they found a hotel sheet hidden in the brush near where the Rodriguez girl had gone missing. There was a blood stain. DNA confirmed it was the girl's blood. This was the closest thing they had to a crime scene.

So then, Derek had a jurisdiction problem. It seemed someone killed the girl in the other city, but dumped her in Portland. Derek wanted the case. He'd already started canvassing the area for witnesses, interviewing whatever leads he could find. He was invested. But jurisdiction went to the city where the crime was committed. Portland transferred the case, along with all the evidence from the dump site. Derek asked his supervisor for permission to travel over there and help the local police. He couldn't let the case go. Wanted to see it solved, yes, to keep his perfect record, but also because the case gnawed at him. With permission, he showed up to help. The department was so small they didn't turn him down, but every lead was a bust. Any time Derek thought they had a minor break, the door slammed shut, and they were at square one.

After a few months, his supervisor called. Said they needed him back in Portland, working fresher cases.

Derek had failed. He tried to be logical and tell himself that it wasn't even his case anymore. It was out of his hands. But logic didn't stick. He dreamed about the Rodriguez girl at night and woke up drenched in sweat, as if he'd experienced the pain she went through. Like it was his pain, too.

The local police department worked the case for a while, albeit less aggressively than Derek would have. Soon, he wasn't even getting updates.

He drove down there on his days off, poked around alone, trying to find something, anything, to learn who killed this little girl. Years passed and there were no real leads. Tips, yes, but they never panned out. The case had been cold in that town for so long and Derek was only wasting time, driving around, trying to discover anything he could. He had to give up. But that wasn't the worst of it. The worst was that soon, he wasn't even working the cases on his plate anymore. The Rodriguez girl kept haunting his dreams. He tried to sock his emotions away. Over time, the booze helped, but then he lost his second marriage.

One night, Derek went to bed and simply didn't show up for work the next day. Or the next. Soon, the booze couldn't black out the pain, the regret. The girl kept showing up, asking why he hadn't found her killer. So, he got his hands on something stronger, something that made it so he didn't even dream. Eventually, Derek couldn't pay his bills, but still didn't care enough to do anything about it. Time ticked by, and he knew where he was headed, and that it was exactly where he deserved to be.

The only thing he cared about was the thing he had to make himself forget: that Rodriguez girl.

CHAPTER 42

Derek stops talking, folds his hands and bows his head as if he's going to pray.

Brooke had assumed there was a story like this in his past. A case he'd failed. But this is baffling because it seems like a normal cold case to her. So many like it where they never find the killer. How could he see it as his own failure? He's a grown man, and it's like he doesn't realize that sometimes shitty stuff happens, but you move forward anyway. In fact, he's been so full of determination to escape since he got here that it's almost difficult to view him as someone who would give up like that. Lose their mind over a single failing.

One thing's for sure: Listening to him speak, seeing his vulnerability, it puts him in a different light. He's a good man, big-hearted under all that machismo.

"Everyone fails. It's not your fault," Brooke says. Her words are careful, much softer than normal.

Derek shrugs, and it almost discounts everything he just told her. "Easy to say that."

"Think of all the good you did. All the cases you solved.

Plus, you did everything you could for her. It's a hell of a lot more than I did for Cody."

She's not trying to turn this to herself, but suddenly that's what's happening.

Derek looks over. His eyes are eager to get the focus off of himself.

Brooke sighs. "This wedding isn't the first time Grace has thrown a curve ball. She gave me a choice once . . ." She waits for a reaction to see if he understands enough to spare her from spelling it out. His face stays neutral. He's waiting for the rest of the story. "Tyson's life or Cody's."

Derek's eyes grow large and Brooke braces for the judgment. The same accusations she's lobbied against herself for years.

How could you do that to a child?

She goes on, "It had to be that way. If I had Tyson killed, it would have been a waste because Cody was playing Larry, who had died young in real life, and so Cody's scene was closer to ending, according to Grace. If I had Cody killed, Tyson would live until after young Grace was married. His scene ended when Albert's did, which I thought would be at least ten years away."

Brooke feels the start of tears, but clenches her fists and hits her own forehead with one. She doesn't deserve the luxury of crying, or feeling sorry for herself about this.

Derek moves to sit next to her on the floor. Both of them, backs against kitchen cabinets. He removes her fist, and she pulls her hand away, puts it into her lap. Otherwise, he doesn't touch her, and thank God, because it's so distracting, the way her insides practically vibrate whenever they make physical contact. The warmth of his body next to hers is everything.

She gets that same surge of solace, like when he was standing close to her earlier. Makes her a little melty, which is a weird mix of emotion right now.

"That's an impossible choice," he whispers.

"Tyson didn't know about it," Brooke continues. "At least, not at first. But Grace made sure he did eventually, and after that, things were different between us. For a long time he wouldn't even look me in the eye. Tyson was a good person, and he didn't understand how I could let a child die. Said he would have died for Cody."

Derek shakes his head. "Again, easy to say that."

Brooke faces him. "What?"

"Oh, come on, it's easy to say that once the deed is done. It's a safe high ground to claim."

What the hell? Derek never knew Tyson. He doesn't know what Tyson would or wouldn't have done. Brooke does.

"Tyson was like that. Sacrificial," she says, trying to hide how defensive she feels.

"How long did he punish you for it?"

The question jars Brooke, and forces warm tears down her cheeks. The concern in Derek's question, yes, but also because it's a lot to switch from defend-Tyson mode into agree-with-Derek mode.

But he's right.

Tyson's harsh reaction over her choice had made her angry enough back when it happened that she had picked an actual fight with him. Their first and only, because Tyson didn't fight. He diffused, constantly diffused everything so that it never turned into a big confrontation. He was terrified of conflict and wanted everyone around him to avoid it at all costs. But Tyson's definition of conflict bewildered Brooke.

He shied away from anything but total agreement, and he got uncomfortable so easily. He hated it when Brooke raised her voice, even in excitement. It seemed he felt threatened by any show of strength. He'd get squirmy, and if it went on too long, he'd leave the room. At first Brooke overlooked it, assuming it was his traumatic childhood, and never having had a family. But soon, she felt suffocated by it. Like he was asking her to change for him. Not change something outward, like Ian had, but change *herself.*

Now, in this moment, she realizes how much worse that is. She didn't see it back then.

So Brooke had held her ground on this one thing with Tyson because Grace put her in the position, and either way, someone had to die. It seemed logical to choose the person who would die soon, anyway. But Tyson's logic said you don't kill a child to save a grown man.

"Not as long as I've punished myself," Brooke finally answers.

The only sound is soft rain on the roof of the cabin. Brooke didn't expect sympathy from Derek. In fact, she thought he'd agree with Tyson, especially after that story he just shared. She wouldn't have mentioned this if she knew he'd be easy on her. It's a little uncomfortable to feel this exposed in front of him.

"It was out of your hands, even though it doesn't seem that way. You should let it go. Forgive yourself," Derek says.

"I could say the same to you. Did they ever catch the murderer?" Brooke jumps at the chance to change the subject.

"Huh?"

"The person who killed the Rodriguez girl. They find him?"

Derek shakes his head. "I don't know." He sighs and runs a hand through his hair, scratching the back of one ear. "Something I've been thinking about now that I'm sober. Maybe when I get out of here, if it's still unsolved, I'll do some looking around on my own again. It's not the same as giving that family back their little girl, but maybe I could find out what happened to her, who was responsible. That'd be something. You know, in the spirit of not giving up."

Brooke tenses. They're not getting out of here. She thought maybe there was something to explore with the perimeter, but Derek is right. One of them would have to test it out, and the risk is too great. They don't even know if the perimeter shuts down. It's all speculation. The reality is Kinsey's gone, and as soon as they satisfy Grace's idea of a wedding, they're both dead.

But Derek isn't asking Brooke to agree with him. He's holding on to hope. Exercising his new skill of not giving up. And who the hell is she to take that away from him? She was in that spot for so many years. It's only been days for him. Plus, Derek solving the case that ruined his life feels super important right now too.

"Yes, I have a daughter," Brooke blurts, going back to the question he asked earlier in the evening. She has to get this out. It just feels right. "Her name is Jessi and she's ten."

Derek inhales sharply, then whispers. "Ten? But you've been here ten years."

Brooke looks at her clasped hands. "She was six months old when Mitch grabbed me."

He shakes his head. "We have to get you out of here."

She's too drained to argue about this again, so she goes along with it. "You too."

Derek moves like he's going to stand up and walk away. She doesn't want him to, so she tries to think of something else to say to keep him close. Draw more consolation from the feel of his warm body next to hers.

But he pulls himself to his feet.

CHAPTER 43

Just like that, it's over. Moment's gone.

Or so Brooke thinks.

When she looks up, Derek's hand is there, palm open. "Come here," he whispers.

She eyes him, and he seems serious, so she gives a little smile, but still hesitates.

"Damn, that smile. Get over here," he breathes, and she takes his hand. But instead of pulling her to stand like she expected, he pulls her into him so that her face is against his chest and his arms are all the way around her back. The affection makes her feel safe, and it's what she needs right now. She's not alone. At least for these few minutes, in his embrace, she's not alone.

Brooke drifts her arms around his back to reciprocate, and her tears make a wet spot on his shirt, but he keeps her in his grip, only moving one arm to place a hand on the back of her head, stroking her loose hair. Avoiding her collar.

It feels good, takes her mind off everything.

Then something shifts inside her and she wants to get

closer, lose herself in him so just for a while, she can feel anything but fear and regret.

She pulls back and looks up at him, trying to determine what his intentions are. He smiles.

"You're beautiful," he says. "A pain in the ass, but beautiful." He gives a sharp exhale and holds her gaze. She puts one hand on his chest and his heart hammers. He wants her. She lets this moment linger. Then he takes her face in his hands, moves down so they're inches away. He stares at her mouth. Is he going to kiss her?

"You're still not my type," she blurts.

"Like hell I'm not."

"But I don't have feelings for you," she whispers.

He flinches, furrows his brows, and he takes a minute, but then says, "I know. I don't have feelings for you either."

And then Brooke plunges toward him, puts her mouth on his, and he meets her with the same strength, sending zaps of electricity through her body. She runs her hands through his hair. He bends down a little, not breaking the kiss while wrapping his arms around the backs of her legs. He lifts her, and her dress slips up her thighs, but his arms are locked tight under her ass. She thinks about how heavy she must be. Nobody has ever held her like this before, it's something that only happens to skinny girls. She tries to cross her ankles behind the small of his back, as if to somehow help bear the weight.

"I've got you," he says. "Let me," then he kisses her again, and she allows herself to relax in his arms, lets her legs hang, and it turns her on even more, so she nips at his neck, and whispers, "What are you waiting for?"

He carries her toward her bedroom, but she leans back. "No. Too much has happened in there. Just here."

"On the floor?" He sets her on her feet.

"Yes." She pulls a blanket off the couch and tosses some pillows on it, then approaches him again. Brooke could go right now, but she doesn't want it to be over too fast. She wants it to last, this feeling of being with someone. The togetherness. That's what she's aiming for. Sex is just a vehicle to get there.

It means nothing.

"Come here," he says again and hugs her, like they hit reset, like he's drawing comfort from her too, making it last longer. When he unzips her dress, she wants to gasp at the way his fingers brush down her back, to her waist. He moves it off her shoulders, and the dress drops on the floor. Then he pulls his shirt over his head and she works at his pants, and God, he really is gorgeous.

Then he's got her bra off and pulls back to look at her. They stand there: her, topless, and him in his boxers. She looks at the spot below his waist, wants him to notice her looking, and then she bites her bottom lip. Before she can make eye contact with him again, he's kissing the pooch of her stomach, pulling off her slip, her underwear. He stands and cups her breasts.

"I love your body," he says, breathless against her cheek.

She runs her fingers up his thigh and along the bottom of his loose boxers, grazing him with tenderness underneath. He gasps.

"Not yet," he says, then spins her around so she's facing out. He holds her back to his chest, one arm bracing her below the breasts, the other hand running down her body toward her pelvis, but it's just a tease.

She arches her back and locks her hands behind his neck, resting her head against his chest, giving him total access without reservation. He runs both hands down the sides of her torso, sending shivers everywhere. Then he cups one breast and kisses her neck. She moves her head to the side, making room. She's suspended here, practically on her toes, and once again, he's holding her weight. It makes her hot all over again.

She whispers in his ear. "I want this."

He whirls her around, lifts her under the legs and holds her straddled against his waist again. They kiss for what feels like a long time.

Then he sets her down on the couch and kneels in front of her. Spreads her knees open and starts with light kisses up the insides of her thighs. She braces herself with fingers scratching into vinyl and lets out a little whine. This must melt him because she can feel the quality of his kissing change, become more determined. He explores with his tongue exactly where she wants it. She won't last and it feels like freedom to enjoy this. Freedom she's not experienced in years. She hangs her head back, closes her eyes.

He backs off.

She looks at him. "What's wrong?"

"Just drawing it out." He smiles.

But she's almost there. She grabs him by the hair and puts his face back. "I don't want to wait."

He pulls back again. "Too bad. You're waiting." Then he kisses her mouth.

It's the same way he always fights her, and maybe it'd piss her off if she wasn't enjoying this so much. Then all she can do is gasp when he finds his way down there again.

She can barely focus, her mind keeps luxuriating in the washes of pleasure, she feels fuzzy. Brooke slips a hand down his chest, trailing fingers toward his waistband. He inhales sharply.

"Nice try," he breathes into her ear and moves her hand back to the couch. Then he hovers above her, kisses her so deeply she thinks that out of context, it might actually hurt.

"Give me what I want, or I'll make you come so hard and fast you'll wonder if you've ever gotten off before," she whispers, pulling away.

"That's the dumbest threat I've ever heard." Then he circles her nipple with his tongue and she leans back into the couch, spreading her legs so wide, just to entice him down there. Brooke focuses on his touch, on the throbbing in her pelvis.

His mouth is down there again and this time, he's not messing around. He works it in steady perfection. She arches her back and cries out. Combs her fingers through his hair and wonders if she could ever love this man. She could definitely get used to this. And he's not what she pegged him as. He has a heart, and it seems like it might be beautiful.

But there's no time to think about it because she's rising. His hands grip her ass, fingers digging into her skin as he braces himself against her. She might have bruises tomorrow, but she doesn't care. She touches the top of his head to get his attention. He looks up, makes eye contact without breaking stride. She smiles.

Then she's climbing, higher, higher.

No limits.

A burst of ecstasy. It feels like being set free.

And he doesn't stop. It happens again, and again, and just when she thinks she's satisfied, there she is at the edge. One last time, and everything inside of her spasms, her whole body tingles, and she doesn't think she can feel anything else. Nothing but this bliss ever again. Then she pulls his face up toward hers.

"Thank you," she whispers. "Now, I'm all yours."

He kisses her forehead and slips an arm underneath her on the couch, flipping her over in one motion. It takes her breath away to feel so light in his arms. He doesn't hesitate at all to take his turn, and she likes that. She even likes how rough he can be, so she braces herself against the seat of the couch and moves her pelvis up, an invitation. He's earned it.

Then he's inside her. He holds still, letting her body adjust, and folds his body over hers, strokes her breasts, kisses her back, and there's comfort again, stillness. Almost every inch of his body pressing against hers, skin on skin. So tender.

Then he pulls back, gripping her hips, and moves. His fingers find the exact right spot on her body, and it's electric again. She's almost at the edge, he goes deeper and each time she wants to moan, but she tries to hold it in, until he whispers, "Go ahead and scream."

But all that comes out is "Derek," followed by a gasp she can't help.

"Oh fuck . . ." he moans, moves faster, his fingers not slacking at all until they both go over the edge.

CHAPTER 44

Afterward, Derek cradles Brooke on the blanket. "Kinsey was right. We probably should have done that a lot sooner," he says.

Brooke tightens up against him. Was the mention of Kinsey too soon? He's not sure. Derek isn't thinking straight. How could he after that?

She doesn't reply right away and Derek's mind fumbles trying to come up with something else to say, but Brooke speaks first. "Nah," she says. "It would have been angry sex. Comfort sex is much better."

"Oh, come on, angry sex can be a lot of fun too. And I meant what I said earlier."

"About what?"

"About how I think you're beautiful. I know I can be a dick, but—"

"This can't happen again," she interrupts him.

It feels like a slap. He assumed she was lying about her feelings toward him the same way he was. But he recovers and makes sure his tone isn't antagonistic. "Why?"

"We're going to die." She sits up and the outline of her

body against moonlight makes him a little breathless. "Plus, I thought we had an understanding," she says. "This was just the equivalent of a long hug for me. I needed someone, and you were here."

"It wasn't good?"

"It was . . . phenomenal."

"So what's the problem then?"

"No problem. Just want to be clear."

Derek is going to force her to say it. Spell it out, because he doesn't believe her. It goes against everything her body was telling him a minute ago. The growing attraction he's been sensing between them.

"About what?"

"That it meant nothing. I don't care for you . . . like that."

"Bullshit."

The word falls out of his mouth, and he winces, expects a fight, but she lays back down beside him and whispers, "Fine. There might be something here, I won't lie. But it doesn't matter. We're out of time."

"And if we'd met under different circumstances?"

She shakes her head. "I can't be with an angry man. I have too much of that inside me. I need someone tender and peaceful to balance me out."

"Someone like Tyson," Derek says, regretting how the jealousy seeps out.

"Yeah, actually," she says, and there's a challenge in her tone. "Tyson brought out something else in me. Something soft. That thing that rages inside of me, it died down when I was with him."

"Because he extinguished it. Shamed you for it. And anyway, why would you want it to die down?" Derek asks. "You've been through a lot, but at the core, that thing inside you that you hate so much, it's what's kept you alive. It's strength, passion, and power. It's you. I like it. I like how you are."

She takes a deep breath as if she's thinking about this, but Derek doesn't know what he's doing. Is he trying to change her mind? Convince her to love him for the hours they have left? There's no point, and yet, here he is trying to make a point.

"Well, whatever. In any case, I'm glad you're here with me," she says, reaching for his hand and lacing her fingers through his.

He nods and lets it go. It has to be enough.

After a while, Brooke stands and pulls her dress over her body. He wants her to stay longer, but he keeps it to himself and watches, because he can't control her. Has to let her go. She takes a step toward the bedroom and turns.

"Come on," she says.

"Where?"

"You don't have to sleep on the couch. My bed is gigantic."

He hesitates, doesn't know what this means. She says she won't be with him, says she won't even make love to him again. Then she invites him into her bed.

"It's just sleep. I won't bite," she adds when he doesn't respond.

He wishes she would though, that's the problem, but at least he knows better than to say it. It's enough that they've had this much interaction without a fight. After great sex, too. So instead, he follows her into the room.

Once they're lying in the dark, under covers, Brooke rolls over to face him. "Would you hold me for a minute? Nothing else, I just . . ."

He pulls her close and her head finds his chest. He pets her hair and wonders again if she's being honest. Because this feels so right. Them together like this. He doesn't have to walk on eggshells around her. She's not afraid of him at all. He loves the very thing about her she's mentioned bothered others. Bothered Tyson. But then again, Brooke said Derek's temper—the reason to walk on eggshells—was why she couldn't be with him.

Well, here he is again, acting as if they have a future. They don't. Unless he can come up with something.

CHAPTER 45

The drive to Portland was wet, and Mina's windshield wipers frantically tried to keep the window clear enough for her to see. But the trip was productive. She made one purchase: a GPS car tracker, like the one she saw on *Breaking Bad* back in the day.

If she couldn't get those people across the street to come outside to confirm everything was fine, and she couldn't get the police out there, maybe she could do some sleuthing herself. Find out where that guy lives, then drive to his place sometime when he shows up at the house across the street. She'll check out his house. Then, depending on what she finds, make the police do something about it.

The tracker purchase required signing up for a monthly service, and inventing a story about a cheating husband. But the guy explained how it worked and Mina asked a lot of questions because she's not very techy. Once satisfied, she hit the wet roads again, trying not to hydroplane on her way back to the rental.

She made record time, returning to Freeport before evening set in. Now she's waiting and watching out the front window. It's been hours. She's got the GPS tracker all set up and ready to go. All she has to do is slap it on the silver Jeep without getting caught. Not that she expects it to show up tonight, but either way, she's ready.

This is a little crazy.

But that's why she hasn't told Brady about what she's doing. He wouldn't understand. In fact, she's a little afraid she'll chicken out. But if this is her chance to help that little girl, she can't botch it. Can't sit back and relax while that girl across the street is in danger. She's out of options. Can't call the cops because they're either in on it, or they're alerting the man, and he's the one putting the brakes on their response.

That sounds paranoid.

Sure. But it doesn't feel like paranoia. Why else would that guy show up at her doorstep when she called 911? He's involved in covering something up over there. Has to be.

So yeah, she's going to follow him. Gather more information about where he lives, what else he does with his time. Anything. Maybe she'll find some clues that open the door for her to help the girl. People make mistakes, and Mina's praying that man makes one soon, so she can capitalize on it.

What if it is paranoia? Mina's brain objects again.

It's true that the only things she has to go off are a creepy guy and a blood smear in the window.

Well, and the girl asking for help.

And that she's never seen either of those neighbors leave the home.

And that the grocery delivery guy thought something was off too.

No, she's not being paranoid. She's being proactive, and even if nothing comes of her little tracking venture, at least she'll know she tried.

The car pulls up to the house across the street. What luck that he'd show up as if on her schedule. A rush of adrenaline hits her.

It's now or never.

Mina slips on her tennis shoes and pulls her arms through her coat.

She watches from her dark living room as he enters the house, and when the door closes behind him, Mina explodes out the front door, pulls her hood over her head. The cover of dark is ideal, and the rain hits pavement so hard that it muffles any noise she might make.

On the far side of the car, she crouches, feeling around underneath, and affixes the tracker, but it doesn't take the first time. She pulls it back to figure out what the problem is and tries again. It stays. This might actually work.

The front door of the house opens. But it's too soon. She's still close to the car, but on the other side, hidden from view of the porch, thank God. Mina peeks around the car to see if he's coming, and the door is wide open, light illuminating the front yard. Then she hears the little girl screaming and crying inside the house. What the hell is going on?

She has to get out of here, but no way she can walk back to her rental. He'll see her, and know that she was in the driveway. Snooping.

More than snooping. Stalking.

Mina stands and walks down the street toward the beach path instead, shoves her hands into her pockets and makes sure to secure her hood.

It's dark. He can't see me. I'm just on a walk.

At night.

In the rain.

Shit.

She looks suspicious, but as she picks up her pace, she tells herself it's fine, she's fine. But she doesn't know if she got away from the car quick enough. He could have seen her. Can't turn around to find out. Instead, she jogs. Has to get to the footpath leading down to the beach to hide. If he pulls up behind her, she could get caught.

Mina can't hear whether he's started the Jeep. Is it running in the driveway? The rain pelts hard all around. She doesn't even know if the car is still *in* the driveway. It could pull out at any moment. What if it already has? But wouldn't she see the headlights if that were the case? Only ten more feet to run. Can't look back to see. Her ragged breathing keeps time with her steps, and once again, she curses herself for being so unfit.

She turns right to take the footpath to the beach, but ducks behind a huge bush to hide and wait. It's only a few feet away from the tiny intersection, but out of sight. Headlights bloom. She watches through open patches in the brush. Seconds pass, and the silver Jeep arrives at the end of 'J' Street. It stops.

The car idles there, but why? There's not a single vehicle anywhere around. Why isn't he going?

Mina listens to the rain, the grinding of the Jeep's windshield wipers. She's that close.

Then she sees it.

A little head silhouetted in the back seat.

No.

Mina chances a closer peek, letting her face show as the car idles.

No. No. No.

It's the little girl. He's taking her somewhere.

Mina hides and tries to slow her heart rate. It feels like it might beat out of her chest. The car turns left toward Highway 101, and away from her.

Her knees wobble from adrenaline.

Mina pulls out her phone and looks up the tracker's location.

It's working. The Jeep is going south on 101, taking her somewhere.

A bad feeling overtakes her. Such a bad feeling. That little girl.

Paxton.

She was planning to track the car. That was it. Gather information, learn the man's home address. Visit later. But now? Now she has to follow it.

Mina shoves her phone back into her coat and runs to the rental, grabs her car keys. Once she's inside the SUV, she sets her phone in the cradle on the dash so she can follow the Jeep. Then she lays her head back, enjoying the dry shelter of her car. Has to catch her breath for a minute even though everything in her is shouting *go*. But she needs to let him get nice and ahead so he doesn't see her tailing. The hard rain hits her Lexus like tiny pebbles dropping from the sky.

She pushes the ignition button and pulls out of the driveway.

CHAPTER 46

Where the hell is he going?

Mina's been following the Jeep for a while now and it hasn't slowed once except to turn off Highway 101 and take a back road toward the forest, away from the ocean. The rain hasn't let up either. Mina has stayed a nice distance behind. So far, so good.

She's trying to corral the stray thoughts about that little girl. Panic seizes in her stomach, sending her brain way ahead to worst-case scenarios, but she's doing everything she can right now.

Just focus on following.

After about thirty minutes on the back road, Mina realizes she hasn't seen another car in a while. No houses. Nothing out here but moss-covered trees and brush. And rain. Torrential rain that her wipers struggle to clear before the next deluge.

Rain blurs the Jeep's tail lights too, but she can still see that steady red ahead of her. Whenever the Jeep's brakes light up, she brakes too. Trying to keep distance. But surely the man can see her headlights, and now that there aren't any other cars out here, what if this tips him off? She taps the brakes a few times to slow down more and watches his red tail lights blink out of sight.

Her phone is still following the tracker.

I'm fine. I got this.

Glancing at her phone on the dash, she watches the Jeep make a turn. It's about a mile ahead of her.

She's making good time, hands gripping the wheel, straining to see through the windshield when her tire hits a pothole and bounces the car off-kilter a bit. Mina corrects her course and puts on the brakes. She stops in the middle of the road, releases a big exhale.

Slow down.

Looking ahead, it's all washboard and potholes now, as if she's come to a part of the road where nobody drives.

The tracker stops moving.

He must have reached his destination.

Mina presses the accelerator more carefully so that she can dodge the biggest holes in the dirt road. She needs a plan. Obviously, she can't pull up behind them. She'll have to park farther away. The rain is still coming down, but it's slowed, so that's good. There are so many trees out here that it should be easy to pull her SUV off the main road and then sneak behind one until she gets to wherever the man stopped. Mina drives past the turnoff, parks her car where the road slopes down into a shallow ditch. As long as the Jeep goes back the same way it came—back toward civilization—they won't see her car farther up the road.

Once she's sure she's parked as far away from the turnoff as necessary, she turns on her phone's flashlight and steps along the dirt road, avoiding puddles until her feet touch the driveway, or whatever it is. Mina checks the phone to make sure the Jeep hasn't started moving again. It hasn't. It's just ahead of her, a quarter of a mile or so.

But she has no service, and that reality is a rock in her gut.

Then a scream rips through the sound of rain.

It's the little girl.

CHAPTER 47

"Did you hear that?" Brooke whispers, sitting up in bed. "Sounded like a kid yelling."

Derek absolutely heard it, and he moves out of bed fast, looking around in the dark as if he's got weapon options. It's an instinct he acts on from years on the job because he's not fully awake yet. No weapons, of course, so he reaches for his pants.

"Stay here," he whispers, pulling them up.

"No," Brooke whispers back, sliding out of bed and straightening her long, white nightgown.

Derek groans. Not the time to argue, but at least she doesn't give him hell when he shoves her behind him to shield her as they approach the front door. One of her hands holds his waistband at the small of his back like it's a handle, and the other rests on his upper back.

They look out the front window into a downpour of rain. It's hard to see in the dark and with the windows draining water down glass like that.

Mitch's truck is in the driveway, and he's wrestling with something—someone—in the back seat.

A tiny figure emerges—a child, has to be—and Mitch yanks them toward the cabin.

"The fuck," Derek mutters.

———

It's a kid. Another kid. No.

Brooke's legs turn to liquid and she can't stand anymore. She plops down on the couch.

"You okay?" Derek is at her side, hand on her head.

"I can't watch another child . . ." She doesn't finish her sentence before words turn to sobs.

"You think that little kid is the next young Grace? For the wedding?"

Brooke nods.

Derek strokes her hair and then removes his hand. Takes a big inhale. He tenses next to her. Fists clench at his side.

Brooke ignores it and looks up at him. "He's alone though. And now we know he doesn't have a remote."

"Just a gun." Derek's jaw ripples. She can practically feel his wheels turning. He's trying to think of how to take Mitch down.

"We need to catch him off guard somehow. I have an idea."

There's no time to get dressed, and it's still raining, but that kid is giving Mitch so much fight that it's taking him forever to get them inside. They keep dropping to the ground, kicking and darting out of Mitch's reach. He can't even get a handle long enough to pick the child up and carry them. Brooke moves into action right away. "Follow my lead. I'll go for the kid. You take Mitch."

Brooke throws open the door and runs out into the rain.

Her thin nightdress is sopping wet right away, but she ignores it, along with the cold, restrictive way it grips her legs when she moves.

"Mitch! What are you doing?" she yells.

"What's it look like?" he shouts over his shoulder.

She approaches the child and when she gets close enough to see in the dark, it's a girl, she's crab walking backward through the front yard weeds toward the Jeep. When Brooke sees her more closely, she stops cold.

The girl wears a metal collar.

"Stop! You have to stop!" Brooke screams.

Too harsh. Have to be sweeter, but she's heading right for the perimeter.

"I want my daddy," she cries. "Take me home!" she hollers at Mitch.

"Hey, baby," Brooke says. Firm, but much softer. The words come out fast. "You'll die if you get to the driveway. That collar will kill you. Please stop moving. Let's go inside and I'll make you some hot cocoa."

Then Derek and Mitch are on the ground nearby. Brooke didn't see how it started. He must have lunged toward Mitch, but the asshole wriggles free of his grip. Mitch gets to his feet and makes his way past the perimeter. Like this is some neighborhood game.

Olly olly oxen free!

He laughs out loud at Derek. "I'll leave you two to deal with this brat. Wedding's tomorrow."

Derek grunts and stands, covered in mud.

She doesn't want to be hard on him, but how could he biff that? She turns to the girl, who is probably about ten.

The same age as Jessi.

Could it be . . . ? Something like hope doused in vinegar

overtakes her and, with a shaky hand, she pushes the girl's hood down. But she doesn't know what Jessi would look like, so it's no use.

"What's your name?" she asks.

"Carly."

"When's your birthday?"

"January fourth."

Brooke sighs in relief. Why did she think this was Jessi? Thank God it's not. But relief is short-lived because now there's a child in the picture.

CHAPTER 48

Mina's mind races, trying to think of what to do next when the Jeep's headlights spark to life near that cabin.

Darting behind the closest tree that's girthy enough to hide her, Mina watches as the Jeep takes the driveway toward the road. Toward her.

Everything feels like a dream. The tail lights in the distance. The drizzling rain. The girl screaming.

Brady.

Brady comes to mind, and she wishes he were here. She misses him. It feels good to miss him.

Mina waits, holding her breath while she crouches as the Jeep approaches, inching as it passes her. It's too dark for her to see inside the truck, so she can't confirm that the girl is there. Maybe he dropped her off. But why? When the car passes by her location, she rushes to another tree farther from the driveway and ducks, hugging her knees in a squat, hoping to hide from the bright lights.

What the hell is she doing right now? She's supposed to be working on her book, but here she is, playing spy games with this creepy guy.

Putting yourself in danger, Brady would say.

The little girl.

She *may be in danger.*

It's easy to talk herself back into this when she thinks of that girl and the blood. The scream from inside the house right before the man came out. Maybe he had grabbed her. Maybe he'd hurt her trying to get her to come with him. And then the second scream out here in the middle of God knows where.

But maybe he's taking her back to her actual home. Maybe this will be nothing and Mina can drive to the rental and get back to work.

Not likely, her gut screams.

The Jeep turns right, just as she expected it would, traveling the road the same way they came.

She waits a few minutes more to be sure he doesn't return for whatever reason, and then she points her phone's flashlight at her feet, and tromps through the tall brush back up the dirt driveway to see what the man came here for.

CHAPTER 49

Derek and Brooke got Carly into the cabin and wrapped in a blanket. They learned she was nine years old, and from Portland as well. Mitch and Grace were holding her and her dad—who was in a wheelchair—at another location.

Derek can't think about this little girl being murdered. But he has to. Has to come up with some sort of plan to avoid it.

Brooke's out of her wet nightgown and into a dry dress, bustling around the kitchen, dumping cocoa powder in a big mug of hot water.

A knock at the door startles them.

Who the hell could that be? Mitch and Grace never knock, besides the fact that Mitch was just here, and left.

"Who's there?" Derek says through the door, switching on the porch light.

"Sorry to bother you," a woman's voice answers. "This might sound really insane, but I was worried something was —going on. I know it's the middle of the night, and I would love to be wrong about this, so if you tell me everything is fine with that man and the little girl, I'll leave."

Derek turns to look at Brooke, her mouth a little O. He

opens the door, and immediately feels the warmth of Brooke's body behind him.

The face on the other side knocks the wind out of him, and he's in such a state of shock that he can't find words at all. Brooke pats his back hard as if to prompt him, remind him to speak. She probably can't see much since he's blocking the whole doorway. But Derek can only stare at this woman, shrouded in a blue Patagonia jacket, rain running off the hood. Blonde curls stuck to her wet cheeks. Against the soft porch light, he registers the same level of surprise in her eyes.

Brooke pushes herself in front of Derek. "We're being held prisoner by a psychopath! Do you have a phone?"

But the woman only gives her half a glance and then returns to staring at Derek. "You," she breathes.

"Mina . . . how? What are you doing here?" he asks.

"You know her?" Brooke's surprised voice goes up in pitch.

Derek nods. "Remember the Rodriguez girl I told you about? This is her mother."

CHAPTER 50

"Her name was Paxton," Mina corrects him, as if that's what matters right now. But it matters. To her.

What are the chances she would run into the officer who worked on Paxton's case? Out here in the middle of nowhere, on the same vacation she's been thinking of Paxton so much. It seems impossible.

Officer Derek keeps staring at her. Mina stands in the rain, arms loose at her sides.

"That little girl. Is she here?" Mina asks, trying to look around them and into the cabin.

"Yes."

One word. One single word is all this guy can manage?

"We have to get her out of here, get some real police involved."

"Look, it's crazy that you two know each other," the woman behind Derek starts, "but the most important thing right now is calling the cops."

"This is Brooke," Derek says.

Mina tries to acknowledge with a brief nod, but it's not

what's important. "The little girl, she's staying in the house across from my beach rental. I think they're holding her and her dad captive. Why are you out here in the middle of nowhere?"

Then Mina notices the collars around their necks. Why didn't she see those first thing? A shiver scrapes imaginary fingernails up her spine.

"What is going on?" she whispers.

"Jesus Christ, come on! Where's your phone?" Brooke almost yells.

"There's no service out here," Mina says. "And we can't call the police, anyway."

"Why?" Brooke shrieks.

"Because he *is* the police. The man. I think he intercepts 911 calls. It happened to me when I tried to get them to help with the little girl. Can I see her?"

Derek stands aside even more so Mina can see the little girl sitting in a chair, draped in a huge afghan, with a cup of hot cocoa up to her lips.

"Hey," Mina says, sticking her head into the cabin.

The girl's face lights up. "It's you. You found me."

She's fine. Thank God.

Brooke sighs loud, her arms folded across her chest. "Where's your phone?"

Mina reaches into her jacket pocket and catches the expression on Derek's face shift from surprise at seeing her to a hardness. "Mitch is a cop," he states, as if to himself. Then he looks up at Mina. "Did he work on Paxton's case?"

"I don't know. I had a . . . mental break after she was . . . found." Does he remember that? "Brady—that's my husband —" she says to Brooke, drawing her into the conversation.

"He was the one who spent so much time in Freeport talking with the police. This is the first time I've come back."

"Wait, what did you say your daughter's name was?" Brooke asks, softer now.

"Paxton."

"But she died in Freeport?"

"They think so," Mina says.

"Ok, get back in your car and drive somewhere that has service. Call the Portland police," Brooke says.

"They won't do anything about it. I already looked into that."

"Well, you need to call somebody to help us, and fast! Go!"

"I'm tracking the Jeep on my phone," Mina says. "No service out here, but GPS still works. Don't worry, he left."

"I *am* worried. We're all in danger!" Brooke shouts. She's frantic, but Derek still watches Mina, like he sees a ghost, like he's thinking about something else.

"Mitch must know me from when I came down here to work Paxton's case. I don't remember him, but that has to be it," he says.

"Oh God," Brooke mutters, then her eyes grow large and she puts a hand on Derek's arm. "What if Mitch has been orchestrating this whole final scene? Pulling in players that he wanted to get even with."

"He's not that smart," Derek says.

Brooke cocks her head to the side. "He targeted you. He knew you when he grabbed you. And anyway, we don't have time to chat about it!" Then she looks at Mina. "Go. You have to go and bring back help before morning. Otherwise he's going to kill Carly." Brooke nods in the little girl's direction.

Mina looks at her phone again to be sure Mitch is gone.

But the Jeep isn't moving. In fact, it's parked right around here. Close. But where? She whips her head around and still can't see it.

The porch light goes out and puts the three of them in total darkness.

"What the hell?" Mina whispers.

"Mina, go. Call the Portland police when you're safe," Derek breathes. The fear in his voice makes her shiver.

Then someone slaps the phone out of her hands.

Mina looks to the right, where the force came from. Sees a gun pointed at her face.

"Jesus Christ, you're a nuisance," the man—Mitch —growls.

She puts her hands up. "I'm sorry."

Funny how it's the first thing that comes to her mind to say. She's anything but sorry.

Derek flinches toward Mitch, but Mitch points the gun at him. "I don't think so."

Derek and Brooke both put their hands up in the air.

"How did you know I was . . ." Mina starts.

"Following me?" Mitch says and holds his smartphone up. "I got an alert that detected a tracker on my car. Knew the whole time."

That's a thing? Why didn't the guy who sold her the tracker warn her about that?

"I was thrilled," Mitch says. "Was going to use little Carly as our bride, then find a new Grace Wakeford for 'J' Street, since that was less urgent. But now? Now this is so much better. I hate seeing the kids die."

Dread crowds Mina's ribs, runs icy fingers up her spine so that the hairs on the back of her neck stand up.

She makes eye contact with Derek.

"Oh my God," Derek whispers. Then he shoves her out of the way of the gun and shouts, "Run!"

CHAPTER 51

Mina stumbles backward, but catches herself and stands up all the way. She can't run. He's pointing a gun right at her.

Then Derek punches Mitch and he falls backward too. Derek is on him, and all Mina can do is watch.

"Run, you idiot!" Brooke yells. "Fast!"

Her body feels stuck, paralyzed.

Then, it's not. It's like something lets go inside of her and she whirls around and sprints toward the driveway.

Her hood falls down and rain saturates her hair and head, courses down her face and she has to swipe it with her hands to see.

A gunshot goes off.

She wants to turn around to make sure Derek is okay. See if Mitch is following her now.

Don't look back. It'll slow you down.

Adrenaline charges through her veins and she's almost through the yard and to the driveway. Long grass and weeds whip her legs, soaking her jeans. Her drenched tennis shoes squidge through the mud.

Mina pumps her arms and pushes her body to the limit.

It's a long way to her car, and she's only a third of the way down the driveway.

Have to turn around and look. Have to.

She does.

It's a blanket of darkness everywhere, and he's not there. He's not following her. Derek and Brooke are no longer on the porch. At least, she doesn't think so. It's hard to tell in the downpour.

Halfway down the long driveway now, Mina fishes around in her jacket pocket for her car fob without stopping. It makes her run a little lopsided, but then she's got it in hand.

No phone. Shit.

Mitch slapped it out of her hands and she didn't have time to grab it. How will she make a call?

Once she's in town, she'll find a phone. Yes, call the Portland police, like Derek said. Call Brady, too.

Mina's almost to the end of the driveway. The road where she parked her car is maybe a hundred yards away.

Headlights flicker on behind her. They're coming from the direction of the cabin. He used the other side of the roundabout to sneak up on the cabin, must have.

She has to get to her car and get the hell out of here.

Mina glances around and then turns left to run through the trees. It's a more direct route and the Jeep can't follow her, but the ground is uneven. She can't see where to best plant her feet, so she has to slow down. It's better than falling and hurting herself.

Mina runs parallel to the road, to her car. Dodging trees and mossy boulders, making her own path.

She doesn't know where her car is, exactly. Can't see very well through the thick cover of trees, only knows she's near it.

Then the headlights blare again, turning from the

driveway to the road. Closer this time. She ducks behind a tree, watches as the Jeep trolls alongside her. It crawls. Even at this snail's pace, the Jeep will get to her car before she does.

The realization is a punch in the stomach. And she lets out a sharp exhale of defeat.

Then a burst of hope.

Location sharing!

Brady tracks her location to a fault. Maybe he saw her heading this way before she lost service. Won't be long before he realizes he hasn't heard from her in a while. He'll check her location, won't be able to see it, and he'll move into action. The thing that annoys her to no end about him might just save her this time.

The Jeep stops on the road. Red brake lights flash, and as Mina makes her way, half-jogging, hiding behind and scrambling between trees, she can see the situation.

The Jeep's headlights are pointed right at the rear of her SUV.

No.

She plops down in the dirt on her ass, not even caring that the ground is wet. She needs a new plan. Can she wait him out? Maybe sneak back to the cabin and get her phone?

Then what? Walk until she has service? She was on this road driving for thirty minutes. That's a marathon to walk. And what if Mitch took her phone and going back is a total waste of time anyway?

She's on foot. He's in a Jeep.

But she's got suitable cover here in this patch of forest. He'd have to venture in on foot himself to find her. He's old, and based on what she's noticed, doesn't seem like he's very used to exertion. Maybe she could make a break for her car. But he would still have a gun! She catches her breath.

Think, Mina.

A few minutes pass. The red brake lights have dimmed. The Jeep must be in park.

He's waiting *her* out. She's not waiting him out, it's the other way around.

Panic arrests her chest, and it makes her feel like she might hyperventilate.

More time passes. She doesn't know how long, but nothing changes. That damn Jeep just sits there, idling.

Then, more headlights illuminate the road and approach the Jeep.

Red and blue lights flash, a little siren blips.

The police. The police are here.

Out of instinct, Mina's heart flares with promise. But it dissipates when she remembers Mitch *is* the police. These officers are probably on his side.

Another cruiser pulls up behind the first one.

Four people, who just look like shadows in the dark, get out. Flashlights blink on. Dogs bark.

Mina has no choice, now she has to go back to the cabin and try for the phone.

She turns and runs again, but she can't go as fast. Her leg hurts. She must have done something to it and not realized it because of the adrenaline.

The rain has let up and the sound of dogs barking accompanies the swishing of wet weeds behind her. Flashlights beam, lighting a fraction of her path ahead, but also threatening to find her.

"Mina!" a man yells from closer behind than she likes. "Mina Rodriguez! Are you out here?"

Something about the way he says it—*do they think I'm lost? That they're somehow helping me?*

Maybe they aren't with Mitch. But she can't chance it.

The barking closes in on her from behind.

"Mina! Stop!" They're so close. She can't go any faster, but pushes her body anyway.

"This way! She's heading toward the cabin," another close voice shouts. The police cruisers both move along the road back toward the cabin's driveway. But there are still cops on foot behind her too, and with dogs. Then it's sheer brightness all around. She shields her eyes. One cruiser blocks the main road, facing her and shining the car's spotlight right on her.

The other cruiser, the one in the lead, turns into the driveway.

She's surrounded.

She lets herself cry.

"Mina?" a man's voice says from behind her. The tenderness in it surprises her.

She whirls around.

"We're here to help. Come with me."

CHAPTER 52

Derek's "Rodriguez girl" is named Paxton.

Brooke knows that name. How many little girls named Paxton could there be?

When Mitch shot that gun in the air, Brooke retreated into the cabin. No way was she going to stick around to catch a stray bullet. Derek was lucky not to take one himself, but it startled him enough to allow Mitch to put Derek at gunpoint while he got away.

Now Derek watches the commotion from the yard, shouting updates over his shoulder to Brooke while she sits close by Carly. The girl seems so exhausted that if it weren't for all the commotion, the anxiety, the fear, she'd probably crash out. Brooke wraps an arm around her and kisses the top of her head. No way anyone is going to hurt this baby girl. Not on her watch.

"She's in the woods now," Derek informs. "The cops showed up! Yes!"

He yells at the cops. "Hey! Over here! They're keeping us prisoner!"

Doubtful that the cops can hear him over the rain. It's

quite a distance, but Brooke doesn't say any of that. He comes inside and says, "The cops are here, Brooke. They'll find us. We're getting out!"

His face glows, even though it's drenched for the second time today.

Brooke gives him a tight smile. "Mitch is a cop too," she whispers, not wanting to burst his bubble, but also, he needs to be realistic.

He must not have heard her because he doesn't respond. Then a few seconds later, he returns to the porch. "Wait. They brought dogs. Why?"

Because they're with Mitch.

He screams at the police, walks out into the yard, waving his arms above his head, trying to get their attention. But it's too dark. The rain consumes any volume he might otherwise project.

Of course, Mitch grabbed the phone off the ground before he ran after Mina. Now, Brooke is only half-paying attention to what's happening with Mina. Because her mind is working at trying to figure out how to keep Carly alive.

Even though it's the other little girl that keeps swimming laps in her brain. Won't let her go.

Paxton.

Paxton.

Paxton.

Derek comes inside the dark cabin. The power is out. Mitch must have cut it when he put them in darkness on the porch.

"They're leaving. The cops are leaving, and Mitch has her," he says, slicking back his wet hair. Then he picks up the living room chair and throws it at the kitchen cabinets.

Brooke flinches.

"Not helping," she says. Her voice is firm.

This time, the chair sort of lands next to the lower cupboards and breaks nothing.

Derek sighs. "You're right, I'm sorry. I'm so sorry. It's just . . . Why her? Of all people? Why does it have to be her? I can't watch them kill her. I can't. I fucking won't."

Does he have feelings for Mina? It annoys Brooke that her mind goes right there. After all, she doesn't care about Derek like that.

Right?

Right. But then why is there a little wave of jealousy creeping up over her heart? When that's the very last thing in the world that should matter.

"Were you guys . . . a thing?" she asks to her own shame.

"What? No!" Derek almost shouts. "She's the Rodriguez girl—Paxton's—mom. She's the mom!"

Brooke says nothing. Waits for him to keep talking.

"I already let Paxton's family down by not finding her murderer. And now I'm going to be forced to watch the woman who lost her baby girl die too."

He drops his body on the couch next to Brooke. Carly's head lays in Brooke's lap, she's asleep now that the outside commotion has died down. Amazing that she can sleep through Derek's outburst. Must be dead-dog tired.

Brooke swallows hard. "I'm so sorry," she whispers, and leans into him, laying her head on his shoulder.

He turns his hand palm up and holds hers, interlacing fingers. Inhaling, like he's about to say something, he stops. Mitch approaches the cabin, and he's carrying Mina, her limp arm dangling.

She's wearing a metal collar.

Brooke looks out farther toward the road, but the other

cops are gone. It's just the Jeep, headlights on, parked in the driveway.

"Good thing the police came to help me locate my 'lost niece.'" Mitch smirks, and Brooke can hear the air quotes in his voice. He walks into Kinsey's old room and returns solo, gun in hand.

"You called them? And then lied to them?" Derek says.

"Grace did. I radioed her about the stunt you all tried to pull. She's got the entire department in her pocket. Small town, you know. But she's funny about anyone knowing what she's doing out here, so yeah I had to lie. Cops thought they were helping a fellow brother in blue locate a visiting family member, and they got to go home feeling good about themselves for doing that, and for making Grace Wakeford happy. Now, where's that wedding dress?"

"Kinsey's room," Brooke mutters, defeated.

"That's right." He walks back in there, but Brooke speaks up again.

"Mitch, let me dress her. Please? Let's at least give her some dignity."

He rubs his cheek. "I'm no perv."

Right, no perv.

"Whatever. Just let me do it."

"Fine. She's all yours."

"You targeted me," Derek stands and says through clenched teeth.

"Who, me?" Mitch feigns surprise.

"Because of Paxton. I worked on her case with your department. I wasn't a stranger on the street to you."

"Told you that on the first day, if you recall. Not my fault you're shit at solving things. You were hard to find though. Took me a whole month."

Derek looks down but balls his fists. He's going to attack Mitch.

No. That can't happen. Mitch has a gun, and Derek has already tried that route and failed.

Brooke moves Carly off her lap and on to the couch so she can keep sleeping, then stands next to him. Puts her hand on his arm, but he stares at Mitch, his breathing picks up. He's going to blow. She takes his face in her hands and turns it down toward hers.

"Not now," she whispers. "Let's make a plan." His eyebrows raise and the tension releases, seems to go out of his body.

But then his face tenses again, his eyes go wide. "Brooke, your collar. It's flashing yellow."

Brooke touches the metal and looks at the charger on the wall.

The power is still out. She whips her face to Mitch. "Get the power back on!" She rushes over to the charger, poised to lock in as soon as the power returns.

He shoves his hands in his pockets and leans on his forward foot. "Well now, how did you get off schedule? You should be fully charged by now."

Derek. She and Derek, getting lost in the moment and screwing on the floor like teenagers. She forgot to charge her collar. Derek's still not on her same schedule, but his will flash yellow soon too.

"Mitch, get the power on. You really want Brooke to die the day before Grace's big final scene?"

Brooke can't believe his composure. No breaking dishes, no streak of f-bombs, no fat lips. Just a sincere and persuasive demand. Maybe there's hope for him yet.

Mitch rolls his eyes.

Derek looks at Brooke's collar again. "More flashing yellow."

"Mitch, please," Brooke pleads softer than she's ever spoken to him before.

"Fine, but only because I can't deal with Grace's rage over losing another one of you morons on my watch."

Like they're children he's babysitting.

He disappears, and in seconds the lights flash on. Brooke hooks up to the charger and sighs in relief. Derek runs a hand through his hair and plops down in his chair again.

"Now give me that one, and I'll take her back to 'J' Street." He takes steps toward Carly.

"No," Brooke says, but she can't physically block him because she's charging.

Derek takes her hand, and she holds on to his strength enough to allow him to speak for both of them. "How long does she have at 'J' Street?"

Mitch shrugs. "Longer than she has if she stays here for the bloody wedding."

Derek levels his eyes at Brooke. "You have to let her go."

Tears fill Brooke's eyes. It's irrational. Of course she needs to let the girl go, doesn't want her to be here, not with what's going to happen. But it feels like so much more than letting go of Carly, this girl she's known for less than an hour.

Derek takes her face in his hands now. "She's not Jessi. And she's got more time than we do. We'll help her, but not right now. Let's make a plan, as you say."

Brooke nods.

CHAPTER 53

Mina wakes up in a bed. Her head pounds, but she tries to sit up, anyway. Her whole body is heavy, so sore. It's bright in the room. Daylight outside.

Derek and that other woman, Brooke, are in here with her. They're talking to each other, and Mina's pretty sure it's about her, but her mind is slow and she can't make out words.

"Take it easy," Derek says. "You okay?"

Of course not.

But if there's a question behind the question here, it's fair. He probably wants to know if she's injured.

"I'm fine." She moves to stand, but the headache hits harder and all she can say is, "What the hell?"

"He drugged you."

Then she notices what she's wearing.

A blood-stained white dress.

There's something restrictive around her neck. She touches it, but Derek takes her hand. "It's a device with a kill switch, don't touch it."

Those collars the other two were wearing. She's got one now too.

Her mouth opens, but words tsunami around her mind, rushing by so fast that she can't reach out and grab any.

"It's how they keep us here," Derek goes on, explaining something about a perimeter and acting out events from the old lady's life. That Mitch took the girl back to 'J' Street. And about a wedding. The reason Mina's in a white dress.

"Why is it bloody?" she asks.

They look at each other and Derek shakes his head, like he's warning Brooke not to speak. But she does anyway. "The last girl died in it."

Mina lets out a little whimper, says, "I need to use the bathroom."

Derek takes her by the hand and pulls her up, wraps her arm around his waist and supports her so her jelly legs can shuffle out of the bedroom.

She registers the hardwood floors, the mid-century furniture, and one chair lying on its side. The refrigerator is old-fashioned. Frigidaire with a big metal handle. Brooke wears a vintage powder-blue dress with a white apron now. Derek's clothes look old-fashioned too. High-water dress pants and a button-up shirt. She didn't interact with him very much after they found Paxton's body—that was Brady—but she remembers the few times she saw him, and he always dressed casually. T-shirt, hoodie, jeans. That sort of guy.

After she's finished in the bathroom, Mina makes her way to the couch. Brooke brings her a drink of water. The chair is upright in the living room now, as if someone tidied in those few minutes. Both Brooke and Derek watch Mina, like she's an unpredictable animal.

"How did you know to follow him?" Derek asks.

"I was worried about that little girl. She never came out of the house. Neither of them did. She kept writing *HELP* in the window, but the cops wouldn't come. Then yesterday I saw blood on the glass and it scared me, so I followed him out here after I realized the cops wouldn't do anything."

"She controls the town," Derek says.

"How?" Mina asks.

"She's loaded. Her husband was big in real estate around here," Brooke says.

"You could have mentioned that sooner." Derek turns to Brooke. "Back when we were pooling information."

Brooke shrugs. "Does it change anything?"

"Speaking of pooling information," Mina says. "My husband pays attention to my location on his phone. There's a good chance he'll see I'm here and try to call me. When I don't answer, he'll worry."

"Mitch destroyed your phone," Brooke says.

God, she's a real bubble-burster.

"It would still show your last known location to the police, possibly to Brady too," Derek adds.

"The *Freeport* police?" Brooke this time.

Right.

How easily they keep forgetting that the police are not their friends.

"We live in Seattle. Maybe he'll go to the Seattle police first," Mina says, even though she knows Brady will go immediately to the police in this area.

There's silence again and Mina has so many questions that she doesn't know where to start. And she's honestly too tired to prioritize them or even explore them all, but she begins anyway.

"How long have you been here?" she asks Derek.

"A few weeks. Brooke's been here a decade."

"No way."

Brooke shifts her weight from one foot to the other and looks around.

"So we're doing this pretend wedding thing and after that, they're going to kill me," Mina states. She doesn't mean it to come off so matter-of-fact, but it does.

Brooke looks at Derek and he speaks up. "Fuck no. We're going to get out of here. It's not over yet."

Mina watches Brooke's response. She's the one who's been here the longest. The one who knows the most about their abductors. The woman bites her bottom lip, refuses to look at either her or Derek after he says that. Her face is crestfallen. Brooke doesn't think it's possible to get out of here. This sends an arrow of despair into Mina's heart.

"Can you tell me about your daughter?" Brooke asks. "What happened to her?"

"Why? I don't see why that matters right now." Brooke doesn't strike her as the type to make small talk, or waste any time at all.

"It might matter."

CHAPTER 54

Mina takes in a big draw of air as thoughts gather in her mind. It's been a long time since she's told the story, but there were a few years where she was talking almost daily about what happened. And it's not like she could ever forget a single detail.

It was the day her life came to a screeching halt. This, even though the weather on the Oregon Coast was perfect that week. The ocean was a dark turquoise, the air so warm you could wear a swimsuit. Paxton had this little pink and orange pineapple-covered one-piece. She wore a yellow hat, and her curls clung to her face, mixed with sunscreen and sea water. The crowded beach was full of sunbathers, people playing volleyball, tossing a football to their kid, or a tennis ball for their dog. A group of college-aged boys played loud music, and Mina remembers thinking it sounded obnoxious, like a car at a red light next to you, reverberating with bass. The pounding surf took the edge off of any melody there might be.

It was Paxton's first time seeing the ocean, and she became obsessed with tide pools. One in particular. A little one near their hotel. They could step out of the sliding door and walk there in minutes. Brady and Mina had to keep Paxton back from touching everything in the tide pool. They didn't want her to disturb the habitat, although as parents, they also couldn't help letting her touch a few things in the name of sensory exploration. Starfish mostly. There were orange, purple, and yellow ones. Brady made a comment about how shocked he was that more people weren't at this tide pool. He was right. It felt like their little secret. Like it was visible only to them, so that Paxton could have this magical experience at the sea. Her last ever experience, as fate had it.

So, that's where the three of them were whenever the tide was out. But Paxton didn't understand the concept of the tide. So whenever it was in, and the tide pool was underwater, she'd cry in the hotel room, so upset that they couldn't go down to see the starfish. Brady tried to tell her it was the starfishes' nap time. That they had to recharge so they were ready for her again later and maybe she should do the same thing. At one point, Mina told Brady it was a bad idea for them to get a room right on the beach. It made it so much harder that Paxton could see the water, think about the tide pool, and cry because she couldn't be there.

On the last full day of their vacation, Brady ran to the grocery store for more sunscreen. They didn't expect it to be so hot, although they weren't complaining. Mina told him to take his time, maybe bring his book and a chair and find a spot on the beach to get some time to himself. Paxton needed a nap, and Brady had been staying home with her full time during the day while Mina worked. He needed the break. Deserved it.

When Mina thought Paxton was asleep, she ran a bath for herself. Even though she was happy to give Brady a break, she was still grumpy about having to be in a dark hotel room in the middle of the day with a napping child. She felt stuck, which was so ridiculous. What wouldn't she give to do that every day for the rest of her life if it meant having her baby back.

Mina turned on the little Bluetooth speaker they brought along and listened to some Billie Holiday and Nina Simone while she sipped wine in the bath. She took her time; Paxton was wiped out and would sleep long. An hour or so passed and Mina came out of the bathroom.

It wasn't dark anymore. In fact, the hotel room was bright with sunlight.

The slider door was open.

The bed was empty.

Paxton was gone.

Mina was in the hotel's white robe, but she didn't even think about that. She ran out the open slider door, wet feet hitting hot sand, and shouted Paxton's name. Over and over again. She went around asking the people on the beach if they'd seen Paxton. *She was wearing a purple shirt and white and purple polka dot shorts. Blonde curls, green eyes.* That's what Mina told everyone. Purple, blonde, green. Purple, blonde, green. Purple, blonde, green. Like she was a recording repeating the same lines, over and over.

Nobody had seen Paxton.

Mina felt untethered from reality. Couldn't grab ahold of anything to anchor her. She wanted to be everywhere all at once in order to find her girl. But she couldn't get anywhere fast enough. What if Paxton returned to the hotel room? What if Mina was always just missing her? But Mina was only one person and so she ran back into the room and called the police, then Brady. Brady came back, and by that time, Mina had gotten dressed and returned to the beach, calling for her girl. It was the only thing she could do. Her throat was strained and in pain from yelling over the volume of the waves. The tide was in, so she couldn't get out to the tide pool. That was her fear. That Paxton had wandered out there alone. Drowned.

Brady took the beach in the other direction, picking up the search where Mina had left off and going farther.

The police showed up and interviewed people, but otherwise, the cops were useless. They kept asking Brady questions about what he was doing, could anyone verify his whereabouts? It was so aggravating that they wouldn't listen. Especially since between Brady and Mina, it was Mina who had let Paxton out of her sight. If there was blame to pass around, it should land on her. It was she who closed the bathroom door for so long. Turned the music up. She who took her damn sweet time out of frustration with sitting in the dark hotel room. Mina was responsible for this, and the thoughts needled into the edges of her mind as they searched for Paxton.

She didn't turn up.

Not that day, not the next, and not weeks later.

Months passed. Brady and Mina wanted to stay in Freeport, keep searching, but she had to go back to work. Bills and collectors didn't care if you lost your most precious love. Still, they didn't give up. Mina started reaching out to the bigger cities around Freeport. When she got in contact with Derek, that's when they learned about Paxton. They'd found her body.

Mina couldn't cope. Couldn't even come close to handling the news. She didn't believe it at first, and denial served as some sort of emotional defense mechanism, but when Mina saw Paxton there, in Portland, in the morgue, she came apart at the seams. It did her in. All those months of stress over her baby girl missing, culminating in the news she was murdered. That night at home, Mina tried to take her own life, and that's when Brady drove her to the hospital.

Eventually, she got herself together. Meds helped. Lots of therapy. Brady had been in contact with Derek, and Derek, bless his heart, had tried. God, how he tried. They felt that Derek wanted to find the lowlife who did that to their little girl. But eight years later, she knows no more about Paxton's death than she did back then.

CHAPTER 55

After Mina finishes the story, Brooke allows a few seconds of silence to pass.

Blonde hair, green eyes.

It's her. It's the same Paxton.

"I need to say something," Brooke whispers.

Derek has situated himself on the chair, elbows resting on knees, head hanging. His usual pose. He tips up his face.

Mina looks over at Brooke, next to her on the couch.

Neither of them speak.

Brooke clears her throat. "I don't know how to say this, so I'll be direct."

She waits for some sort of response, but neither of them give her one. "Paxton was here."

"The fuck," Derek mutters, stands. He clenches his fists like he's going to have another outburst. "Here? In the cabin? But how?"

Brooke doesn't answer him. Instead, she watches Mina, but the woman's face is a total blank. She blinks fast, but otherwise, nothing, until her mouth morphs into a slow frown, and sobs shake her body. She puts her face in her hands and when Brooke tries to offer comfort—a touch on the shoulder —Mina flinches away.

Brooke looks at Derek and he paces. His jaw muscles ripple and his knuckles are white from balling up. "That goddamn bastard." Derek slams a fist on the kitchen island. His voice climbs in pitch. "I'm going to kill him. I'm going to wring his dirty neck—"

"Please," Mina squeaks at him.

He comes back to himself. Shakes his head and sits his ass back down. "I'm sorry, Mina," he says. "Go on, Brooke."

"I only put it together last night when you said her first name, Mina. I never knew Paxton's last name, and the only thing Derek ever called her was 'the Rodriguez girl.'"

Derek pipes up. "I didn't forget her name. It was just . . . too painful to say it. I'm sorry. I can't believe she was here." He mutters, like he might go off again, but Mina speaks up.

"Tell me everything," she says, her gaze steely now. "And I mean everything."

Brooke takes a deep breath. This story will be painful for her to tell, but she's doing it anyway.

"Paxton was an adorable little girl. Those blonde curls— like yours." She motions to Mina's hair, unruly waves hanging past her shoulders. "Those dimples, too. Green eyes, like you said. She was something special, and the moment I saw her, I fell in love with her." Brooke pauses to read the room. But there's no response from either of them.

Mina shakes her head, trying to snap out of it, wipes her nose. "Please keep going."

Tears threaten to push through, but Brooke can't cry right now. She has to share this, for Mina, for Paxton. It's not about her, so she clears her throat. "I'd been here a couple years when Paxton arrived. She was the first kid cast member. I was determined to make her life as full of joy as it could be under the circumstances.

"We grew close. She called me Auntie B." Brooke watches Mina's face for any signs that she's crossing lines. That she's saying too much, but Mina only sits there staring at her, allowing the tears to course down her face.

"I made her favorite cookies as often as Mitch brought me the chocolate chips for them. I asked questions about her parents to keep their—I mean, *your*—memory alive in her mind. She told me about how the three of you had been at the beach. How she named all the starfish she saw. How a man had cracked open the sliding door of your hotel room and said that the starfish were out, and did she want to come look real quick?"

Mina gasps, covers her mouth with a hand.

"Goddamn bastard," Derek breathes.

Brooke stops. Watches again for signs she should shut up. Mina cries. Brooke finally looks at Derek, and he stares at her, eyes glistening. Mina motions with a hand for her to continue.

"Well, the man playing Albert at the time was a total douchebag. I didn't trust him at all, so Paxton was never alone with him. Ever. Even at night, she slept in my room with me instead of in her own room. We only have a few toys and children's books here, and Paxton soon had those stories memorized. So, I tried to recall my favorite fairy tales from childhood to tell her when she got bored with the books. Help her fall asleep. Funny thing was, she'd heard so many of them already, and she corrected me when I got them wrong. Which was often."

Mina's laugh is a whisper, but it turns back to tears.

"She was such a character. I thought to myself that whoever this girl's parents were, they had loved her well because she was so confident in herself. I knew her parents must be overcome with worry. The same way I was—"

Brooke clears her throat to bully the tears back.

Don't go there. This isn't about you. It's not about Jessi.

"Brooke," Derek whispers, like he realizes why this is so hard for her to share.

Brooke puts a hand up. "I need to get this out, please."

He folds his hands again, but the expression in his eyes is pure compassion. She can sense he wants to come over here and hold her. She'd lose it if he did that.

"But all I could do in response to the hellish situation was keep Paxton close to me," Brooke goes on. "Love her as well as I could. Love her like I loved my own little girl." Her voice cracks at that last sentence and she takes a breath to steady herself. Doesn't glance over at Derek at all for fear that she'll break.

"I wasn't anywhere close to a replacement for you, her parents. She talked about you all the time. About her daddy, who stayed home with her while her mommy worked. How he took her to the park. How she loved to swing, and about how he'd do underdogs that made her go so high, she got a tickle tummy. And she told me about you. About how pretty you were. That one day she wanted to grow up to be just like you."

"Oh, God," Mina whispers and covers her mouth again.

"I'm sorry. Should I stop?"

"No!" She puts a hand on Brooke's knee. "No, please keep going."

"Since it was summer while she was here, Paxton and I caught bugs in the yard together. She had the silliest laugh and no matter what my mood was, I couldn't help but crack up when she got going."

"Like chirping," Mina says. "That's what Brades always called it."

"Yes!" Brooke smiles and gives a gentle laugh. "Chirping. That's exactly right."

"For a few months, we had each other. And when Grace came that day . . ."

Brooke breaks off to stifle a sob. She blinks hard, sending tears down her face. "I'm sorry. . ."

No response.

"Keep going. I have to hear. I don't care how ugly it is," Mina whispers.

She swallows hard. "When Grace came that day . . . I don't think she was planning it. Things just spiraled. Because Paxton was young. That's it. That's the only reason it happened. Because she was too young to understand why she was being sent to her bedroom when Grace came. Too young to avoid throwing fits about it. That sweet girl disrupted things in a good way. Like she wasn't designed to smile and nod and give people what they wanted just because they asked for it."

Mina nods wildly, but says nothing else.

"I've always been such a rule follower, and I used to think that was why I've made it so long here. Why I survived. But now, thinking about Paxton again, my perspective has changed. It's not only following the rules. It's the strength inside." She looks at Derek when she says the next part. "The strength it takes to keep fighting, and the ones who aren't afraid of their own strength. They're survivors. The way Paxton was, it's how I am, too. It's what's kept me alive for so long." She takes a breath and looks at Mina. "If Paxton were older, able to understand, she'd be alive too."

Derek's face is soft. Her heart expands with affection

for him.

"Tell me how it happened. I have to know," Mina says, almost impatiently.

"Yes, Grace arrived one day, and it was quick. I promise to God, it was immediate. No suffering. Once I saw Grace coming at her with those dead eyes, I told Paxton to think about her mommy and daddy. About how much they loved her. About how I loved her, too. And then . . ."

Brooke can't hold back the wall of sobs trying to crash through, and she can't speak through them either.

"And then Grace slit her throat," Mina says, monotone.

Brooke nods. "How did you know?"

"It was her cause of death."

Brooke wishes there was more to share, but there really isn't.

Derek stands, wipes his nose, and puts his hand on Brooke's head, pets her hair, but says nothing.

"You've given me a gift," Mina says. "Two gifts. You loved her when I wasn't there, and now I know how she spent her last days. Thank you."

Mina's face is still. It's red and puffy from crying, and she wipes her nose with the back of the long-sleeved wedding dress. But there's a tough determination in her eyes.

When Mina goes back into the bedroom, probably to clean herself up, Derek comes over and holds Brooke.

"Jessi," is all he says.

She falls apart against him, crying. She failed Paxton. Cody. What right did she have to see Jessi again?

Then, to her own surprise, there's something Brooke wants to do. It's the right thing. Her gut screams this truth. And she has peace.

They can get out of here. They can, and she knows how.

CHAPTER 56

"That's your idea?" Derek almost shouts, a one-eighty from the lovey-dovey moment before this. But he can't believe she made a big deal about this idea and it's that. The same idea they already talked about and he shot down before.

Brooke nods.

Mina walks into the living room.

"No," Derek says. "Hell. No."

"Not asking for your permission. I want to. I owe it to Paxton and Cody. It's time. And maybe I won't even die. Maybe the perimeter will shut off and I'll walk right out. But there's only one way to know."

Derek paces around the living room. He has to think. Has to keep his anger in check, but this woman can be so goddamn infuriating. And he cannot lose her. "No," he says again. "You owe it to Jessi to walk out of here alive. There's another way. There has to be."

"Who is Jessi?" Mina asks.

"What is it then? This *other way* you speak of?" Brooke's voice steadies, and they both ignore Mina's question. She

257

doesn't even stand. There's no challenge, not like her usual posture when they argue.

Derek hangs his head back, stares at the ceiling. "I don't know. But there has to be one."

"My husband will have noticed my location sharing is off. That's still on the table," Mina adds.

"But it might just make him call the Freeport police, remember?" Derek says.

"And he might be too late," Brooke adds.

Mina looks at her feet.

"I'll throw Cody's collar across the perimeter and if the humming dies down, I'll step over," Brooke says. "If I make it, you two follow. We could do it right now." She stands, and Derek tackles her back to the couch. Mina moves to get out of the way.

"No," he says right in her face, through clenched teeth. She tries to wrestle him off, but he's got her wrists and she can't budge out of his grip, so she gives up.

"Who is Cody?" Mina asks.

They both look at her. What an enormous chore to explain, but Derek gives her the quick and dirty version any way.

"Jesus," Mina whispers. "But I agree with Derek. Let's find another way."

"Get off me. Please!" Brooke cries out. "You two are clueless! There's no other way. We don't have time for your optimism and brainstorming sessions!"

"Don't run. At least wait until we have a solid plan," Derek says, only pretending to entertain her idea so that she will trust him and wait. Buy him more time to come up with something. Anything other than that.

"Fine. I need to get Cody's collar and try to charge it,

anyway. We don't even know if it will turn on. May I have your permission to do that?"

He lets her go and ignores the sarcasm.

Brooke smooths her hair and rubs her wrists.

"Sorry," Derek whispers, when he realizes he hurt her again. She ignores him and walks into Cody's room.

There's a noise like sticks breaking, and soon Brooke is back, holding the metal file in one hand and the collar in the other. "Doesn't seem like anyone has tampered with it. It's exactly like ours. A little blood-stained, but that shouldn't matter." She plugs it into the charger and notices the whole room holding its breath to see if it'll work. Green lights appear.

She and Derek exhale at the same time. It's charging.

"Even if we did this, I don't have the keys to my car anymore," Mina says. "What are we going to do? Walk the entire way? We're so far out here. But we could wait until they come back, then take the Jeep."

"Hell no, we aren't waiting for them to come back," Brooke says.

Derek groans. This is insane, and it gets more insane by the minute. But he'd rather escape and take his chances walking through the forest than attempt to overpower two people with both a gun and the ability to kill them with the push of a button. If they're going to do this, they have to do it before the killers show up.

"We can't overpower those two, but they could be here any minute, and they have all the town's police. Remember the dogs?" He directs the question to Mina.

She nods, folds her arms and looks down again.

Then, like he summoned the beast, the Jeep pulls up. Derek goes to the window to see.

"It's Mitch. And he's alone again," he says.

"We have to kill them both," Brooke says, as easy as if she announced that she's making tacos for dinner. "It's the only way now. We kill Mitch today. Now. And we take Grace on with his gun when she arrives."

"Then we try with Cody's collar," Derek adds.

Brooke nods and hands the metal file to Derek.

It's the plan he's been mulling over, or some variation of it, but who cares if she gets the credit for it? And they can figure out the part about who walks over the line first later. Right now, he has to take Mitch down. He can't fail again.

"I won't be in the same room as that bastard," Mina says, starting for Kinsey's old bedroom, but Brooke catches her by the arm. "Stay. It'll be better if you cooperate."

CHAPTER 57

Mina doesn't want to share air space with that monster. He's the one who lured her baby out of her safe bed and brought her here, where she was murdered in cold blood. It is something that Paxton wasn't alone when it happened, that she had Brooke, but still. Thinking of how scared her girl must have been absolutely kills Mina's soul all over again.

And now, this man is coming. She has to face him when all she wants to do is claw him to shreds and feed him to the sea.

"I don't trust myself to act calmly," Mina whispers and shakes loose from Brooke's grip.

"Mina, please stay," Derek says. "Go stand over there, in the kitchen, so that you'd have to get past both Brooke and me in order to get to him. We won't let you."

She nods and goes over near the sink, embarrassed about how stupid she looks in this hideous blood-stained dress.

Derek reaches for Brooke, holds her hand and hides the metal file behind his back like it's a gun.

Mitch comes in with a silver lighter in hand. He's flicking it on and off, making a show of it.

The gun is in his waistband, and he's wearing a woman's necklace, a fancy gold chain with a big square dangling from it, which seems weird. Brooke and Derek make eye contact and exchange a look that Mina can't read.

"I imagine you've all figured it out by now."

"That you're a flaming prick, yes," Derek hisses.

Mitch laughs. "Oh, come on now, mystery solved for you two!" He wags a finger at Derek and Mina.

"And you," he says to Brooke, "you got to find out more about your little friend. Even meet her mom."

What the hell? Did he know Mina was Paxton's mom this whole time? Mina can't keep in the sobs. Her body is tired, shaking from the events of the past twenty-four hours. Add to that all the crying she's done. It's overwhelming. She bites her tongue, though, plants her feet in place even though her heart is screaming inside to end him.

"You designed this whole thing," Derek says.

"Can't take credit for all of it. You? Sure. When I found out this was going to be Grace's last Albert, I needed it to be you. So poetic." He points at Mina again. "Her? I saw her name on the rental agreement, and I was as surprised as you all are. And her following me out here? Well, that was just dumb luck. The Universe likes me, I guess."

"You're a fucking beast," Brooke yells, and lunges toward Mitch, clawing him at the neck, exactly like Mina wanted to do, but it happens so fast that Mina startles. He drops the closed silver lighter, and it goes skidding across the wood floor.

In a few steps, Derek pulls Brooke off, holding her tight in a hug. Brooke resists for a second, trying to get back to attacking Mitch, but turns and melts in his embrace.

Mitch touches his neck. Blood. She got a piece of him and

it elates Mina. Just to see him suffer a bit. He whips his head down and pats his chest with fury.

"Give it back," he growls at Brooke, pulling out his gun.

She smiles and breaks away from Derek, holding out the necklace he was wearing. "What? This?"

Mitch steps forward, gun pointed at them.

"You can't shoot us, dumbass. If Grace herself refused to kill me the other day, how do you think she's going to handle the news that you did?" Brooke says.

He stops, but doesn't lower the gun.

Instead, he cocks it and aims at Derek. "I like my chances if it means I can finally end this one."

Everything slows and the charge in the air tells Mina he's not messing around. He might shoot Derek.

Mitch pulls the trigger, but nothing happens.

He looks at the weapon, and open-mouthed surprise replaces rage. The gun seems jammed, or it doesn't have a bullet or something.

Derek has him on the ground in half a breath. He takes the gun, stuffs it in his waistband, pulling out the metal file.

Why is he doing that?

Mina panics. Why put the gun away in favor of a stupid tool?

Derek motions with a nod toward the kitchen table. "Sit down."

Mitch looks behind him, toward the front door, like he's considering running away again.

"Unless you want a brand new metal piercing through your jugular, sit the fuck down."

"The gun, Derek. What are you doing?" Brooke asks.

Instead of answering her, he looks at Mitch. "Brand new Glock 19, huh?" He pulls it out and turns it over. "Didn't bother to break the thing in? Pretty big risk. Failure to feed is an actual issue unless a new gun's done at least 150 rounds. Too bad for you it happened now and not when Grace shot it. Guess the Universe isn't quite on your side. But don't worry, I'll make sure to break it in after I get out of here."

Derek approaches Mitch with the metal file, and Mitch puts his hands up, so he restrains him by the wrists.

"Can you get that yarn and tie him up?" he asks Brooke, who disappears and reappears fast.

Derek shoves Mitch into the chair while Brooke works behind him, tying up his hands.

When she's done, Brooke shouts, "Now. Let's do it now."

"Slow down," Derek says. "We have the remote. If Grace shows up, I'm sure I can handle her even if I can't rely on this gun. She doesn't know it's jammed. Let's see if we can find out more about the perimeter before we risk anyone's life using up our one Hail Mary." He points to Cody's collar.

Mitch laughs.

Derek's fist connects with Mitch's face so fast it makes Mina jump. His head hangs, chin to chest, and he's lights out.

Brooke and Derek pick their fight right back up as if Derek didn't just knock a guy unconscious.

"No. This is it. This is our chance," Brooke says, backing toward the front door.

Derek yells, "Damn it, woman! Stop!" and tackles her again. This time he brings her down, so she's on her stomach, and he sits on her ass, puts his knees up, resting elbows on them. He shakes his head, runs a hand through his hair. It would be a funny scene if everything wasn't so goddamned scary right now.

She yells at him to get off her.

"I will," Derek says. "I want to see if he'll confirm our

plan when his life is on the line. Any chance you can stay in the cabin for a minute longer?"

"Ok, yes. Fine."

"Promise?"

"God, yes, I promise!"

Derek rises and picks up the metal file he dropped in order to tackle Brooke. He hands it to her, slaps Mitch's gray-stubble cheeks to wake him.

"You stupid asshole," Mitch groans as he wakes. "She doesn't know I came out here, and she's probably on her way."

"Why did you steal her remote? Now she's defenseless," Derek asks, and doesn't wait for him to reply. "Does the perimeter go off after a collar detonates?"

"Grace will be here soon. All's I gotta do is wait you out."

"*All's we gotta do* is shove this tool through your flesh," Derek says, pointing to the metal file, now in Brooke's hand. Mina doesn't know what's worse. Derek's rage and strength or the cold, hard stare of hate on Brooke's face. She'd be equally scared of both if she were Mitch.

"Tell us what the flaw in the perimeter is!" Derek yells as he moves into the monster's face.

"Why would I do that?" Mitch spits on him.

Derek wipes his face and moves back.

"I don't know. Maybe because living to kill another day appeals to your psychopathic sensibilities?"

Mitch sighs. His shoulders drop, chest deflates. "I got nothing to live for."

CHAPTER 58

Mitch seems open again. Like the time Brooke seduced him. Like the time he mentioned the flaw in the perimeter after Kinsey's death.

As much as Brooke could not care less about him, his perspective, what his life was like, this is the thing to ask right now.

"Why?"

Mina stares at her, tilts her head to the side, as if trying to figure out what is going on, but she needs to wait. Brooke has an idea. Derek's eyebrows raise, and he nods.

"You don't deserve to know. Not after that stunt you pulled." Mitch spits on the ground this time.

"You don't deserve to be alive right now, yet we're managing," Brooke replies.

"Fine, just for shits and giggles, I guess I'll tell you. Her husband ran the town. He got me on with the police. Grace wasn't always insane, but soon she became obsessed with buying the properties she grew up in, reliving her life. Gerry —her husband—humored her at first, bought her the places, paid to have them restored. But then she wanted to staff them with what she called 'cast members.' I was doing side jobs for him and he paid me to manage the cast members. It was above board, if not totally crazy.

"Well, long story short, Gerry got uncomfortable with what she was doing out here, and he was afraid of how it would look when people found out. Grace grew tired of dealing with the employees and all their workplace demands, requests for raises. So, she enlisted her son, who was this bigwig engineer in tech, to create the collars and the perimeter. Gerry found out and threatened to sell her properties if she didn't stop. So, she killed him. If I don't do what she says, she'll kill me too. She cut me up real good when I tried to fight her one time, years ago." He points to his chest.

The scars. Has to be.

"This son. Is there a way we can talk to him?" Derek asks. "Find out how to shut this whole thing down."

"Unless you can talk to ghosts. He's dead. Grace owns the company and the patent now."

"What? Her son is dead?" Brooke asks.

"Grew a conscience like his dad."

Derek looks at the ceiling. "Holy shit."

"If I do what she says, I get paid well," Mitch goes on. "She's had me by the balls this whole time. That's why I did what I did. After a while, you shut down any thinking or feeling. It's the only way to stay alive."

"So just because she destroyed your life and threatened you, it's fine to kidnap and murder children and dump their bodies for a living?"

"How would you escape if you could?" Derek asks on the heels of Brooke's question, playing along as if Mitch is the victim he claims to be.

He shrugs. "Kill the old woman, I suppose."

"Why haven't you then?" Derek asks.

He smiles that lopsided, menacing grin and gives a hard shrug. "Weren't you listening? Tried once. And now, I'm not as young as I used to be and I guess I like the money."

"Because you're a psychopath too," Mina shouts out of nowhere.

He's in on it. He enjoys this little kingdom of torment he's built, even if there might be a looming threat. It's not real to him. He's not scared of her.

"You let Paxton's case go cold," Derek says, as if he's realizing it. "Jesus Christ, you faked a crime scene so Freeport could claim jurisdiction and you could bury the case."

Mitch flattens his lips. Brooke can't tell if he's trying to hide a smile, or what.

"Grace's idea. She was afraid of getting caught."

"He won't help us," Mina says. "He's wasting time, hoping Grace shows up to save him."

"Yep." Brooke moves toward Cody's collar, still on the wall, but Derek grabs her arm to keep her from it. Then he reaches for her hand, holds it. "Not yet, please," he begs.

She squeezes her eyes shut and hates that she's going to give in, but she does.

Derek gets in Mitch's face again. "Does the perimeter shut down when a collar detonates?" he repeats.

"She'll be here any minute now."

Derek puts a hand out, asking Brooke for the file. She gives it to him. He takes it to where Mina stands in the kitchen. "If you aim for right here,"—he points to a spot on his own neck, a protruding vein, pumping hard—"it'll be quick. Up to you if you want it to be quick or not. But first, I have one more idea to get him to talk."

Mitch's face falls.

Mina's smirk tells Brooke the woman is going to enjoy every moment of this.

CHAPTER 59

Walking into the kitchen, Derek grabs a small towel and opens cupboards.

"What are you looking for?" Brooke asks.

"A juice pitcher, something to hold water."

She nods and joins him, pulls out the pitcher she uses when she makes lemonade, hands it to him. He turns on the faucet. This will work. It has to.

When the pitcher is full, he says to Brooke, "I need you to hold his face up toward the ceiling." He walks over to Mitch.

She stands there.

"Come on!" Derek says. Anger swells inside of him, and he's not mad at her, but he's coming across that way. He hopes she knows it's not her. "I'm getting an answer out of him. Period."

To his surprise, she doesn't argue, or get upset. Instead, she rushes. Brooke holds Mitch's face from behind, tries to tip it up by the chin, but he fights against her.

"Harder," Derek says.

Brooke wrenches up his face. Derek lays the towel over it and trickles the water.

Mitch sputters and coughs at first, but then he thrashes in silence.

"Ready to talk?"

Mitch nods.

Brooke lets go of his head.

Derek removes the towel. "Does the perimeter shut off when a collar detonates?"

Mitch spits water in his face, coughs loud, gasps for air. He laughs. The bastard actually laughs.

"I was in Iraq, you bastard, you think I can't handle a baby's attempt at hazing?"

Derek punches Mitch in the face without even a breath of hesitation. Saliva and blood go flying.

Mitch laughs again, and there's a maniacal tone to it this time.

Derek's about to throw another punch when Brooke says, "This isn't working. We have to be more aggressive."

"What do you have in mind?"

Brooke looks toward the kitchen, at Mina, holding the metal file. She moves around to stand next to Derek, facing Mitch.

It happens so fast that Derek almost gasps. Brooke takes Mitch's pinky finger and cranks it back with so much force that he screams. It's broken. Brooke broke his finger.

"Does the perimeter shut off when a collar detonates?" he repeats.

"I lied about the perimeter. There's no flaw."

Derek's heart drops. But the humming had stopped after Kinsey's collar went off. That was real.

"I'm not fucking with you, so don't fuck with me," he says, and Brooke reaches for his next finger. Mitch tries to ball up his hands but she pries it loose, smearing blood all over her own hands. Mitch glances out the window. Derek follows his gaze.

It's Grace. She's here. Brooke lets go and steps away.

"Looks like I'm saved."

A streak of metal zips in front of Derek's face. Blood next. So much blood. He gasps and backs away as his mind clenches around what the hell is happening.

Mitch's neck drips red, rivering blood, and his mouth gapes open and closed like a dying fish.

Mina stands next to Derek, holding the handle of the metal file, and it's buried inside Mitch's neck. The exact spot he showed her. She pulls it out.

A gush of blood.

It's over in seconds.

He looks at Mina, but shock keeps him from speaking. He reaches for the metal file and she allows it to roll from her hand into his. She staggers back.

"I got tired of listening to him talk," she says. "Only enough time to make it quick."

It's not what Derek would have done. Mitch may still have been useful, but now it's over.

"The second she comes through that door, I'm taking her down," Derek says, pulling out the gun to use as a threat, and pressing his back to the wall, so that when Grace walks in, he can surprise her. The first thing she'll see is Mitch, dead in a chair. It should throw her off a little and give him an advantage.

"Turn off the lights," Derek shout-whispers at Mina, who is closest to the kitchen. She does it.

Brooke takes Cody's collar off the charger and slides it underneath the couch, but within reach.

Minutes pass and it seems Grace should have gotten to the door by now. Can she tell something is wrong?

The door knob turns.

It's quiet except for the creak and the sound of wind through the trees outside.

And Derek's heart beating in his ears.

The door cracks ajar about an inch.

"Mitch?" Grace says, still on the other side.

Derek is ready to pounce, his body sending that go urge, but he resists. It's not time yet.

The barrel of a small gun appears through the open slit in the door.

Fuck.

He didn't expect her to have a gun. But he has to see this plan through either way. He's the only one in a position to overpower her. And this is their chance now that they have the remote, and Mitch is dead. He grips the Glock 19, shoves it into his waistband again. It no longer works as a threat when she has a working gun.

"What is this? What happened to Mitch?" Grace asks. Derek breathes in and out as Brooke and Mina put their hands in the air. Her arm and part of her body comes through the doorway, and he's still hidden from view.

Now. It has to be now.

Derek lunges for her. But before he can make contact, the gun swings in his direction. She saw him somehow, and he can't stop his momentum. Somewhere deep inside his mind, he registers that this won't turn out how he hoped. Before he can knock her to the ground, the gun goes off.

CHAPTER 60

"No!" Brooke screams and rushes to Derek.

He's shot. Oh God, she shot him.

Brooke touches around his shoulder, where red expands to soak up fabric. He's not dead. And he's awake, lying on the floor.

She pulls a blanket off the couch and presses it against his wound.

A switch flicks on in her gut. The stacked-up rage of ten years gathers strength like a volcano deep within. Everyone she lost when she went missing. A daughter she'll never know. Innocent people she saw die. People she loved.

I won't lose Derek. This ends now.

Grace bends and picks up Mitch's Zippo lighter, but before Brooke can do anything, the old woman's in the kitchen near Mina.

"This isn't the final scene I envisioned, but let's make it cinematic all the same," she says, and flicks the lighter on. She holds it in a threat beneath the kitchen's strawberry-print curtains. "Back in the day, these used to be quite flammable, did you know that? It was hard to find authentic drapes. But I did it. Because I wanted this to be real. I wanted it to mean something."

A fire. She's going to light the place on fire.

Grace touches the flame to the hem of the curtain and it ignites right away, flames licking up the length.

Mina slinks toward Brooke and Derek, like she's trying not to attract Grace's attention.

Grace notices and points the gun at her as she crosses into the living room. "Stay right there. Don't worry though, I'm giving you three a choice. Burn alive, or cross the perimeter and end it fast. I'll wait on the other side and watch the show. For as long as I can, at least."

She's at the living room drapes now. They dissolve when she lights them up, and embers drop on the couch, which catches fire. Heat pulses against Brooke's cheeks. Cody's collar lies under the couch, but it won't be long until the flames reach it too. She has to get it, and get Derek out of here. She wraps the blanket around Derek's shoulder and he cries out in pain. Grace stands at the front door.

"I've never been one for locked doors, so you can see yourself out if you'd like," she says.

Brooke moves to stand, but Derek grabs her forearm and pulls her back. "No," he whispers. His voice is ragged. "Let her go. We'll try your plan once she's gone. She still has a gun."

What the hell is he talking about? She's not leaving. Didn't he hear? They have to do it now, before the fire pushes them past the perimeter. Out here in the forest, fire travels fast. Too fast. And if Grace isn't leaving until her darling final scene is over, well, Brooke has no choice.

She doesn't argue with him, instead, touches his hand to remove it from her arm. Pushes his hair off his forehead.

Grace turns her back to them.

The door clicks shut behind her.

Brooke stares at Derek.

He shakes his head.

Screw him.

Brooke grabs the metal file from the floor, and reaches under the couch to get the collar, puts it in Derek's good hand, squeezes his fingers around it. She stands. "Get him outside," she barks to Mina.

Mina nods.

"No, Brooke, don't go after her," Derek says. "She'll kill you."

"Not if I fuck her up first."

CHAPTER 61

It's not just the curtains that are flammable in this cabin, it's everything. The fire spreads so much faster than Mina expected it to.

She rushes to Derek's side, shouting, "Brooke's insane!"

He smiles. "I like that about her." Then he grimaces in pain.

Mina has to get this huge man out of the cabin somehow. "Can you walk?" she yells over the roaring flames.

He nods. "It's just my shoulder. I think I'll be all right. Help me up."

Mina takes the collar from him, so he can use his good arm. She loops it on to her elbow like a purse.

She slips her shoulders underneath Derek and braces herself for his weight.

When he tries to stand, she stumbles, but catches herself. The fire crowds them and almost smothers the doorway. They both cough hard. She has to hurry.

Derek yells out in pain, but he's steady on his feet and his bad arm hangs limp, a blanket tied around it. He takes her hand and they walk out the door into the yard.

Grace has her back to the cabin, swaggering, and she's almost to the car. Mina watches as Brooke runs straight toward her.

CHAPTER 62

Grace walks through the weeds, the gun hanging limp in her hand. She must not have heard Brooke open the door between the sound of the fire cracking, and the perimeter's low humming. In fact, she's almost at the perimeter when Brooke closes in on her. It takes all of Brooke's willpower not to shout out some battle cry. Make her fury known, release it. But she's only a few feet away and can't lose the element of surprise.

Grace stops, turns, as if to evaluate the scene and congratulate herself, and right when she seems to realize what's happening, she makes a move toward lifting the gun, but Brooke has already launched herself at her.

Go for the gun.

The words jump into Brooke's mind in the split second before making contact with Grace.

Brooke's impact knocks the gun out of Grace's hand, along with sending the metal file she held careening across the yard. Both land in the tall weeds, hidden.

She's on top of the woman, straddling her so Brooke's

legs pin Grace's arms down at her sides. Brooke punches, screams, scratches.

She looks around for the gun again, but can't see it. Remembers that goddamn knife at Grace's hip and pulls it out of its sheath.

She presses the blade to the woman's neck, mirroring how the blade was pushed against her own neck only yesterday.

Grace's eyes are empty, scared, and now she's just a frail, old woman.

"I kept you alive all these years," Grace hisses.

"I kept myself alive, you bitch."

Brooke runs through all the reasons this woman should die right now.

Tyson.

Cody.

Paxton.

Kinsey.

All the others.

Ten years of Brooke's life, stolen.

Jessi, grown.

Derek, shot.

She pulls the knife across Grace's neck in one rough motion. Stares at the blood torrenting out.

It's not until there's a hand on her shoulder that Brooke comes back to herself.

"You did it," Mina whispers.

Grace's eyes are wide open, her entire chest, blood saturated.

Brooke pops up to her feet.

She shakes. She just killed someone. Someone who deserved to die, yes, but *she killed her*. Problem for later.

Right now, flames engulf the cabin and travel outward toward them, like sloppy rays of sunshine.

"Where's Derek?" she asks.

"There."

Mina points to the far side of the property where Derek stands by the perimeter, his back to it. He's holding the collar and facing her.

No!

It's supposed to be her. It has to be her. She has so much to make up for. She runs to him. "Wait!" she screams. "Maybe the flames will die out. Buy us more time."

An explosion from the house sends a blazing inferno into the sky, catching the nearby trees on fire and startling her.

"Our timing really is shit," Derek says, smiling.

"The fire department will see it and get here fast, right?" But even as the hope-laced words leave her mouth, Brooke registers how fast the flames are coming at them now. The explosion sent rainfalls of fire farther out into the yard, doubling and tripling piles of growing fire. The hungry flames eat weeds. They can't wait for rescue.

Brooke tries to take the collar from him, but all he has to do is raise it so it's high out of her reach. She pushes his chest, and he cries out in pain from his shoulder. She backs off.

It might be fine. Cody's collar might turn the perimeter off and whoever goes over first, is just . . . fine.

In theory it sounded like a workable plan, but now, faced with the reality, it scares her like crazy.

"I'm sorry for hurting your shoulder," she says. "But you have to let me do it. Let me toss the collar and step over first. I owe it to everyone I watched die here."

"You owe it to your daughter to return home. Plus, I'm

pretty sure I can still overpower you if you try anything, even with only one arm." He smiles again.

Why is he so calm about this? So smiley. It makes the thought of losing him tunnel despair throughout her whole body.

The fire rages so hard now, that nothing will slow it. Unless the fire department was already pulling into the driveway, which it's not. Whatever exploded—a propane tank? Who knows—has sped up the process. Heat rips toward them, gaining ground by the second.

Mina screams from behind, and Brooke can't see her, but she imagines Mina is trying to hold off the flames.

How?

With what?

She's about to turn and see when Derek puts his hand into his pocket and pulls something out.

Her hex bolt ring.

Brooke's jaw drops. "You had it?"

"I'm sorry." He hands it to her.

She wants to lash out, but can't conjure the energy for it right now. Instead, she cries. Relieved to have it back.

"You're getting out of here and you're going to find someone peaceful, like Tyson," Derek says, touching her hair. "Someone who deserves you. Just be sure he appreciates your strength too and doesn't try to change you."

Brooke lines the ring up on her left ring finger, but stops to find his eyes. He's watching her, facing the house and she's facing the perimeter and the orange flames color his cheeks, glowing in his eyes. The fierce heat pounds against her back. Mina approaches them.

Brooke puts the ring on her right hand instead, and says, "Derek, I lied—"

"There's no time! We have to go. Now!" Mina shouts.

Brooke turns toward the cabin and the flames are almost to the perimeter. The inferno intensifies by the second, rumbling so loud, signaling that the uncontrolled blaze will be right where they're standing soon. Brooke can't hear the perimeter humming anymore. How will they know if it goes off after they trip it?

There's only one way to find out.

When Brooke whirls around to face Derek again, his back is to her.

"Wait! I can't hear the humming! What if this doesn't work?" she cries, but the collar has already left Derek's hand and it's flying like a frisbee. It sparks in mid-air and lands on the driveway, black and smoking.

Brooke inhales and holds her breath. Derek lifts a foot to step over the perimeter. She closes her eyes.

CHAPTER 63

Brooke feels the pressure of a hand holding hers, and when she opens her eyes, it's Derek.

Mina is across the perimeter waving both arms at her.

"Let's go," Derek says, smiling.

He came back over to get her, and she doesn't need to be asked a second time. They hurry over the perimeter and when Brooke's feet crunch the gravel driveway, she cries, but she keeps going. Has to get away from the heat and flames. This is the farthest away from the cabin she's been in a decade. And now? Now she's free.

Her collar clicks, and she gasps.

Kinsey's collar had clicked too.

But when she touches it, she finds it's loose. Nothing more than an unclasped necklace, Mina's is already off, and Derek pulls his off too.

It's over. Unbelievable. She hurls it back toward the house and they run to the end of the driveway. Mina rushes ahead, already having chosen to make a right on the main road. She points because she knows the way. The fire is still behind them, but they've put legit distance between themselves and it. Brooke can't stop looking at Derek. His eyes glisten.

"We did it," he says.

Brooke collides into him for a hug, but she knocks against him so hard that he yelps in pain.

"Oh! I'm sorry," she says, touching his hurt arm.

He bends and kisses her forehead. Light as a whisper.

"Derek, I want *you*. If circumstances were different, I would still want to be with you."

He smiles. "I knew it."

She rolls her eyes, but leans into him.

"Hey!" Mina calls out from ahead. "Here comes somebody!"

It's a car.

And farther behind the car, sirens, and lights blare. A firetruck. And the police.

Brooke gasps because her first instinct is fear. Grace owns —or owned—the whole town. She killed Grace. What if these people aren't here to help? What if they see her as a murderer?

Derek takes her hand, squeezes.

"It's Brady! In a rental car!" Mina shouts. She's jumping up and down, waving her arms in the air. The car pulls over and the emergency vehicles speed by. Mina runs to the car and a thin, dark-haired man gets out and they embrace. He lifts her up and swings her around in a circle.

CHAPTER 64

Brady has never looked so good and Mina's never been so thrilled to see him in her life.

He seems more than a little surprised when she jumps into his arms. When was the last time they even touched? He falters for a second, but gets with the program and lifts her, spins her around. She kisses him, and it feels good, like home. He sets her on the ground.

"Meens. Are you okay?" He looks at her bloody dress. Fair question, probably no other question behind it.

"Yes, it's not my blood. And it's a long story for another day, but I'm fine, other than exhausted and so ready to go home. But Brades, I have to say—about us, I'm so sorry for everything."

He takes her face and swallows hard. "Yes or no only. Understand?"

She nods, and a tear runs down her cheek and on to his warm hand.

What if he doesn't forgive her? What if now that she's ready to be with him, to truly appreciate him, he wants to step back?

"Do you still . . . love me?" He chokes on the words.

"Yes. God, yes! That was never the issue. It was just losing Paxton, and then losing myself and—"

"Yes is enough for me, Meens," he whispers. "Let's leave the past behind and move forward together. Build a new life."

How could she have been so hard on him all these years? Why did he stay and endure it? She'll never take him for granted again.

By now, Derek and Brooke have caught up to where they're at and Brady and Derek shake hands. A reunion of sorts. Brady seems baffled at the odds of running into Derek out here, but once they move past that, Mina introduces Brooke.

"She knew Paxton," Mina says, smiling.

Brady looks at Brooke, eyes wide. "How?"

"I'll tell you all about it, I swear, but first, let's get out of here."

"Yes, we have to call the police about that house on 'J' Street. Get Carly and her dad out of there," Mina says.

"And I have to find Jessi," Brooke says to Derek.

"Hell yeah, you're definitely doing that. And afterward?"

Brooke tilts her head to the side. "What do you mean?"

"What's next for us?"

"I guess we start living."

BONUS EPILOGUE

Want to check in on the survivors a few months later? Scan the QR code to read the bonus epilogue called "The Reunion."

ACKNOWLEDGMENTS

This story was so much fun to write that I powered through the first draft in a month. Then, I spent many (many!) months revising it with the help of some truly amazing and talented people.

Starting with Noelle Ihli, my first reader, sounding board, and dear friend. Since this is my first thriller, it felt right to dedicate it to you because you've helped me so much as an author. Thank you for your brain on my stories during the early developmental stages. Your suggestions and tweaks are always spot on!

Thanks to all my amazing beta readers: Anna Gamel, Jeanne Allen, Faith Gardner, Lisa Hunter, Chris Nelson. Each of you contributed one or more pieces of early feedback that I used to improve scenes. Having friends and loved ones who will read my manuscripts and tell me honestly what isn't working without sparing my feelings is liquid gold. I don't take it for granted.

Thank you to my editors, Patti Geesey and Maddy Leary, for your amazing keen eyes. You both caught so many things even after I thought the thing was polished to death.

(Reader, if you find typos that somehow snuck past all the eagle eyes, feel free to spam my Instagram DMs about it! We're only human around here.)

Maddy, thank you especially, for reading as a beta and

suggesting a few plot tweaks early on that really brought the story to the next level! And then, for reading again as an editor. Seriously, so grateful.

Thanks to my dad, retired detective Jim Dresback, for being my go-to human Google for all things police work. I'll only take credit for anything that's glaringly wrong.

Thanks to the thriller/horror Bookstagram, Booktok, and Facebook communities, for being so enthusiastic about this book and for tirelessly sharing your love of scary stories with the world.

Thank you to my family, Chris, Cam, and Jonny, for your love and support.

And thank you, reader, for picking up this story. I'm a reader too and I know how many amazing books are constantly clawing for our measly twenty-four-hours-in-a-day. So honored that you chose to spend time in mine.

XO, Steph

Printed in Great Britain
by Amazon

43319043R00172